THE DRAGON AND
THE HERO

With the throbbing lance telling him that the dragon was very close, Galen spoke the name imperiously. "Vermithrax!"

The dragon rose.

Galen could not be sure where Vermithrax came from, only that one moment he was looking into the flames of the lake, and the next he was gazing into the eyes of the dragos. So shocking was the suddenness of the beast's appearance that he did not have time to react before he had been fixed by its mesmerizing star. Only the lance leaped and surged; the lance sang in his hand.

Galen himself was lost by what he saw in the dragon's eyes. Immobilized, he watched those eyes. Slowly Vermithrax's head tipped back, slowly its mouth opened.

In the last second before the flame poured forth, Galen raised his shield.

DRAGONSLAYER

Paramount Pictures Corporation and
Walt Disney Productions

Present
A Barwood–Robbins Production

Executive Producer Howard W. Koch

Music by Alex North

Written by Hal Barwood & Matthew Robbins

Produced by Hal Barwood

Directed by Matthew Robbins

DRAGONSLAYER

A novel by Wayland Drew

Based on the screenplay written by Hal Barwood & Matthew Robbins

A Del Rey Book

BALLANTINE BOOKS • NEW YORK

Contents

CHAPTER ONE

Cragganmore

THE TOWER WAS SQUARE AND THICK. IT SQUATTED defiantly on its hilltop, its narrow windows and arrow-slots facing north and south, east and west, like elongated and blinded eyes. Once the keep of a proud fortress, it was surrounded now by rubble and by ruins, and it itself was crumbling inexorably. Centuries of rain and frost had nibbled its masonry. Parts of its roof had collapsed. Its sills and timbers were soft with rot.

A windless hush surrounded the tower, and filled the vast bowl of land around its knoll. The last sunlight lay on the broken roof, but the valley below was blanketed by heavy dusk, and the quicksilver river had darkened and vanished behind its screen of trees.

The sun set reluctantly. It touched the horizon, bulged, began to move beneath.

It was the eve of the spring equinox; the following day would be given half to light and half to darkness.

Motionless, clinging upside down on the coarse bark of an oak, a small brown bat watched the setting of many suns. All were in the composite eye of a fat beetle, two inches away. The beetle was smug and drowsy, watching the sun; it did not know it was about to die.

It had been careless. So still had the bat been, so perfectly did the bat's color blend with the brown and

1

mossy hue of the bark, that the beetle had not seen it.

Both hung motionless, insect and predator. Then, as the sun shrank finally to a mere bead, the bat's left wing unfolded with only the slightest silken whisper, moved over the drowsing beetle, enfolded it. The insect screamed, a sound heard only by the bat. It struggled briefly under the membrane, before it was crushed against the bark. When the bat's keen mandibles closed upon it, it was still twitching, although it was quite dead.

The bat was ravenous. It had eaten nothing for two days and two nights. During the days it had slept, exhausted, but during the nights it had traveled, launched on a lone flight across the darkened land.

It did not know why it had left home. Nor had it any reason to recall what it had seen on its long flight. But some things it did recall. The tiny dots of sun in the eye of the unfortunate beetle, for example, had recalled other dots—the fires of lonely villages and encampments flickering in the vast darkness of the undulating land. Some had been larger than others, villages aflame. And the beetle's dying screams had recalled other sounds as well, the screams of torn animals, and men's cries for help from the borders of random fields, and sometimes the shrieks of women. And the beetle's mangled corpse had recalled other corpses, both fresh and blackened, littering the battlefields over which the bat's silent and inquisitive wings had borne it. Looking down now through the deepening dusk at a silver band of river, the bat recalled other rivers, some with weird shapes moving on and in them; some quite empty.

The edge of its hunger blunted, the bat uttered cries, the plaintive cries of a creature searching for another of its kind. There came no answer, and the bat's flickering ears received only the hum of myriad evening insects. The bat yawned. Its claws clenched in the oak bark and its back arched catlike. Its wings unfolded and stretched with a sound like the rippling of soft silk. Then, in an indolent movement, it released its grip and glided down and out through the oak leaves and into the evening air. Ahead rose the stone tower where, the bat's instincts told it, there would be fine fare—worms lifting pale snouts in the stagnant moat, fat and witless fireflies, thick salamanders nudging through dank masonry.

Nor was the bat mistaken. As it neared the tower it was stricken by the splendid odor of decay, an odor so delectably rich that the bat swooned, clasping its skin wings across its abdomen and gliding along a little updraft. It was an odor that caressed an ancient memory in the base of its medulla, an odor of the death of creatures that the bat's kind had not seen for generations. Hungrily the bat glided down, heading for a dark area in the expanse of wall that it knew to be an opening. Beyond that opening the succulent grubs would be moving in rotting beams.

The bat grinned in anticipation.

But suddenly it veered out, terrified. The gray beauty of the evening had been shattered by a flash of light so brilliant that it hurt the bat's eyes. Like lightning, it was accompanied by a thunderous crack, but instead of jabbing talons of fire at earth, or flickering in a liquid wash through distant valleys, this lightning had shot out from the window of the castle. Its shape was ghastly. It was like the bat itself but with drooping tail, and elongated neck, and yawning, awful jaws. In the bat's sudden desperate efforts to avoid those phantom jaws, it uttered a string of cries like the shrieks of the beetle which now lay torn within it. The next instant, however, the vision vanished. The iridescent wings and arching neck dwindling down into the starlight gleaming on the membranes of the bat itself, in terrified zigzag flight down the valley, away from the castle.

A paler and steadier light replaced the lightninglike flash. It came from a charcoal brazier just inside the second-story window of the tower, a brazier whose magical flaring up had so frightened the bat.

Had the bat flown into the room it would not have found what it expected. Here and there in the remotest corners, dripping water had leached lime from the ancient stones and formed grotesque and bulbous stalactites; but for the most part the room was dry, darkened by the smoke of countless fires. From the ceiling hung not only candelabra but also the mummified cadavers of small animals, and strange instruments which could have been the tools of torture or sorcery. Books and scrolls bearing arcane symbols lay open on elevated reading desks, and shelves of other scrolls lined a wall. Passageways and staircases, ascending and descending, led off from the room at odd angles; in fact, this was less a room than the heart of a labyrinth, which could be reached in many ways.

In the center stood an old man. His feet were braced apart under a fawn robe of coarse cloth. His eyes and his outstretched hands flickered with lambent fire. If the chimera of the dragon had not frightened the bat, the man would have done so, for power emanated from him. He was Ulrich, the master of Cragganmore, most powerful of sorcerers. It was he who had ignited the brazier with such force as to send a dragon's fiery image hurtling into the night. The specter had startled him; he saw in it a premonition, and he had paused before lighting the other fixtures in the room.

Now he turned. *"Omnia in duos. Duo in unum. Unus in nihil. Haec nec quattor, nec omnia, nec duo, nec unus, nec nihil sunt."* He laughed, his old voice like stone on rusted metal. His bent fingers flicked infinitesimally, and, as they did so, ensconced candles on both walls flared and hot wax rippled down to thicken the stalactites beneath. The flames lit strange bulges and concavities about the room and stirred odd occupants to life. On its oaken pedestal, a gyrfalcon raised its head and gazed intently at the window, sensing the bat's passage. On a ledge above, three pigeons stirred uneasily, watching the man, but did not take flight. To one side, so still that it could have been a statue, a stately heron slept, balanced on one splayed foot. A raven, stark white, crouched motionless on one of the chandeliers. "Ulrich," it said quietly, "Ill wrought." Its voice was like a timeless and exotic stringed instrument.

The old man ignored it. He turned to a circular ta-

ble in the center of the room, already occupied by a
stone bowl that sat upon it. He moved with difficulty,
turning in a series of small cautious steps in the way of
old men, supporting himself on a gnarled cane. Although a sinewy power still showed in the movement
of his shoulders, he was clearly very old, and weariness
hung upon him like the folds of the gown itself, weighing heavily on his neck and his shoulders, and drawing them down and forward. His gait was constricted
and shuffling, as if he had been hobbled. Furthermore,
it was obvious that with the lonely passing of the years
he had grown careless of his appearance; indeed, he
had abandoned personal attentions almost completely,
and now when he bent to gaze into the stone bowl of
still liquid he was startled by the reflection of a grizzled and repugnant old man, looming toward him as
if out of his very past. He appeared like someone from
his own childhood, one of the countless wanderers who
traveled the forest paths in those days, grim, dogged
and limping, men who had long since forgotten the
object of their quest and for whom mere movement
had become the reason for being. Was he like one of
these? Yes, like the senile celebrants he had once
chanced upon in the alder thickets, in a spot once
sacred, practicing among their dolmens rites made obscene by forgetfulness, he was old. His was now such
a face as he remembered—the hair gone, the eyes
liquid oysters in pouches of flesh, the mouth dribbling
into a caked and yellow beard, the skin pocked and
blemished. Was this indeed *him?* Yes. The thing in the
bowl had nodded, *yes.* And this fact was all the more
astonishing because at that very moment he glimpsed
behind this specter a beautiful vision, a fleeting vision
now in white robe, now in trousers and jerkin, a beautiful young girl who, before she had vanished in the
shadows of the bowl, had turned for a last long look.
Could it be, really, that she was there no longer, that
she had passed beyond the power of even his recall?

Again the grim head nodded: "Yes!"

"What solace, then?"

Hearing his voice, the birds mewed in response and

moved restlessly on their perches. A breeze whispered through the darkening corridors. *Power*.

Ulrich smiled and shook his head ruefully. Ah, if it were only that simple. If only the mere acquisition of power could compensate for the loss of that which made men human. For some, he knew, it did; but not for him. He required more. All his life he had required more. And now, as the visions began to form and dissolve in the viscous liquid of the stone bowl, he acknowledged again that it was not power that had seduced him all those years ago but *knowledge*. It was the incessant, insatiable itch of curiosity that had drawn him into the solitude of Cragganmore.

What solace? The bleak comfort that the world was not as most men perceived it to be, but that it was still, after the long and lonely decades of inquiry, an utter mystery.

Sighing, he leaned his cane against the table, straightened himself as far as possible, and prepared to conjure over the bowl. It was the eve of the vernal equinox. Twice a year, at the equinoxes, he probed forward and backward into the mysterious regions of the stone bowl farther than at any other time. Strange and unpredictable things happened in the liquid of the bowl. Time there was not what human beings imagined it to be, and often Ulrich would launch himself on what he believed to be a voyage into the future only to find that he had entered a time before he had been born—indeed, before the world itself was born. He always began, however, by requesting some vision of the present and the bowl responded by giving him a key, by showing him how—at least until the following equinox—past, present and future would be one.

So now he commanded, "The Present!" and made the adept and requisite gesture above the bowl. The bowl responded. It shuddered slightly and its liquid at first darkened, as if it were drawing in upon itself, and then quickly lightened, presenting a clear scene. The room in the vision was similar to the one in which Ulrich stood, but much smaller and without attendant birds. The oaken table in the vision was like the one before which he stood, and the stone bowl was identical to that in which Ulrich's vision was occurring. The boy leaning over that bowl, however, was having no success in conjuring a vision of his own. Under a disheveled shock of flaxen hair his brow was creased in exasperation, and as Ulrich watched, he attempted twice more, clumsily and futilely, the gesture that Ulrich the Master had performed so smoothly, each time afterwards peering into the unresponsive bowl. At last he brought his fist down hard on the table, and although the old man could not hear what he was saying, it was clear that his adolescent patience was exhausted.

"Oh Galen, Galen." The old man shook his head. "My dear boy. My poor muddled apprentice. That is *not* the way. I've told you a hundred times!"

"Ill wrought," said the white raven, who had fluttered to the old man's shoulder. "No luck. Never rich."

"Get away, Gringe." Absentmindedly, Ulrich shrugged his shoulder and the raven glided off, muttering. The other birds stirred and shifted on their perches. The falcon had turned toward the window, alert to high sounds passing—an owl's shriek, the shrill hunting cries of bats, and an unidentifiable sound that was either enormous and distant or infinitesimal, vibrating like a minute insect against the falcon's tympanum. The bird crouched immobile, listening. But the sound was gone, crowded out by the old man's voice.

"Rerum gestarum memoria . . ." Ulrich was saying, and then, after a momentary hesitation, "The history of Galen."

"History, mystery," said the white raven, shuffling in the shadows beyond ancient stacks of books and manuscripts, "Galen may learn . . ."

"The lad may learn," Ulrich was saying, but the words merely echoed in the memory of the old man, and it was a younger self who was actually speaking them in the depths of the bowl, the Ulrich of fifteen years before, his scalp richly tonsured with white hair, his beard glistening, his stride vigorous. He was speaking to himself as much as to the fretting father and mother who accompanied him, and he was musing over the child Galen who had just created, by exuberantly shaking his fists, a bevy of monsters, strange and furry mammals that panted affectionately toward him, tongues lolling, some ambling on eight legs, some on six, some undulating serpentlike.

The mother shrank from them in genuine fear.

"Do you see, sir?" the father asked. "He does it whenever he wants to."

"I can see that," Ulrich said, nodding. "He has the Talent."

"But it's not a talent, it's a curse!" The mother wrung her hands, beginning to weep. "How can it be a talent to create monsters? He does it even at night. He *dreams* them!"

The father nodded blankly. "And then they just wander away. Out. Into the world. Who knows where? How do they survive?"

"Dreams," Ulrich said. "Other people dream that they are fed."

"Awful!" The mother shuddered and the father embraced her comfortingly. "Why has this happened to us? Why? The *other* children are all normal."

Ulrich regarded the parents silently and with profound pity. He had no answer to that question, "Why me?", although he himself had asked it countless times. He leaned forward and took the child's tousled head between his hands. "Such talent!" he said. "If only . . ." He did not finish the sentence, but fell into a reverie from which he was finally drawn only by the mother's broken sobbing and the father's plaintive question, "Can you . . . can you *cure* him?"

Ulrich made his decision then, a decision influenced by the fact that in all the long and lonely years of his sorcerer's quest he had never seen such a natural and exuberant talent as that which sent these strange creatures tumbling about his feet, and by the fact that he deeply feared the bending of such power to evil ends, and by the fact—most poignant—that he had no heir to whom he might pass on his knowledge of the ancient, dwindling Craft. "Cure him? No. That I cannot do. I can merely govern his power. But . . ."

"Oh thank you!" The mother seized Ulrich's hand.

The father's brow creased. "Will it . . . cost much, this cure?"

"Nothing. But later, when the child has become a boy, I will want him to come here, to Cragganmore, to live. I shall want to teach him. That is my condition."

Sighing, drying her eyes, the mother nodded.

"And you understand," Ulrich added, raising a warning finger, "that it will be dangerous. It is always perilous to meddle with such power. If I should miscalculate . . . If I should cast too strong a spell . . ."

"Oh," the mother whispered, "you couldn't make a mistake. You're a sorcerer."

Ulrich smiled sadly.

"Done!" the father said. "Agreed."

Ulrich frowned and sighed heavily, remembering.

All visions vanished. The liquid in the bowl lay still, reflecting only the flames from the braziers and the sconces, while the old man dreamed back, his tongue working at the bearded corner of his mouth. He had indeed erred, suppressing that innocent power; the charm, a dangerous one, had twisted serpentlike upon him. It had flawed Galen's gift, leaving him bemused and easily distracted. Later, when Ulrich had begun the formal training, following the precepts of his master Belisarius, he found that the boy lacked interest and concentration. And in fifteen years —what failure! what shame!—Ulrich had not brought him even to the First Degree. After all this time the lad still could not levitate, could not transmute, could not foresee. He was unable, in other words, to perform the most rudimentary tasks. Very soon, Ulrich feared, the boy would be called upon, and then he would need help; yes, would need much help.

Stiffly, massaging his hip, the old man straightened up. He groaned and sighed. The birds stirred expectantly, watching as Ulrich shuffled toward a second table, smaller and raised on a dais at the center of the room. On it lay an object covered by a white silk cloth. It was cunningly embroidered, this cloth, colored with arcane symbols intertwined, and as the magician approached, it began to shimmer with a light which was not a reflection but which radiated intermittently from the embroidery and from the object beneath, brightening and fading with an unnatural rhythm.

When Ulrich lifted this cloth—rather, when he caused it to rise by a touch at its edges and an upward gesture—a marvelous and subdued luminescence briefly pervaded the room. The night birds blinked and stared at the object that had loosed such weird light. It appeared to be a stone, gold-set and hung on a golden chain. To the gyrfalcon's eye it was the size of a small mouse scurrying through November stubble.

"Ill wrought!" muttered Gringe, shrinking in the far shadows of the room. Ulrich took it, enclosed it in his cupped hand, momentarily containing the light, and then gathered up the golden chain so that the amulet nestled among its coils like a small egg. Then he released the strange glow again from his cupped palms, just as it began to fade.

Seen close, the object was almost colorless, its tints of blue, white, and rose so subtle that they vanished and reappeared, like shifting and magically layered seas. An infinitesimal spark lay captured in its center, and this was the source of the undulating moonlike radiance in the room.

Ulrich bore the amulet to the table where the bowl lay, its liquid trembling slightly at his approach. He carried it with utmost reverence; candlelight glinted palely in the swaying gold of the chain. Holding it as he addressed the bowl he whispered, *"Nunc, illo tempore!* And now, the old, old time!"

Again the liquid swam with visions. This time they took longer to form, and they churned the bowl with a darker and deeper turbulence than before. Tiny splashes reached for Ulrich's hands as if seeking to draw the amulet he held back into the darkening vortex of the bowl. Indeed, a vortex *had* formed, rotating clockwise, revealing the very bottom of the bowl which seemed at that instant, even as Ulrich watched amazed, to open farther into huge dark spaces speckled by random fires.

Ulrich found himself again gazing into the Past—
not merely the few millennia of human history, but
the time for which there were no records but enigmas
buried in the earth, buried in the troubled myths and
dreams of men. At first it appeared as an undulating
mass of plasma, gray and black and purple relieved
by streaks of pale white, then brown, then orange,
then finally yellow, broadening and fluctuating until at
last what appeared were the irregular horizontals of
sky and earth and water. Through these moved the
first life, amorphous and ponderous shapes, lifting
monstrous snouts through the scum, dragging themselves down hopeless paths. Then, later, gaunt frames
were lifted on updrafts of ceaseless storms, coupled
clumsily, spilled young; they died and were swept
away to become rock at last, flesh liquefied, bones
pulverized by pressure.

Ulrich watched wearily. He had long known, had
long understood. But what now occurred within the
bowl was new to him, and despite the clamoring pains
in his back and legs he eagerly leaned closer to watch.

He saw a man first, a man clad in skins, poised in a
sorcerer's stance that Ulrich knew well; it was the
stance taken when attempting a spell beyond one's
reach—determined, yet wary and defensive. Even as
the vision clarified, the spell passed from that other
sorcerer, leaving him drained and weak, and at the
same time the scene shifted so that Ulrich saw the
effects apparently through the eyes of his fellow.

The charm had been directed at the earth and had
entered it. At first it seemed that only a minor tremor
would result; bushes shook and pebbles rattled down
a rocky grade. But then the agitation grew, and very
soon the earth, which was in places like a scaly hide,
undulated rhythmically. Fires pocked its surface in
cones and opening fissures, and tiny rivulets of fire
snaked down the slopes. Streams of water vanished in
sudden steam.

Even as the sorcerer reeled back from the heat, a
fissure wider than any others spread magenta lips, and
from between them a creature emerged. Two sets of
talons came first, and then a leg, and then the mem-

branous tips of incandescent wings. It was a winged
lizard, cowled heavily with a ropy brow. The head
was bejewelled with ruby encrustations, the snout surmounted by a gray-brown shield. Its thick tongue was
pure scarlet, like a gross red pepper. Embryonic horns
knobbed the skull. As far as Ulrich could see, it had
two legs only. The end of its tail was clenched in the
corner of its mouth. Shreds of a membrane hung upon
its scales, and from it there spread the stench of unearthly amniotic fluid. Its eyes had opened and were
apparently sealed open, utterly unblinking. The slit
pupils were horizontal, and looking into them was like
staring across the horizons of time itself.

Around and beneath, the earth gradually subsided,
the trembling diminished. There was still the hissing
of steam on hot rocks and a deep complaining as the
last small rockslides occurred and the land composed
itself. From the far distance came the fear-and-
mourning cry of a strange bird. Incredibly, Ulrich
heard these sounds distinctly, although what he was
watching was but a vision.

Then the small dragon roared. It was a monstrous
sound, like the scream of a gutted horse, and the
sorcerer recoiled from it just as Ulrich recoiled from
the vision in the bowl. Again came the roar, and
again, more jubilant as the man was driven back, and
the beast lifted scrawny arms in triumph. Fleeing, the
man turned to face Ulrich, and Ulrich saw the frozen
mask of horror and despair that was his face, and saw
too, as clearly as if it were graven on the stone of the
bowl the thought that was in his mind: *Have I done
this? What have I done?*

Ulrich was profoundly shaken by this vision. He
gripped the table, and he found that he had trouble
breathing, and that a strange, circling pain was teas-
ing the center of his chest. But there was more to
come. Before the images vanished forever, he saw
the skin-clad sorcerer a final time. It seemed that
some years had passed. The man was thin and hag-
gard and perhaps very close to death. His energies
had clearly been almost totally drained from him. He
was kneeling and he was offering to a boy, whose

hand was outstretched to take it, the very amulet Ulrich held, which shone with eerie luminescence. But
the sorcerer was looking at neither the newly crafted
stone nor the boy. He was pointing into the distance,
and following his line of sight Ulrich could see approaching, very low above the horizon, the awesome
silhouette of an airborne dragon.

"So," Ulrich said, nodding slowly. "So."

The liquid in the bowl clouded, calmed, cleared, lay
inert.

Ulrich's back ached miserably. Groaning, he held
the amulet in one hand and leaned on the table with
the other. His knees had stiffened, and he performed
a little shuffling dance to stimulate his circulation. He
muttered wordlessly. He had never really learned to
curse, although as a youngster among the fens he had
tried hard, in Latin, and in Celtic, and in Anglo-
Saxon too.

"Old rick," said Gringe, the white raven, scrabbling
across the flag floor to safety under the table.

"Avaunt!" Ulrich shouted at him, lifting his gnarled
oak cane. "Get Galen!"

"Galen may win."

"Get him!"

The raven made several obscene sounds in quick
succession.

"Gringe," Ulrich raised the fist with the amulet. "I
warn you!"

The raven complained more, but he was going. One
eye on the amulet, he was already scurrying past the
aloof falcon and fluttering from chairback to window-
sill and away into the night. A moment later Ulrich
heard him chattering below at Galen's window.

In another moment a soft knock came on the door,
and Galen entered diffidently. "You wanted me, sir?"

"I sent Gringe for you," Ulrich said, still staring
morosely into the bowl.

Galen nodded, rubbing his neck. "I was practicing
the new spell you gave me, and when I didn't answer
right away, he came over and pecked me."

"Um. The fact is, he's never forgiven you for turning him white."

"I know. I apologized, though. It was an *accident*," Galen said, louder than necessary, frowning at the raven, who had reappeared on the window ledge.

Gringe blinked mournfully.

Ulrich gestured impatiently. "Nevertheless, you *were* impetuous. I told you not to try that charm; I warned you there was a coda to be attached to it, a danger . . ."

"Well . . ."

"But you went ahead anyway. You experimented. And Gringe got in the way."

"I . . ." Galen shrugged and offered a palms-up gesture. He had no excuses. He was a slim boy, eighteen now. He had an honest jaw and broad-spaced confident eyes, the green-blue of forest pools. His head, bowed deferentially now in Ulrich's presence, was covered with curly and disheveled flaxen hair. His shoulders were broad, his stance elastic. The open-handed gesture had revealed calluses and black, broken fingernails—the hands of a laborer.

"And so," Ulrich asked, still gazing at his bowl, "did you master the new charm?"

"No, sir."

"The gesture? Did you practice the conjuring gesture for the present *exactly* as I showed you?"

"Well, sir, I thought so. I *did* try."

"But, obviously, you didn't get it right."

"No, sir." Galen sighed. "As a matter of fact, Ulrich—" He brushed back his hair resolutely. "I'm not sure I *am* a sorcerer."

"Nonsense!"

Galen shrugged. "Oh I know that you believe that I am, and it's true that I get an occasional charm right; but usually they go wild and something crazy happens. A tree grows fur, or flowers start laughing, or somebody passing by, like Gringe, gets turned a different color." He shrugged again. "Last week, when we had that thunderstorm?"

Ulrich nodded.

"Well I went down to the tarn and I tried to calm the waters—a simple little charm like that! And what happened? Fish! Dozens of fish came crowding up and rubbed against my legs like cats!"

"You must try *harder,* Galen. You must discipline yourself! You must concentrate!"

The boy grimaced. "I know, sir. But I *do* concentrate. I *do.* And there *are* times when I feel almost that . . ."

Ulrich leaned forward, eyes narrowing, "What?"

". . . that I am going away from myself. Up, somehow. And I feel that if that could happen then I could do *anything.* Anything would be possible."

"And what happens then?"

"Well, I don't know exactly. Something brings me back. I see something. Something ordinary. Maybe a bird, or a glimpse of the river or somebody walking past—and then, well . . . it's lost."

Ulrich covered his face. "I know," he said. "I know."

"But the odd thing is that right away I feel better. I feel . . . human again, and being a failed sorcerer doesn't bother me so much. It doesn't seem to matter, except that I let *you* down."

Ulrich brushed this away, shrugged wearily, and did a little shuffling circling walk. Then suddenly his old fist began to pump the air in agitation. "And yet, you had the *Talent,* Galen!"

Galen looked up quickly. "I did? When?"

Ulrich's hand faltered. "When you were small," he said, speaking more carefully, "I saw that you had . . . potential. That you might be capable of grand events. I . . . I would like to think that that was still true."

Galen frowned dubiously, and when he looked up his face was pale. "The fact is, sir, I'm frightened. I don't understand the power. I think . . . I think I would like just to be human, and to let the power go."

Ulrich dropped his hand and drew himself to his full height. "Go? Go *where?*"

"Back where it came from, I guess."

"But it comes from you, boy! From *you!* And if you eschew it, relinquish control of it, you will make monsters; you will loose monsters on the world! Do you not recall the first condition of the Regulae: *whosoever has accumulated the power through fortune, or zeal, or labor, let him beware that the safety of it is his forever . . ."*

"Yes," said Galen. "I remember it."

"Then . . ." Ulrich was breathing deeply. His anger had flown, and in its place had come a stealthy reptile of dread deeper than any he had known. ". . . then you must never talk of abrogating your power. *Never.* You must control it, and contain it, and use it. You must . . ." His voice trailed off.

He had almost said that the young apprentice must use his power for the forces of Good, and once he could have said that and meant it. But now, although he believed in Good, he was much less certain how to attain it. He had known too many charms to go awry in the name of Good, to twist like snakes and cause pain, loss, and tears. Time, he knew, was the culprit; time and circumstance and chance, but mainly time. All his efforts had sought to transcend that ambivalent whirl of time and to enter a purer ether, where intention shone like crystal, and was never tarnished by action. Gravity he had conquered, but time he had not, and the evidence of his failure was there, in the aching back and legs, the bent shoulders, the seamed and blemished face, the uncertain hands.

He sighed deeply.

Power. What was it, after all, but a conjunction of coincidences which he had not, for all his study and magic, begun to fathom? Rather, the more power he had attained, the more the conundrum had deepened, broadened, grown away from him in labyrinthine passageways; and, having no alternative, he had descended deeper into those passageways until it seemed that he had lost his grasp on any thread connecting him with the healing simplicities of sky and earth and water. . . .

"I know," the boy was saying, still musing. "I know there is *something* there, but it's not like *your* gift, Ulrich. I'm not a great sorcerer like you, or like Belisarius, or like any of the others."

"You might have been," Ulrich said softly. "You might still be."

"Well, maybe. I don't know. What's the point of having power, after all? Is there anyone to help? No, I think . . ." He paused.

"Go on."

"I think that if it weren't for you, Ulrich, I'd stop trying. I'd travel. Maybe I'd go south, or maybe west with the next longship to come up Raggenfirth to the tarn."

"Simpleminded stuff!" Ulrich snorted. "Diversions for bumpkins!" But for the fraction of a moment he had been thrilled by old longings of his own.

"Think of it, sir! I have heard that beyond the Western Isles, where the Christians are, there are mountains all of ice that fall into the sea and go voyaging themselves."

The gyrfalcon moved restlessly. It canted forward on its perch and lifted its wings, staring as if it shared the boy's free vision; but it did not take flight.

"I have heard those stories," Ulrich said. "But do not believe them."

"They are true! I have heard . . ."

"You have heard? From whom? What do you know? No, Galen, you must stay with me for a little time yet. For only a little time. Then you will be free to make your own decisions; to use your power as you see fit."

"What do you mean—only a little time?"

"Come," said Ulrich, taking the boy by the arm and leading him to the conjuring table. "Look, and you will know all that I know now." He gestured with the hand that still contained the amulet.

The substance in the bowl again flickered with life, pale green, but the images that formed within it were less substantial than those which had appeared before, for they were the intimations of what was yet to be. Galen stared entranced, for the first thing that he saw was the very stone that Ulrich held. For only a moment it retained its present shape, and then slowly and inexorably it began to expand with terrible force, fragmenting in myriad pieces, each of which shattered, infinitely expanding, to ever-smaller particles, and finally to drift down in a cool and universal rain, which quenched all fire within the vision, leaving only the shifting greens, turquoise, and blues of a water world. Yet, at the heart of the vision, even as it lay at the heart of the amulet in Ulrich's hand, there remained a gleam of fire.

"What does it mean, Ulrich?" Galen whispered.

The old man shook his head. "Well, see for yourself . . ." He again indicated the shifting scene within the bowl.

Ulrich was there himself now, and it seemed that he was flying, for he was borne magically up and farther up. Above him, the colors were no longer ultramarine, but had shifted to vivid yellow and orange, and the space above him flickered with a steely luminescence. For an instant the surface of the water suddenly contracted, drawn into the vortex of itself, and then erupted violently in an uncontrollable turbulence of tiny clashing waves and waterspouts. In the same instant the old sorcerer cried out and shuddered so violently that Galen feared he might collapse. Then all changed—the cataclysm passed, and the image which faded in the bowl was that of a transparent Ulrich, smiling beatifically, soaring ever higher as the water calmed. . . .

"Out of time," the old man whispered.

"But what does it *mean*, Ulrich?"

"It means that I am going to die. And quite soon, although I do not know how or when. *That* knowledge is always hidden. But it means also that it will be a perfect departure. A time when all things will converge. And you, Galen, you will be part of it! You will know beyond all doubt what must be done." Ulrich had begun to rub the amulet delightedly, and he was about to say something further when he paused, listening."

"But, Ulrich, you *can't* die! That's terrible!"

"Nonsense. Of course I can. It's not terrible at all. It's rather interesting, the thought of being transmuted back into the elements again, beginning a thousand journeys. Besides, when you get old, my son, things are, well, different—you'll see—and death begins to look more like *you*, like a brother and an old friend."

He shook himself. "In any case, I know it's coming soon. And I know, although I do not know how, that *you* will be involved in my death . . ."

"I don't *want* you to die!"

The old man was far away, oblivious to the boy's distress. "Shh." Ulrich placed a hand on the boy's shoulder. He was staring over Galen's head, far over the tears that the apprentice was wiping away with an embarrassed knuckle. "Listen!" Ulrich said.

Galen raised his head, turning it right and left like an alerted animal; but he heard nothing, nothing beyond the mutterings of Gringe, who had hopped onto the conjuring table and was peering into the bowl in a mimicry of Ulrich; nothing beyond the restless movements and the soft, reptilian inhalations of the other birds.

"It has begun," Ulrich whispered. "It is starting now."

"But . . ."

"Listen!" The sorcerer placed the boy's hand on the amulet. "Use this!"

Then, with his hand cradling the amulet, Galen did indeed begin to hear, although at first the sounds were so slight that he mistook them for the coursing of his own blood. But then they came again, unmistakable, although still muffled by the forest and by distance: the tinkle of a bridle; the fall of horses' hooves on a humus path; the weary fragment of a sentence, "Visitors," Galen said.

Ulrich nodded. "Pilgrims, traveling through the night. Bearing a request."

Galen strode toward the door. "I'll get my sword! I'll waken Hodge! They won't take you, Ulrich, not without a fight!"

"No, no, my son. There is no threat yet. These will be peaceful and harmless men, ordinary men caught in the coils of circumstance as are we all, beset by difficulties from which they believe I might free them. Perhaps . . . perhaps . . ." There was a scuffling of sandals on the stone stairway, and a thudding on the door of the tower chamber. "What is it, Hodge?"

The door opened and an old retainer entered. He

was bent, and grizzled, and his skin was the color of smoked-tanned leather. "Torches, sir. Comin' up through the forest. I seen 'em because I couldn't sleep. I were havin' a dream, a terrible dream about yourself, sir, beggin' your pardon. So I got up and I was all atremble, and I says to myself, 'Hodge, yer old fool,' I says, 'it were only a *dream!*' 'Well, then,' I says to myself, 'if it were only a dream and there were nothin' of the truth about it, then why should it bother a body so?' I were that shaky, sir, and that much bathed in the cold sweat of the night, the dream were that awful, sir, indeed it were . . ." Hodge's pale eyes glazed over and he stood for several seconds lost in recollection, arms dangling.

"And so?" Ulrich said, frowning at Galen, who had begun to twist his toe impatiently against the flagstones.

"And so I roused myself," Hodge said. "I says to myself, 'Get up, yer old fool! Get up an get about somethin' useful to occupy yer brain and yer poor bones!' That's what I said, and that's what I did, fer I got up and I begun to draw the wood and light the fires for mornin'. And then," Hodge crouched, one hand shielding his eyes, "then I seen 'em, sir. Comin' up through the forest. I seen 'em over the wall. Comin' this way!"

"I know, Hodge."

"Ten, maybe twelve, sir!"

"Yes, Hodge."

"Unless I mistake myself, sir, they were . . ." He paused, listening, and at the same instant the sound reached the three of them at once, a querulous raising of voices. ". . . they were chanting, sir."

They all turned to the window, then. Across the river, they saw a twisting line of torches winding through the mists and along the path toward the castle, their fires, like fallen bits of the great orange dawn, lighting the horizon beyond the hills. Indeed the pilgrims were chanting; first, a clear and youthful voice like quick water on rocks, and then the responding chorus, more muddled and weary, milling and eddying behind. It was a fearful, small, and human sound, a sound to keep back the surrounding night.

Gringe muttered on the window beside the three watchers.

Slowly, with what Galen thought was a trace of a smile, the smile of the warrior who welcomed an approaching battle although he knew it would be his last, Ulrich waved his hand. The raven launched itself soundlessly from the ledge, and drifted out into the cool dawn, vanishing and reappearing against the white and dark of the landscape, gliding down toward the frightened travelers.

CHAPTER TWO

Journeys

GRINGE GLIDED LOW ABOVE THE HEADS OF THE STAR-
tled pilgrims, so low that their torch smoke smudged
his feathers. There were thirteen. A few were singing,
but most slept on their trudging horses. "What?
What?" he heard them asking, waking, as he raced
over the trees, "What bird? What white bird?"

"Foul!" he answered, sweeping back, "Follow!"
And he was gratified by nervous laughter.

"Why," someone said, "it's only a raven! A white
raven! A freak!"

Within a few yards the tunnel of trees broadened,
opened, and the crumbling battlements of Cragganmore loomed ahead, silhouetted by the first of the
dawn. Candlelight spilled from one of the upper windows, and the Urlanders, arriving at the edge of the
moat, could plainly see the silhouettes of a watching
man and a boy. They went no farther than the moat,
for a querulous challenge halted them: "Who are ye?"
It was old Hodge, bristling in rusted armor, brandishing a spear which—though they could not see this—
was bent and woefully dull. He was peering through a
crenellation directly above the drawbridge. "What
seek ye at Cragganmore?"

There was a flurry among the pilgrims. Those who
had remained asleep suddenly awoke and began mumbling and asking foolish questions. A great deal of milling ensued, during which a single name was spoken

22

more often than any other—"Valerian? Valerian?"—
at first questioningly, and then assertively: "Valerian!
Valerian will speak for us!" A slim youth was brought
forward through the little crowd. He stood on the grassy
edge of the moat, swatting at the clouds of mosquitoes
the steamy horses had aroused, and peering up at the
indistinct, dome-topped figure of old Hodge among the
battlements.

"We are Urlanders," he said, "from the town of
Swanscombe, three weeks' journey beyond the moun-
tains. We seek Ulrich, Magister Ipissimus, if this be
Cragganmore, for we have a petition for him alone."
The clear young voice sang like a flute in the dawn, and
in the window far above Ulrich heard clearly.

"Humph!" he said. "I guess at it!"

"Ye be men of peace, then?" Hodge asked from below.

"Oh yes . . . yes of course . . . wouldn't be here otherwise . . ." A chorus of similar comments ran through
the crowd. "Yes," answered the young voice again,
suppressing a cough, "we are men of peace."

"Yer never know," said Hodge, his helmet beginning
to bob slowly as he worked an unseen turnstile, and
the bridge, creaking, began to descend. "Yer just never
know. Countryside teeming with rowdies. Charlatans!
Imposters! Aye, and vagabonds and vandals too! But
ye look peaceful enough, and too foolish to have harm
in ye, comin' up through a night forest where there
might be a dozen to cut yer throats for the clothes on
yer backs. There be some force protectin' ye, is the way
I see it!"

"Well, we're not Christians, if that's what you
mean," said an indignant, older voice from the crowd.

"Didn't say ye were," said Hodge, continuing to
crank. "Wouldn't accuse yer without good reason. Just
said ye was real lucky." He leaned over and spat neatly
into the moat. The drawbridge bumped down the last
foot, and Hodge waved them in. "Stayin' long?"

The youth was the first to dismount, and to lead a
horse across the echoing drawbridge. "Not long," he
called up to Hodge as he passed beneath, "at least, I
hope not. I hope . . ."

"In that case," said Hodge, wiping the sweat out of his eyes, "I'll leave 'er down till yer go. Just shut and bar the gate behind yerselves. Follow me!" He descended the rickety staircase beside the wall and headed across the courtyard, making snurfling sounds that to the travelers' ears sounded like suppressed laughter. They glanced uneasily at each other.

Like the rest of the castle, the courtyard was unkempt and moldering. Rank weeds flourished, overgrowing chunks of masonry fallen from the upper battlements. A little path wound through the shambles, and in single file the pilgrims followed Hodge to the oak door of the great hall. "Leave yer horses," Hodge called back over his shoulder, gesturing vaguely, "let 'em browse."

Those with horses loosened their girths and reins and then followed the others into the dim hall, coughing and flapping their arms for warmth. Inside, however, it was even cooler than outside, for there were no windows through which the rays of the rising sun might have penetrated; and although birch logs lay in the great hearth, they were unlit. The pilgrims clustered at one end of a massive oaken table, peering in wonderment around the hall. The huge granite blocks that formed the walls supported—and were supported by —immense oak beams, blackened by age and by the smoke of countless fires. Thick with dust and cobwebs, escutcheons, banners, broadswords, and battleaxes adorned all the walls. Hodge had mounted the steps of an entranceway at one side of the hall, and he had pulled off his helmet to reveal an unkempt mat of gray hair. He now cleared his throat and rapped the butt of his spear on the flagstones for attention. "Welcome to Cragganmore, home of Ulrich, and home before him of Belisarius, and before him of Pleximus." Hodge patted the mass of masonry at his side. "Legend says that this fireplace was in an ancient fastness from days of the Celts, and that its mortar was ground from the bones of three faithless wives of Maeve, wives who had betrayed him with young warriors, and that it was with great regret that he had them slain, for they were beautiful to behold and their voices were like fresh streams." Here Hodge paused for effect and looked somberly at each face in turn. "On winter nights, when the fires are stoked here, their voices may be heard again, freed by the heat, singing the songs that drive young men wild. I have heard them. Aye. That I have." Hodge chortled and his glance darted around the room, settling at last on Valerian, who flushed. A strand of drool escaped the corner of Hodge's mouth and dribbled down his beard; he brushed it away with the back of his hand before continuing. "Now, on your left may be seen the great coat of arms . . ."

A white speck fluttered in the dark hallway behind him and, before those watching had time even to gasp, it had burst out into the room and settled on the railing beside Hodge's shoulder—a bird. "Drivel," said Gringe. "Make soup."

"*Soup?*" Hodge's eyes bulged in outrage. "Here be Hodge, in the midst of greeting guests, just at the start of the tour, and you say . . ."

"No Gringe, Ill rich!"

"Oh. Well, in that case. If *Ulrich* wants me to." He looked over the small shuddering crowd of pilgrims. "And I do see that they be cold. Very good. Soup it is. How many . . ." He counted quickly. "Twelve."

"Thirteen," Valerian said. "Malkin's with the horses."

"Excuse me." A tentative hand rose amidst the group. "It's not . . . not lentil soup by any chance, is it?"

"No," said Hodge, "it's marmot."

"Oh good. It's just that I'm allergic to lentil. Anything but lentil."

Grumbling, Hodge set out toward the kitchen, leaving Gringe to watch over the shuffling little group. "Ulrich will be along," he called over his shoulder. "Getting dressed."

Indeed that was what Ulrich was doing, with Galen's help, in the tower room. So stiff was he from the conjuring and visions of the night that he could scarcely move, but he insisted on standing erect while Galen brought his cape and drew it over his shoulders.

He peremptorily waved away his canes. "Do you want them to think me decrepit? Useless?"

"But you can hardly walk," Galen protested. "Look at you!"

"Boy," said Ulrich sternly, "do you believe I *need* to walk?"

"No, sir. But I thought . . ."

"Listen, now! You will precede me and greet our guests and make them welcome. And you will do that in such manner that they will know that they have come to the house of a sorcerer. Do you understand?" He held the boy's shoulder firmly. "You will use the power that is yours by nature, Galen, as well as that which you have acquired."

"But . . ."

"But nothing!" Ulrich raised a monitory finger. "Very soon, *very* soon, you will be alone, and you will win respect by your own merit or not at all. In an emergency, in a *real* emergency, when you are acting for others besides yourself, then special help may be given. But, for the moment . . ."

Galen nodded dubiously.

"And remember, my son," the old man continued soberly, "that no matter what happens before this day is done, it is for you to carry on, despite how pitifully small your knowledge is. When I am gone it is *you* who will succeed me. *You* are my heir, neither Hodge nor anyone else. *You,* Galen, only!"

"If you say so, sir," Galen replied. He was disturbed. Rarely had he heard his teacher speak so intensely. "But I'm not ready to . . ."

"When the need is there, you will be ready. Now, no more talk of the sea, or traveling to the silken lands of the East, so long as there is a Great Thing needing to be done."

"Yes, Ulrich."

"Yes." Ulrich rested his hand on the boy's shoulder for a long moment. Then he smiled. "And now, now let us not keep our guests waiting. You first, and I shall follow."

Head bowed respectfully, Galen backed away from Ulrich until he was through the door; then he hurried down the stairs. Visitors of any sort were rare at Cragganmore, and only twice since he had been apprenticed to Ulrich had travelers as young as himself arrived. Usually those who came were supplicants—aging councillors gnawing their beards, or fretting parents—or else renegades skulking along the edge of the woods and easily frightened off by a fireball conjured around their shins. So now he was particularly anxious to meet Valerian, whom he liked already, although he could not say why, and to hear more of Urland, for he had already heard strange tales. So eager was he that he almost burst indecorously into the hall. At the last moment he stopped running down the corridor, composed himself, and gestured to Gringe, who was still perched on the railing just inside the hall and who had been watching his approach with a baleful eye. He smiled ingratiatingly at the raven. "Announce me!" he whispered. But the bird turned a disdainful back and uttered a single raucous and unintelligible cry, like the grinding of oak branches in a wind, which startled the pilgrims and caused them to huddle together.

"Greetings," said Galen, entering with what he hoped was a friendly wave. "Welcome to Cragganmore."

They stared at him. They saw a gangling boy of eighteen, with an ingenuous face, big hands, and a patched cloak that was much too big. "Oh no," he said, guessing their thoughts. "No, no. I'm not Ulrich. Ulrich's coming. He sent me to greet you. I'm his apprentice. I'm Galen."

"Magic, not talk!" said Ulrich's voice, but Ulrich was not there. Only chortling Gringe, preening his wing, was there.

"Well," said Galen, "let's have some light!" In a sweeping gesture he included all the stubs of tapers that Hodge should long since have replaced—on the table, in the iron candelabra, in the wall sconces. *"Habeamus lucem!"* He spoke confidently, for he knew he could do this, if nothing else. It was a game. Something revolved inside him, a huge tickling sensation in his stomach, like a sudden recollection from long ago, from beyond the lost threshold of childhood. It gave him a childlike delight. He laughed. Instantly the candles flamed, guttering and dribbling wax as if they had been burning for hours, and the brighter room seemed also warmer. Galen glanced surreptitiously at Valerian and was gratified to see that the other youth was impressed, watching openmouthed. "And, let's see, how about some music!" Again he gestured, this time at the little musicians' gallery where once, he knew, flutists and lute players had entertained through nightlong banquets. Again he felt the sensation in his belly and knew exultantly that he had done it. After a moment, ghostly music drifted from a time long dead, the kind of music that would be played when the feasting was finished, when the jugglers had entertained and been thanked with their flagons of mead, and when at last, with the guests settling back in their chairs, the poet would move to the dais and begin to tell of heroic deeds and of times commensurate with the dreams of men. It was music to introduce a saga, and to contain it, as the perfect sphere of an egg contains the finished creature, even its decline and death; and it held its listeners spellbound, staring toward the phantom players.

Before it faded, Galen turned to the cold logs in the fireplace and whispered—too fast—"*Habeamus calorem.* Let us have heat!" But he felt nothing but the keening music still, and he knew, even before he had completed the charm, that there would be no fire. Some few of the pilgrims had heard and turned questioningly toward him, so that he knew he must repeat the order or be discredited, and with that knowledge there came flickers of panic. Once more he concentrated on the inert logs, and this time when he spoke —"*Habeamus calorem!*"—it was with a voice augmented, a voice which contained the resonant power of Ulrich's voice as well; and the logs flamed, and the hall warmed, and when he turned, Ulrich himself, resplendent, stood beside him.

He stood as he had been when Galen had first come to Cragganmore—Ulrich erect, and virile, and unbowed by age. Ulrich! his beard afire and his eyes issuing their cool challenge to all the world. "Welcome," Ulrich said, raising his right arm, and instinctively the little group of pilgrims bowed deeply. Then he descended the steps and took each one by the hand, beginning with the two foremost—Valerian, and Greil. Valerian introduced the others: Malkin and Regulus, and Rixor, and Henery son of Henery, and Devlyn Major, and Stepanus, and Mavour, and Harald Wartooth, and Marcellus Minor, son of Marcellus of Ur, and Adamaeus Brittanae, and finally Xenophobius the muleteer, who glowered and mumbled even as he shook Ulrich's hand.

"Friends," Ulrich declared when he had greeted them all, "you are welcome at Cragganmore, and as for the business which brings you hither I guess at it, and at its import for myself. But of that later; for now, let us break the fast of the night, and warm ourselves, and forget the perils through which you have passed and those which are to come."

And so they did. Hodge returned chortling from the kitchen with a vast steaming tureen of gruel, and he brought bread and cheese as well, and they feasted. When they had finished, it was full day, and Ulrich signaled for his bowl to be removed and leaned back in his chair. Within a moment, silence had fallen around the table, and one by one the pilgrims turned expectantly to Valerian. The youth rose, opening the satchel which he had worn slung around his shoulder, and Galen was struck immediately by his graceful deportment, by the fineness of his features, by the casual loose drape of his tunic, and by the clarity of his voice.

"Lord Ulrich," Valerian said, "the reason why we have come can be plainly told. For longer than anyone can remember, Urland has been terrorized by a dragon, a dragon that has settled in a cave on a mountainside overlooking the town of Swanscombe."

"And why," Ulrich interrupted, his white beard jutting, "has it stayed?"

"It has stayed because . . . because of a . . . pact."

"Ahh," Ulrich replied. "Again I guess at it. I guess that it is the same *accommodation*—" he said the

word as if it left a bad taste "—that many villages
have made in years past, with the Monstrous."

"At every half year," Valerian continued, faltering
slightly, "at every equinox, spring and fall, we . . . that
is, the people of Urland offer the dragon a young
woman, whose name is drawn by lot."

Ulrich was nodding slowly. "A woman not more
than eighteen years of age, *pulchra et casta integraque
filla,* a pure and beautiful virgin, isn't that the wording
of the old code?"

Valerian nodded. "It's not followed perfectly, of
course. There are those who . . . who have tried to escape the lottery by marriage or other liaisons, and
those who have resorted to disguise and dissembling
and—" The youth blushed. "—other devices to escape. But the fact is that the dragon doesn't seem to
care whether the victim is a maiden or not. In the past
few years, there have been several married women
given to it. Even mothers."

"It has taken my daughter," said Greil.

"And mine," said Malkin.

"And my niece," said Henery.

"But, in return," Ulrich said, his gaze touching each
face in turn, spreading responsibility in equal glances,
"in return it leaves the village alone." One by one
they nodded ashamedly, none able to hold his gaze
except Valerian. "Ah yes." Ulrich sighed. "It is an old
familiar tale, although I have not heard it these many
years."

"There are those of us," Valerian continued softly,
and again Galen admired the youth's cool resolve,
"who agree that it is a shameful bargain. That it de-
grades us all. That it has continued long enough. That
it should end now."

"Already too late for some poor soul," said Malkin.
"You've forgotten today is the equinox."

Valerian hung his head, nodding. "We were de-
layed. Nevertheless, we shall not be too late for the
next, and we shall end the peril for good."

Ulrich was smiling. "Brave words," he said.

"With your help," Valerian said. "That is why we
are here, of course."

"And do you come with your king's blessing?"

The little group frowned and shuffled. Valerian spoke with bitterness. "No. Casiodorus does not know that we have come, or he would have sent his horsemen to bring us back. He does not believe, as we do, that there can be a power as great as the dragon's, or that it might be possible to destroy the beast. He speaks of balances, of compromises, trade-offs. For him the lives of two girls each year is little enough to pacify the beast."

Ulrich laughed. "And has anyone asked the dragon's opinion? Perhaps it's glutted."

"It's no laughing matter, sir."

"No, no, of course it isn't, but I tire of these rulers who make their own solutions, create their own problems, perpetuate themselves and their ilk. Your king and his lackeys sound like the type . . ."

Malkin protested querulously. "Casiodorus isn't a *bad* king, sir . . ."

"Just weak."

"Weak, yes, but he acts according to his lights, as they say. He does what he thinks best . . ."

Ulrich waved this all away with a weary hand. "Of course, of course. And according to tradition, I daresay. It's always easiest. But tell me, why do you come to me? I have never done battle with a dragon. I'm certainly no hero, like Beowulf or Sigurd, or any of the others. Why me?"

Again they shuffled uneasily, glancing hopefully at Ulrich, and Valerian said, "It's because . . . because you're the last."

"Nonsense!" The old man seemed shocked.

"No, sir. You are."

"What about Grom?"

"Dead. Doing battle with a great serpent in the Tarn Bayrenrich."

"Poor Grom! Well, Prospero then."

"Out of business. Abandoned his power once and for all. Vanished into the crowd."

"Ha! Doesn't surprise me. The Merridyd sisters, then."

Valerian again shook his head. "One dead and the

others entangled in equivocations and brews. We hear they've lost almost all their power for the Good, and have given themselves over to gold and wickedness."

"Yes, that is the temptation, the great danger for sorcerers. Well, what about Elexvir, or Hunneguendo, or Scam, or . . ."

Valerian shook his head firmly. "Dead. All dead. We've checked. No, you're the last. You are our last hope."

The old man sat quiet for a long minute, and the others waited anxiously for him to speak. At last he said, "I didn't know. The years pass, you lose touch . . . Perhaps in the Western Isles? Someone new?"

Valerian shrugged and shook his head.

Ulrich lowered himself slowly into the chair at the end of the table, looking more serious than Galen had ever seen him look. "Tell me about this dragon."

"Better," said Valerian, "I'll show you." He motioned to Xenophobius the muleteer, who came shuffling forward, frowning at Ulrich, and deposited a knapsack at Valerian's feet. "Relics." Valerian opened the sack and drew out first a handful of fire-blackened stones, ordinary enough except that they exuded such a foul stench that Ulrich's nose wrinkled.

For an instant Galen thought he saw a flicker of fear in the old man's eyes, but then Ulrich waved the stones away. "Dragon breath? You're going to tell me *that* is dragon breath? Pah! Nonsense! Mere fetid swamp gas. Take it away, Galen! Into the moat!"

Not wanting to soil his hands with the odor, Galen scooped up the pebbles in a scuttle from the fireplace, bore them to the window, and dropped them. For a long time after they had sunk, the moat's slime bubbled and seethed, and Galen watched it fascinated.

"And bone," Valerian was saying, back at the table. "A victim."

Ulrich peered at the cracked and fire-blackened part of a hand. He shrugged, unconvinced. "People die. They die in many ways. They *all* leave bones."

"And—" Valerian dug deep. "—these." He spread on the table three glistening translucent disks, each roughly triangular and about the size of his hand.

They bore the same odor, but their shimmering beauty made the stench seem less foul. They attracted everyone who gazed upon them; the pilgrims clustered around the table, Ulrich leaned close, and Galen, drawn from the window, felt a chill as palpable as fingers moving on his spine.

"Dragon scales," Ulrich said softly. "Unquestionably."

"I gathered them," Valerian said. "Near the mouth of the cave."

"A very old dragon. Very, very old." Ulrich was musing, running a finger over one of the surfaces. "Observe the striations, like ripples in the bottom of a lake. If you were to count them, you would know *how* old."

"Hundreds," said Greil.

"Many hundreds," said Malkin.

"When a dragon is this old," Ulrich went on softly, still touching the scale, "it knows pain, constant pain. After a time it comes to know only pain, to believe that it itself is pain, and that it exists only for the sake of the pain. There comes a point for such a dragon when, after years of yearning for an honorable adversary, it passes beyond that longing, grows more dependent on its young—yes, even for its food . . ." The old man's voice grew even softer, and at last he lapsed into a reverie all his own, a reverie so profound that he seemed at first not to hear Greil's whisper to his neighbor:

"*This* is a dragonslayer? Why, he talks as if he knew the thing, liked it! Does he not know that the beast is evil?"

"I know," Ulrich replied after a long pause, looking not at Greil but at the scales still. "I know that there *is* something called evil. And I know that there are imbalances to be . . . righted. And I believe that it is possible for a creature, like man, to be inhabited, or to be debased, or perverted." He shrugged. "Or simply to live too long, so that the world changes, and, in just being what you are, you come to seem evil. Oh yes, my friend." His stern wise eyes turned to Greil, who dropped his gaze. "I know that condition which the simple and the unfeeling call evil, but speaking for myself, I prefer to think of it as infinite sadness."

He fell silent, and for a time they all stood quietly, gazing at the relics on the table and particularly at the last one, which Valerian had brought forward while Ulrich was speaking. It was a red-gray chitinous hook, a foot long, serrated along the inside edge. "I don't know what this is," Valerian said.

"I know," Ulrich replied. "It is a dragon's claw."

There was a long silence. At last Valerian cleared his throat. "Will you help us, sir?"

"I have not decided."

"You are the only one who can."

"So you say."

Again Valerian coughed discreetly. "The old scrolls relate that dragons and sorcerers go back a long way together."

Ulrich fingered the great claw. "That is true," he said.

"In fact, according to some accounts it is said—forgive me, sir—but it is said that dragons are the creatures of sorcerers, the results of their unbridled lust for power, and of incantations gone awry."

Ulrich looked sharply at the youth. "So it has been alleged," he said.

"It is said further that all of those who accept the power of sorcery also accept responsibility for the alleviation of great suffering."

"Some do and some don't," Ulrich replied. He was still looking intently at Valerian.

"Please," said Greil softly, "you are our only hope." The others added their murmured requests.

Ulrich's hand still rested almost affectionately upon the claw. His gaze had drifted above their heads, and beyond—far beyond—the boundaries of Craggan-more and time. At last he inhaled deeply. "I shall have to think," he said. "Summon mead . . ." He had almost reached the stairway to his conjuring room when he turned back absentmindedly and pointed with the great claw. "Galen," he said, waving the thing, "you'd better come with me."

He began to labor up the stairs, using the right foot

to climb each step and drawing the left painfully up behind it. "Supplicants! Petitioners! My life has been filled with them. Always wanting something that they think they can't do for themselves."

"But this isn't a little request, is it, Ulrich? This is different, isn't it?"

The old man laughed abruptly. "Oh yes," he said, leaning against the door of the conjuring room, "this is indeed different!" Inside, he began to poke and point with the claw among great stacks of scrolls and folded parchments. "Now then, Galen, I shall need your help. Bring that one out. And that. And that one up there."

He soon had a mound of documents spread on the table. All were very old, so old that some began to crumble even as he unfolded them, becoming indistinguishable from the dust with which they were covered. On many, the ink was scarcely discernible, so faded had it become, or so blended with ancient water stains. Galen saw quickly, however, that all dealt with dragon lore. Here were various enormities, horned and smooth, two- and four-legged, tailed and tailless. "Each is different," Ulrich was saying, tracing details with a palsied finger. "All mortal, thank goodness, and most dead. The question is, which of them remains?"

Galen looked with horror at the drawings as Ulrich discarded them. He had never seen anything so loathsome. He could not imagine that nature had produced such creatures, or that the natural world, otherwise so sensibly ordered, had room to contain them. "Sir . . ."

The old man was lost deep in the drawings, his thumb gingerly running across the serrated edge of the claw.

"Ulrich?"

"Hm?"

"That boy, Valerian, said that . . ."

"Hm? Well, what?"

"Well, he said that sorcerers *created* dragons."

"He is not the first to say so," Ulrich replied, peering close at a very old and frail document.

"But *sorcerers,* Ulrich! Making monsters? That's not possible. Is it?"

"Bring me my glass," the old man said.

Galen stood still. There was a terrible emptiness in his stomach. "Tell me, Ulrich. It's not possible, is it? Not sorcerers."

Ulrich straightened very slowly, and his hand found Galen's shoulder, although he did not look at him. "It *is* possible," he said.

"But . . ."

"Earth and air, fire and water. Of all men, only the sorcerer controls the elements; of all creatures, only the dragon. Sorcerers are human. They have made mistakes. They will make others." He looked at Galen. "*You* will make others."

"But you, Ulrich. *You* would not do such a thing."

The old man sighed heavily, and his arm encircled Galen's shoulders. "I have made mistakes," he said. "Spells have gone awry. But more powerful magic than mine made dragons. The question is whether mine is sufficient to confront this dragon, perhaps the last."

"The last? Do you know it, Ulrich?"

"Nothing is certain, but I believe so. Hurry, now. Bring me my glass and we shall see. Ah, yes," he said, when Galen had found and brought the big magnifier, "do you see here? Do you see this? These claws with the undersides like teeth?" He tapped the drawing, which flaked at his touch. "Vermithrax! The Worm of Thrace! Who would have thought that it had found its way this far, across the seas and mountains? Vermithrax, the very worst of them! Ah, my boy." The old man's eyes gleamed. "What a history of death has washed across *that* claw."

"Will you go, sir? Can you kill it?"

"That I do not know. It is very old, but very dangerous. It has more than made up in cunning, stealth, and venom for whatever the years may have taken from it. Perhaps it is barely possible that I could master it. But I am not anxious to meet with Vermithrax. Indeed, I am not anxious. Yet . . ."

Galen felt his heart leap. He had a sudden inspiration; perhaps, after all, he would not need to travel far for his adventure. "Let *me* go," he said. "Let me do it!"

"You, my boy? Why, you alone would not last two minutes with this dragon. No. I must do it. I alone. Come, let us go below and tell them."

"You accept the challenge," said Greil as the Urlanders rose to greet them.

Ulrich regarded him. "I accept the responsibility," he said quietly. "It is a case of need: a sick land, a sick king, a hurt people. I will go." So saying, he summoned Hodge to join him, and placed his other arm around the old man's shoulders.

"We are ready when you are," Valerian said.

"So be it. We shall depart within this half hour." As the Urlanders rejoiced, he drew both Hodge and Galen very close to him. "And so we shall take an unexpected journey together, my old friends. We shall have one more adventure." He glanced brightly at each in turn.

Galen was about to respond, but at that moment there was a pounding on the oaken door of the hall, an imperious pounding that silenced the Urlanders' jubilation. Then immediately it came again, louder, and Galen heard curt voices and raucous laughter in the courtyard.

"Vandals!" exclaimed Hodge, lurching toward his rusted armor. "In broad daylight! I should have raised the bridge!"

"Shhh." Ulrich held him and shook him with gentle reproof. "Don't blame yourself, old friend. It is perhaps a blessing in disguise. Open the door."

Grudgingly, Hodge shuffled across the room and obeyed. The door echoed his complaints, creaking open. Silhouetted by the rising sun was a formidable figure. The man filled the doorway. He was clad in light armor, including helmet, and his chain mail with its leather underpadding accentuated his massive physique. He had to stoop and turn slightly to enter. He came in, one hand on the hilt of a great sword.

"Tyrian!" Valerian exclaimed.

The man was clad in charcoal black, except for

the crimson coils of a winged serpent emblazoned on his chest. Black too were his beard and his extraordinary, bushy eyebrows. A small silver dragon's head rode the crest of his helmet. He moved with feline grace. "I don't wish to intrude," he said, his smile fixed and watchful.

"You have intruded," Ulrich said.

"So it seems. In that case, permit me to introduce myself. I am Lord Tyrian, Centurion to His Majesty Casiodorus, King of Urland."

"And no friend of the maidens of Urland," Valerian said. The youth's face had lost its color, and he was trembling. "No friend to Urland! What do you want, Tyrian?"

"Nay, young master Valerian." Tyrian chuckled softly. "The question is more what do *you* want. Why have you come to this . . . this *magician?* What seek you?"

"That is none of your affair!"

"But indeed it is my affair. The peace of the realm is my affair, my responsibility." His brow darkened ominously. "I sense that this peace is threatened."

"Do you call it peace, what reigns in Urland now? A dragon in our midst?"

"A pacified dragon. Yes."

"Pacified by the sacrifices you *supervise,* the lotteries *you* arrange! Hateful!" Valerian's voice broke strangely.

"The lotteries in which you participate. *All of you!*" Tyrian flung his hand away from his sword hilt to include the entire group of Urlanders, and Galen glimpsed terrible fires at the heart of his sudden rage. "What hypocrites you are! What fools! To maintain for all these years a compromise that works, and then, now, to sneak off in the night to seek the aid of this old man." He dismissed Ulrich with a flick of his hand. "Whose weak magic will do nothing more than aggravate the dragon and loose the wrath of Vermithrax on all of Urland. Fools!"

"Perhaps," said Ulrich softly in the silence that followed. His voice was thin, like the call of a distant bird. Outside, horses stamped and whinnied, and warriors laughed among themselves. "But there are many kinds of power, and some that do not fade with age."

"Or perhaps even with death?" Tyrian asked, openly sneering now.

"Perhaps."

"In that case, let us put it to the test, for I see no power here, but a pitiful old man." He drew a dagger from the sheath at his hip.

With a hoarse cry, Hodge lunged toward the sword which he had stood in a corner, and Galen and Valerian both seized stout clubs of firewood. Instantly, other armed figures darkened the doorway at Tyrian's whistle; but what might have been a massacre never developed, for Ulrich had begun to laugh, and they were all frozen by his laughter, which was shrill and whistling, like a hawk's cry far away.

"Death?" he said. "Death is the *only* test you can devise? How you reveal your fears, my friend! Had you asked me to change your sword to gold, or to heal some illness of mind or body, or to relieve the suffering of the poor and luckless in your land, then I might have been afraid, and wavered, and so compromised the charm. But of death I have no fear at all. Strike away!"

"No, Ulrich!"

"Nor should you be afraid, Galen. For shame, after all I have taught you? *Ad lacunam igneam,* there I shall be always, where opposites are resolved. As for you, sir . . ." He turned again to Tyrian and moved slowly, arms spread as if to embrace him, through the few paces that separated them. "I will give you the test you wish, and the results you wish, although you yourself will not see them all, for you will long since have been lost in a labyrinth of your own contriving, deeper, and darker, and more convoluted than any dragon's lair. Strike. You cannot hurt me. Not ever. Strike!" And again he began to laugh softly. Galen was also smiling. After his initial alarm he understood that Ulrich had some wonderful trick prepared, something that would make a fool of this bully Tyrian. Perhaps the dagger would go limp. Perhaps it would glance off the invisible shield Ulrich had drawn around himself. Galen was amused too at Gringe, who launched himself squawking at Tyrian's inflamed face, causing the man to fling up a protective arm and brush the bird away.

But then, suddenly, Galen stopped laughing. In one lethal movement Tyrian had his dagger and plunged it into Ulrich's heart.

For a moment it seemed that some magic more powerful than the dagger had indeed prevailed, for Ulrich did not flinch or cry out, and it appeared that he might turn back to them and continue talking as calmly as if the violence had never occurred. But then his knees sagged with awful slowness, the hem of his garment touched the flagstones, and the old sorcerer crumpled silently to the floor. Tyrian's dagger pulled free, streaming blood.

"Old fool!" Tyrian nudged the body with his toe. "And *this*," he said, addressing the horrified Urlanders, "*this* was the man that you would send forth as your champion? A dottard who could not defend even himself against my steel? A senile dolt who was not afraid, even of death? Think what Vermithrax would have done to you had it been pricked by the trifling magic of this dabbler. Think! And admit that you were wrong! Admit it!"

The Urlanders shuffled in fear and dismay. Greil and Malkin nodded, as did Xenophobius the mule-teer. "Never wanted to come anyway," Xenophobius muttered.

Only Valerian shook his head, although he was very pale. "No. No. Some good will come of this."

"No good will come of it! Nothing will come of it! Now, get on your way home and be quick! My men and I have other business here in the village, and when we have finished, we shall overtake you. See to it that by then you are far down the road to Urland!"

He glowered at them all, then spun on his heel and left as abruptly as he had come. They were left with Ulrich's corpse and the rumbling of hoofbeats falling on the drawbridge, fading along the path from Cragganmore.

Galen had been too shocked to hear or see anything since the falling of Ulrich. He felt that the dagger had pierced *his* chest, stopped *his* heart. Dread like nothing he had known gripped him, stifling any outcry, stifling even his breath. He wanted to run to the old man, but his muscles would not obey him. When he did move, it was with the stiff, tottering walk of old age, a walk that was a pathetic mimicry of Ulrich's own, just as the laughter—Hodge's mad, incredulous laughter, which was all that he could hear as he approached the body—was also an echo of Ulrich's. Galen leaned over and touched Ulrich's head. "They've gone," he said in a very small voice, "You can get up now."

But the old man's body was already cool, and there was no doubt that he was quite dead. Blood seeped through the slash in his cloak and spread in a widening pool on the floor. His expression was ineffably calm, even amused. For a long time Galen knelt beside the body, his hand on the old man's head. When at last he heard someone speaking to him, he realized that he was sobbing uncontrollably, and shaking. Someone put a cloak around his shoulders.

"I'm sorry," Valerian was saying. "We should not have come." Only much later would Galen recall that there were tears in Valerian's eyes as well.

Galen shook his head. He could not speak.

"Could we help? I mean, there'll have to be a burial and . . ."

Again Galen shook his head. He had trouble concentrating on what Valerian was saying to him, for it was mixed and overlaid with Ulrich's voice, which was with him still: *"Nihil est mori.* It is nothing to die . . . It is a resolving again into the elements . . . the beginning of many journeys . . ."

"How could you have been so *wrong?"* Galen asked, gently shaking the corpse. "How could you not have *known!"* But there was no answer in the enigma of Ulrich's smile.

"Maybe he was just old," said Valerian, kneeling beside him. "Maybe he really was senile. Maybe he had lost his touch."

"Maybe," Galen agreed at last.

On the steps at the side of the hall Hodge was snorting with convulsive laughter.

"What's the *matter* with that old man?" Greil whispered.

"Nothing," Galen said, getting up and drying his eyes. "That's just the way he is. He sees humor in things other people don't think are funny at all." He leaned on the oak table. "I think, now, that you had better go. I'm sorry Ulrich couldn't help you. I . . . I know he wanted to . . . I know he would have tried, at least, if . . . if . . . Well, perhaps there will be someone in the Western Isles."

Valerian shrugged despondently. "I don't think we'll ever go to the Isles." The others were already filing out, nodding condolences to Galen, whispering commiseration. "We won't ever get away from Tyrian and Casiodorus again—not for a trip like this. No, Ulrich was our last chance."

"I'm sorry."

"I'm sorry, too," Valerian said. "Truly." He looked up from Ulrich's body to Galen and offered his hand. Galen took it. It was smaller than his own. Then Valerian was gone, following the dejected little band of Urlanders across the drawbridge and back westward along the forest path.

Galen, Hodge and Gringe were left alone with Ulrich's body. The raven was muttering among the rafters, making little keening sounds that could also have been laughter. Hodge shuffled across the room.

"What shall we do, Hodge?"

The old man blew noisily into the rag that served him as a handkerchief. "Ye gather yer things, young Galen. Hodge'll look after the old master's body."

"But *then* what shall we do?"

Hodge looked up in astonishment. *"Do?* Why, what sort of question is this from a sorcerer? We'll go west, to Urland, where there is a dragon to be slain. Gather your things, now!" The voice was Hodge's, the tone was Ulrich's. Galen moved like a waking sleepwalker toward the stairs.

CHAPTER THREE

The Blight

URLAND, FROM WHICH THE TRAVELERS HAD COME, lay far to the west, beyond a craggy chain of mountains, and beyond the River Ur. It was a wild land, bounded by its two great rivers, The Ur on the east and the Varn on the west. Its terrains were various. Northern Urland was heavily forested, the region of elk and elusive stalking cats. Only a few areas there were cleared, surrounding the agricultural villages of Turnratchit, Verymere and Nudd. To the south, the land had been twisted by primordial upheavals. Ancient mountains rose from the plains in erratic linkages of valleys and plateaus. In the extreme south, where the narrow Swanscombe River angled from east to west and joined the other rivers, the terrain was especially jagged and mountainous. Narrow paths wound through the valleys below the bleak dwellings of the hillmen; even the valleys were narrow and rocky, and only a very few spacious meadows were to be found. In one of these, nestled among the mountains on the bank of the Swanscombe River, lay Swanscombe itself, the principal village of southern Urland.

But it was not alone the ruggedness of the terrain that distinguished south Urland. Between the village of Swanscombe and the col of Morgenthorme, the ancestral royal residence to the north, lay a region swept by dark winds, shunned even by the most ravenous animals and the most desperate men. It was devoid of natural life, except for tough and stunted lichen sheltered in crevasses, scurrying lizards, and occasional drifting ravens. If the wind had not moaned sometimes among its boulders, it would have been utterly silent.

This was the Blight. It had not always been a place of devestation, although the time when it had been as green and flourishing as the rest of Urland was not within living memory. That was before the dragon. There were men in Swanscombe and other Urland villages who claimed they could recall hearing their grandfathers say that *their* grandfathers had witnessed the coming of the dragon and the blighting of the region around the caverns where it had settled, but no one knew with certainty how long the dragon had been there.

The dragon, Vermithrax, was the principal resident of Urland. Basking on the ledge at the mouth of its cave, or deep and somnolent in its earth, Vermithrax dominated all the lives of Urlanders. Even as the pilgrims approached Ulrich's tower at Cragganmore, many leagues distant, Vermithrax released a subterranean roar which shook the Blight and caused the residents of Swanscombe, without looking at each other, to move closer together.

Deep underground, Vermithrax itself did not move. Only its hide moved, twitching and flickering over its great length. Its immense yellow eyes stayed forever open, even in sleep, their horizontal pupils slits of the deepest black. Inside the creature, the fire had been merely dampened; it never died. Throughout the dragon's slumber, flames rose and fell in the labyrinthine recesses behind its nostrils, and it exhaled wisps of smoke. It lay with the tip of its tail secured between scaly gums.

Immediately below it lay a surface which glimmered constantly with weird and lambent flame. It was a lake of fire. It seemed impossible that creatures lived in that water, and yet shadowy figures did move beneath the surface, perhaps the hulks of real beasts, perhaps mere shadows of the dragon's imagining.

Vermithrax dreamed, and remembered.

In its memory, dead times lived again. In those lost dawns, the sky was dotted with the wings of dragons gliding from their crags to soar in hot new days. In Vermithrax's memory, their shrill cries bounded and rebounded among the cliffs until they fell in splinters of sound to the valley floors below.

In those days, there were only the green forests, the silvered rivers of the land, and the abundant deer herds shying like a single creature as the hunting shadows fell across them. Enough for all there was then; more than enough, and the sated dragons coupled at noon, shrieking their pleasure at the sun.

The change came so slowly that for a long time no dragon noticed. At first, it was the mere flickering of a few scattered fires in the night, no longer the dragon's own, occasional palls of smoke by day, and men scattering with other creatures back to their earths. But then the game diminished, got small and quick. Often it dodged away from the dragons' fire-gout and escaped. Feedless moons passed. And the men grew bold, crept sometimes toward the very heart of the labyrinths where dragonets were hatched, and stabbed between the thin scales on the underbelly. Pests! But there were more and more of them, and their earths spread and took root, always beside water. They conspired with other creatures, gathering them in, feeding, breeding, and slaughtering them. Sometimes they rode on them, and then the attacks grew swifter and more threatening. A few times dragons died screaming, and their killers sang.

Vermithrax could well recall the first attempt on its own life. A young and careless dragonet, it had been basking in the noonday sun on a high ledge. It had no reason to fear. Generations of dragons had freely used the ledge, drowsing with open eyes in the dragon manner. But suddenly Vermithrax had seen a foreign movement at the edge of its vision. A man's head had appeared above a large boulder and disappeared instantly. Vermithrax tensed. Its talons clenched in the granite. Again it caught a fleeting movement—the point of a weapon above the boulders—and a second later the man himself burst from his cover, screaming a fierce war cry. He was young. His eyes were wide with fear. Sweat streamed from him. His weapon was a lance that he had leveled at Vermithrax's neck, and behind which he had flung his full weight.

But the weapon never reached Vermithrax. As the man lunged, so did the dragon. It was too young to be capable of throwing a flame. Its claws and teeth were its only weapons. It sprang with a lean ferocity—straight up. Its wings gave one powerful sweep as it attacked, and a moment later the hero lay shuddering in death, pierced by Vermithrax's claws, lacerated by razor teeth.

After that, except at the equinoxes when it felt strangely compelled to seek out female prey, the dragon avoided mankind and all its works. It was years before it was assaulted again. On that second occasion, it had been drawn far from its normal hunting grounds to the southeast of Urland, and in the evening had by chance flown above a village. It veered away, but too late. There arced up to meet it a projectile that shrieked like a wild owl past its head and tore away a membranous portion of wing. Simultaneously, the heavy thud of wood on sinewed wood rose from the compound below. As it began to tumble, Vermithrax glimpsed in the midst of clustered men a rocking, squat implement such as it had never seen before, with a single vibrating arm upraised.

Terror followed. The dragon foresaw itself crumpled like others it had known who had lost their concentration, or suffered seizures, or had unknown accidents befall them. Its left wing would not function properly, and Vermithrax was almost on the ground before it recovered and, with an enormous effort, swooped out of the tumble, the torn edge of its wing flapping. High and safe again, it had circled angrily and watched the frenzied reloading of the machine. The scene was suffused with a crimson haze of rage, and when Vermithrax at last dipped its wings and began its swoop, torrents of flame leapt from its nostrils like twin rivers, and the roar sent frightened rooks flapping in the valley.

On the first pass, the dragon incinerated the cata-
pult crew; they flared with liquid sounds, engulfed in
a wash of fire. With a flick of its head, it caught two
more, smaller ones, as they ran screaming toward the
river—caught them but did not kill them, so that they
were still scrabbling beside the path and mewing piteously when the dragon descended again, this time not
fast, but with the aroused majesty of its species, the
gouts of flame sweeping in wide arcs as its snout
swung, consuming the tortured unfortunates beside the
path, consuming those others who were running shrieking from their huts, consuming the huts themselves in a
conflagration that spread through the cornfields and
which, despite the later rains, would smolder for days
amidst the forests. The destruction of the village was
complete; Vermithrax saw to that, for it made yet one
final pass through the smoke and mayhem, from east
to west this time with again that terrible swinging of
its head. Then it rose, aided by the heat from its own
fires, its anger spent. It rose, above the crests of the
hills and above the emptied valley, and in the dusk it
turned away from the sun. Its shadow, even with the
frayed wing, was magnificent on the countryside below.

Shortly after this incident, Vermithrax had come to
Urland, its belly empty, its spirit hot with hate and
loathing. The Blight then had been a high, craggy,
boulder-strewn bowl among the mountains above
Swanscombe, but Vermithrax had been attracted to it
by its spaciousness and by the honeycomb of passages
beneath it that led to the lake of fire. It had come low
across the shadow-bound village of Swanscombe with
a sound like the whirlwind, casually gouting its pain
and frustration. In seconds, with sweeping washes of
flame, it defoliated the area within a half-league radius
of the ledge on which it had perched; and, when no
immediate challenge arose, it had twisted about, lithe
as a monstrous snake, and vanished into the central
passageway of the labyrinth.

The dragon's arrival paralyzed the village. During
the first day no one was to be seen, and by evening the
complaints of cattle with swollen udders echoed in the

hills. After dusk on the first night, furtive villagers scampered along the laneways close to the walls, to gather in the village's central meetinghall, the Granary. In the meeting that ensued, several hot-eyed young heroes offered to do battle with the dragon for the preservation of the village, and at last one of them, Baeldaeg—a splendid young warrior, eighteen years old, and the best runner and wrestler in all of southern Urland—was chosen by lot. For the remainder of the night he girded himself for the coming conflict in the stoutest leather, the finest iron, the largest shield. His lance and sword he adorned with talismans given him that very night by hopeful maidens. At dawn he went forth to challenge the beast, with the bolder villagers following at a respectful distance.

Legend said he was magnificent. Legend said that he repeatedly challenged the dragon as he advanced on its lair over the still-smoldering uphill grade. His weapons glinted in the new sun. And, when his challenges seemed to bring no response from the beast, he resorted to taunts, filling the air with jibes and insults that reverberated among the cliffs and boulders. Legend said that when the dragon actually appeared, Baeldaeg was laughing scornfully.

Seconds later he died.

The dragon exploded screaming from the cave's mouth, a taut, taloned, leathery ton of reptilian horror, gouting its fury at the presumptuous thing directly in its path. The young hero had no chance even to brandish his sword. He was caught in a single dollop of fire and turned to charcoal on the spot.

The villagers scattered, scampering under boulders as the dragon swept low overhead, caught two of Swanscombe's houses in a sweep of flame, and set ablaze a tract of forest on the mountainside that burned for two days. Then it veered to the west. What else it set aflame in its rampage the villagers would not find out for weeks, until rumors and tales drifted in from the devastated areas; but late into the night, long after the dragon had returned to its earth in what they were even then beginning to call "the blighted land," they heard it roaring amidst the caverns.

That second night another meeting was held in the Granary. This time there were fewer volunteers to do battle, and at last it was decided that the names of all the men between seventeen and thirty-five would go into the pot for the lottery. The oldest woman drew. It was the name of a man just over thirty, Angenwit, father of two children. His wife screamed and fainted. Angenwit himself gazed comtemplatively at his name on the broken tile. He was no coward; in fact, he bore the scars of many a clash with Roman skirmishers and with brigands, and he was a skillful armorer. All night there was the sound of metal being fashioned in his shop, and when he emerged at sunrise to do battle he bore a stately shield, an elongated bowl sufficiently large for a man to lie beneath, cunningly interlaced with strips of beaten iron. It was said later that he hoped to throw himself beneath this shield until the dragon had passed over and then to stab upward into the soft underbelly of the creature, but no one could confirm that this was indeed his plan, for his wife had been in a swoon throughout the night, and he had walked alone to the Blight, leaving the village without a ceremony and refusing to speak to anyone on the way.

Once there, he issued a single, manly challenge to the beast, as befitted a Saxon warrior somber in his years, and he waited, his lance braced against his instep for the onslaught.

He did not have to wait long. The dragon had been restive throughout the night, stalking the corridors of the labyrinth and the shores of the lake of fire, and when dawn came it was quite near the entrance. It had heard the warrior even before he issued his challenge, and it responded at once. Again the agility of the creature awed and amazed those who had been bold enough to creep to the edge of the Blight. Two strides from the mouth of the cave it was airborne, plummeting toward Angenwit, the edge of one great wing torn and flapping. The onlookers scarcely had time to gasp before the dragon was upon the man. It disdained to use its fire. Instead, its talons dropped and closed, twisting the spear like a reed, splintering and bending the brave shield, and piercing and crushing the man in an instant—so fast that he had no time even to scream his fear or to call the name of his god. Another instant and he was no longer human; he was merely strands of skin and liquid that streamed briefly from the spread talons as the beast rose shrieking its triumph, and turned again to assault the village. This time, ten houses burned, and the Granary itself was damaged.

That night, the third since the dragon's coming, the king himself arrived from Morgenthorme. His horse, and those of his troop, had muffled hooves so that they made only the slightest echoing in the darkness on Swanscombe bridge. Only his presence could have drawn them to the Granary. In the light of the shaded torches he looked very old and tired, and he waited for perfect silence before he spoke.

"I know of your misfortune," he said. "I am here because your misfortune is also Urland's."

"Easy for you to say," muttered a man at the back. "You haven't lost a son!"

"I am here," the king replied with dignity and forebearance; "I tell you again that this evil has befallen me and my land as surely as it has befallen you!" He gazed at the man who had spoken, and he waited for a response, but none came. "I have consulted my scholars, and they have delved for two days among the scrolls at Morgenthorme. They have told me that there are three ways, and three ways only, to deal with the monster Vermithrax." A hubbub arose at the mention of this name, and he waited for it to die down. "Yes, it is Vermithrax itself that has come to afflict Urland and Swanscombe. The first of these ways is by physical attack—the hero's way. There is always the chance, of course, that this will succeed, but the cost of failure is high, as you well know." He gestured ruefully at the damaged roof of the Granary, through which they could see stars. "Enraged, this dragon will destroy indiscriminately, will wreak limitless havoc. It is, as you know, the most vengeful of dragons. Therefore, I urge you not to choose this course. Send no more heroes. Prevent those who travel from afar to test their mettle against this beast. Swanscombe and Urland will pay for their failure and fail they surely will. *This dragon is Vermithrax!*" The king paused, waiting for the advice to sink home.

"From the second way I would also dissuade you. Nevertheless, you should know of it, for the knowledge might one day prove useful. For that reason I have brought my foremost scholar, Giard, who, from long study, comprehends this course and will explain it."

With this, a very old man hobbled forward and began to speak with obvious pleasure, frequently rubbing his hands together, hands as creased and dry as the parchments among which he had spent his life. "I must tell you," he began with a respectful bow to the monarch, "that this is not so much a course of action as a possibility. But to understand what *might* be done —not now but at some future time when the circumstances converge—" He chuckled softly. "—you must know what is written in the oldest tomes of the origins of dragons. Is it true? you will ask me, and I shall answer, I know not; I know only what is written.

"It is written that dragons are not natural but result rather from the abuse of power, or from the careless use of power. It is written in the oldest scrolls, by one who claims to have heard it from another who saw it happen, that a sorcerer created dragons with a careless spell, and thereby loosed the great balefulness on the world; for, although they are androgynes, yet they breed. It is said further that all sorcerers share the guilt of that first one who erred, just as they share his charms, and that no honest sorcerer can therefore resist an appeal to confront a dragon. Our second option, therefore, is to search for a sorcerer."

At this there arose a restiveness and grumbling in the hall. "A *real* sorcerer? . . . Where would we find one of *those?* . . . Fakes and charlatans enough, but a *real sorcerer* . . ."

"I know. I know." Old Giard closed his eyes patiently and waved his pale hands. "They are rare, but nevertheless might still exist. Perhaps in the north. Perhaps in the Western Isles. . . . It is unlikely, but if you search, you may rid Urland of the pestilence by

that means." He was about to step down, but turned
back to his audience, raising a finger. "One further
thing. It is said also that there is a *stone* . . ." He
mused, remembering, his hand to his mouth, indifferent at first to the incredulous mutterings of the villagers. "No, no, not an ordinary stone, of course. In fact
not a stone at all—the old manuscripts refer to it as
res, a thing, but from the description. . . . Of course,
it is not all that certain that it exists, the two allusions
that I have found are so old, so vague . . ."

The crowd had grown restless, and the king's centurion bent forward and touched his elbow. "Hurry
up!"

The old man gathered his thoughts and concluded.
"It is called *res potentissimum,* the most powerful of
things, and it is said that it was made by that man
whose carelessness made dragons. It is said that, overcome by shame and guilt, he poured all the best of his
craft and gathered power into it, so that the whole of
the Old Sorcery is magically concentrated there . . ."
He stood silent, lost in contemplation.

"And?" the crowd asked.

"Where is it?"

"Does it exist?"

"How does *that* help?"

"But perhaps the very knowledge . . ." He shook
his head slowly, and raised his empty palms to the audience. He had no more to say. He stepped down
leaving the crowd disgruntled, so that, even after the
king stood again, it was several minutes before they
fell silent.

"There is, alas," the king said, speaking with difficulty and with frequent pauses, "little solace in these
scholarly pursuits. No, the third alternative is the only
one I can recommend to you, because it alone has a
chance of success. Tomorrow is the equinox. We
know that dragons are most active then, although we
do not know why. And . . . and we know, too, that
they are insatiably fond of the flesh of young women,
particularly maidens . . ."

The king was unable to finish his sentence, or to
continue looking at the hopeful, upraised faces before

him. But he did not need to finish. The significance of
his suggestion swiftly dawned on the villagers. In the
long silence that followed, when they found that they
could not meet each other's gazes, they knew the first
twistings of shared guilt, and they took the first steps
to enclose that guilt in ritual.

"I believe," the king said at last, "that there is no
other way."

Vermithrax slept that night on the ledge at the
mouth of its cave.

Just before dawn, it became aware of movement in
Swanscombe. At first it was so slight that the dragon
did not rouse itself, allowing it to play like a distant
insect on the edge of its vision. When at last Vermithrax's eyes focused, it saw that a small snake of
light had detached itself from the village and was
winding through the sparse woods and along the gul-
lies toward the cave. The dragon's head lifted; its
tail flicked. It watched the little serpentine line draw
closer. At the head was a group of horsemen on
mounts. Some of the horsemen were armed, some
were not. In their midst was a striking pair—a warrior all in black, and a female clothed in white. Behind the horsemen followed several knots of villagers,
each clustered about a torch. The dragon's gaze lin-
gered here and there as it passed down the line; but it
was to the white-gowned figure that its eye always was
drawn back.

When the procession reached the edge of the blackened area, it fanned out and stopped. Alone, the
horses of the black warrior and the white maiden
came forward, stepping gingerly among the ashes and
flinching under the man's prodding. Their whinnying
stirred the dragon's digestive juices, and it inched forward. A strand of saliva spilled between its jaws and
hissed into the granite. Spasms ran through the muscles of its wings; its legs quivered. It was on the verge
of slipping from the ledge, gliding the intervening half
league, and engulfing both man and woman in a wash
of flame. But it hesitated.

About half-way to the mouth of the cave, the
horses balked. The warrior dismounted and lifted the

white-gowned figure from her saddle. Vermithrax noticed for the first time that the woman's arms were bound behind her back. It watched with increasing interest as the warrior led her to a charred trunk and tied her firmly, facing the cave's mouth. Anticipating what would now occur, the dragon emitted a fiery breath that jetted at least fifty feet beyond its ledge. The black-clad horseman retreated slowly backwards, grinning the fixed and ghastly grin of frightened warriors. The woman swooned; her head fell forward on her breast, and long black hair shrouded all her features. The horses cantered clattering down the stony hillside.

With a gentleness almost tender, Vermithrax glided off the ledge and alighted on a knoll a few yards from the woman. Some fresh movement of the air, a sound like shredding silk, aroused the girl, and she raised her head and looked into the eyes of the dragon. She did not cry out—she was far beyond screaming or struggling against the rawhide thongs; besides, as she gazed into those unmoving eyes, wonder replaced her fear. She found herself staring through the corridors of centuries, down, down and back to the first pulses that were the start of time. It seemed that she herself was the sole end toward which all life had blindly surged. The grime and tears on her face, the blood congealing on her wrists and hands, the torn and besmirched smock she wore, all these ceased in the instant to have significance. She felt pure, radiantly beautiful, and wise beyond all comprehension. Incredibly, she smiled.

And Vermithrax, in a transport of admiration and baleful desire, opened its thin-skinned dragon lips, and sighed . . .

From their distance, the villagers saw a lolling tongue of flame, heard a sound like a great bird passing overhead in the night. In a little while they returned singly and in pairs to Swanscombe, and they did not speak, and they did not look into one another's eyes.

Later, when the sun had reached its zenith, the sated Vermithrax raised its head and uttered the long, sorrowful dragon cry of triumph and of loss, staring wide-eyed into the heart of the sun. Again and again it cried, but there came no answer except for echoes rebounding among the crags.

Much later—the legend did not say how long, it could have been a year or ten years after the first coming of Vermithrax to Swanscombe—the dragon mated. At sunrise when the sun was a mere bead on the eastern horizon, another dragon swept down the Swanscombe valley, and Vermithrax rose exultantly to meet it. Male-female, female-male, in that amorphous condition in which polarities are sensed merely, existing unformed for future convolutions of the species, they yearned toward each other in the pale clear air of morning, circling slowly, uttering high-pitched cries. When they met at last, cowled by the shifting curtains of the sun, not even the falcons which had accompanied them to that pitch, like lilting bridesmaids, were witnesses to the union, and the villagers in the valley far below saw nothing but the swirling sun itself. Certain it is that they mated; and it is probable that the decades of dragon gestation began for both.

Many years later, at the very hour when the Swanscombe pilgrims approached Ulrich's Cragganmore, Vermithrax lay deep within its earth beside the lake where weird flames played across the surface. For many hours the dragon had not moved. Only its hide moved, twitching and flickering over its great length. But then, imperceptibly at first, its lower regions began convulsive undulations that grew gradually quicker and sterner. Giving birth, Vermithrax saw amidst the visions of the burning lake the image of a bent old man gripping a boy by the shoulder. In the other hand, the old man held an object that the dragon could not discern before the vision faded into a conflagration which, to the dragon, was indistinguishable at that moment from its own agony. Into the cradling safety of its coils it produced three glistening and translucent eggs, cowled in a single membrane.

CHAPTER FOUR

The Pyre

SUNLIGHT AS PALPABLE AS WATER FLOODED ULRICH'S conjuring room. Galen entered, crossed to the window, and for a long time stood numbly there, letting the sun warm him, gazing out across the countryside. In the far distance to his right, across the river and beyond the tangled wood, rose a plume of dust that he knew was Tyrian's patrol making its way toward the village. Closer, on the road to the west, he caught glimpses of the doleful band of Urlanders as they retreated, appearing and disappearing among the trees.

Countless times during his childhood he had stood at this very spot in front of Ulrich's window and looked out over the green land that had seemed always full of purity and innocence. The meanders, the gently curving slopes, the canopies of great oaks touching the horizon, the occasional tended field and cluster of cottages with their lazy smoke—always before the serenity of these things had filled him with ingenuous peace. But now, although nothing in the landscape had changed, it was not the same for Galen, for he knew that in it lurked agents of madness, instruments of Evil.

His gaze was drawn away down to the moat by a rumbling on the drawbridge. Hodge emerged, wiping his eyes on his sleeve at one moment and chortling with some irrational merriment the next, leading a mule hitched to a tumbril cart on which, covered with

56

the purple silken cloak he had used for grand occasions, lay Ulrich's body. Galen watched as the old retainer led the mule down the path to the little lake of Cragganmore, maneuvered the tumbril so that the corpse could be lowered gently into a waiting boat, and rowed out to the islet where, according to Ulrich's wishes, a funeral pyre had stood waiting these many years.

Behind him, the birds mewed softly—the pigeons, the gyrfalcon, the heron—restless on their perches. One by one Galen released them, letting fall the tiny silver leg bands crafted years before by small folk gone forever. One by one they responded, lifting their legs experimentally and, finding themselves free, spreading their wings and rising silently into the room and through the window. Every day at this time, Ulrich had released them, and so they had soared through the noon and the afternoon to return at dusk, each in accordance with its own agreement with the magus. This time, however, each bird in its turn glided toward the lake of Cragganmore and circled, crying and spiraling ever higher above the corpse of Ulrich. The falcon went last; with one sweep of its great wings it flew through the window and glided across the tarn, and Galen could hear its plaintive, falling cry of farewell as the bird rode higher and higher, became a mere speck at the edge of the cloud, and vanished.

Sighing, Galen turned back into the room. There was nothing to hold him now. Into his knapsack, which he had brought to the conjuring room already packed with his few belongings, he gathered those potions whose use he knew—dried herbs for the curing of simple ailments; unguents and potions for the soothing of skin disorders, vialled substances whose combining produced explosive results—all of these he gathered with increasing misgivings, for he seemed to be weighing himself down. He could see himself becoming one of the odd, ragged old men who roamed the byways selling charms, curatives, and, for Christians, pieces of the True Cross, and he had almost decided to leave all charms and potions to rot in the ruins of Cragganmore, when he opened a drawer in the conjuring table itself, directly beneath the now-still liquid in the stone bowl.

There lay the amulet.

In the shock of Ulrich's death he had forgotten the stone, but now it lay before him, its center glowing like a small moon at the bottom of a sea. Its gold chain coiled around it, and it was this chain that, after a moment's reflection, Galen took. Gold! Now *there* was a good companion for a journey and the means by which many a man had preserved himself; Galen knew *that* much of the world. But what could he want with the stone itself? Whatever weird power it contained was not his to possess. Besides, it was extremely heavy for its size. He knew that from the one time he had held it, watching the strange vision in the bowl. No, he had enough. He shut the drawer and was turning to leave when he was halted by a high clear sound so like the falcon's cry that he thought at first the bird had returned. But the sound came from *inside* the room, not outside, and although it seemed to be in every corner at once, its source seemed to be the alcove where Ulrich had kept his clothes. Puzzled, Galen investigated. There, incredibly suspended amid the robes, hung the amulet! He hurried back to the conjuring table and pulled open the drawer. The stone was gone! Nor was it, he saw, any longer in the wardrobe alcove. Yet the high-pitched ringing continued, centered now on another table at one side of the room, a table covered with various vials and earthenware containers. Unerringly, Galen selected one of these and picked it up. The jug hummed and pulsed between his palms, and it was clear, to Galen's astonishment, that the amulet was *inside,* although the neck of the container was much smaller than the stone itself.

Gently he replaced the jug on the table. "All right," he said. "All right. I understand." The pot shattered. The amulet lay glowing dimly amid the earthen shards. He reached out and took it; at the touch of his fingers it moved of its own volition in his palm, and the singing ceased. It felt cool and wonderful. Holding it, Galen suddenly knew what he must do, and he knew how Ulrich had planned to help him, despite his incompetence—with the amulet. He would journey to Urland! And he would meet Vermithrax in combat there, and defeat the dragon.

Anticipating that victory, he extended his clenched fist toward the conjuring bowl. "I am Dragonslayer!"

At that the liquid convulsed. It boiled. In seconds it had generated a luminescent cloud of steam that swiftly formed into the image of a massive dragon, gouting pale fire. Galen's ears filled with its roar, and his nostrils with dragon-stench. Terrified, he shrank back against the wall of the conjuring room, aware that the amulet had begun to pulse against his palm. For an instant he feared that he might suffocate or be vaporized by the dragon's hot breath. But almost as swiftly as it had formed, the vision vanished, and Galen was left alone with the suddenly emptied bowl and with his racing heart, was left alone with the amulet, which had grown calm once more.

He swallowed hard. "Well," he said, "at least I'll *try*."

Still shaking, he discarded the gold chain, strung the amulet on a leather thong, and hung it around his neck. Then, with a last look around at the conjuring room where he had spent so many hours of his youth under Ulrich's patient tutelage, he left. He walked down the stone stairs, through the banquet hall where the old conjurer had died so foolishly, and out into the sun of the courtyard. He did not look back. He crossed the drawbridge and went down to the shore of the lake where Hodge was squatting, staring pensively at Ulrich's unlit funeral pyre on the little island. "Good, ye be here at last," the old man said, gesturing toward the island. "Start the fire."

"But I . . . I don't know if I can do it."

Hodge stared up at him, gaping incredulously. "Not *do* it! But of course you can do it! You're a conjuror!" And his faith seemed so complete and so simple that Galen could not face the prospect of disappointing him.

"Well," he said, "all right." He summoned his concentration and gestured; it was, after all, like the charm that he had used to light the candles that very morning after the Urlander delegation had arrived. *"Flammam habeamus,"* he said in a very small voice. Deep inside he felt the revolution that told him the charm was correct, had succeeded. They saw a small flame—so small that it seemed at first a mere reflection of sunlight on the water—flicker amidst the tinder in the center of the pyre. Slowly it spread until Ulrich's body was encircled in a ring of fire.

Galen and old Hodge sat on the bank together and watched.

The pyre burned the rest of the day. It burned with unearthly hues—pinks, and crimsons, and multicolored blues—at a sedate pace, as if Ulrich himself were controlling it, as if it fed on mixtures of gases from the air and the earth that no other fire had savored. The two watched silently, as the day waned and the sky grew darker, and the colors in the tarn deepened and grew ever richer, until it seemed that the fire on the islet and the fire in the lake were one.

"Saved my life, he did," Hodge said. He laughed his wheezy, coughing laugh, and his laughter seemed so incongruous to Galen that again he wondered whether old Hodge were entirely sane, or whether the tides of time and circumstance had gently eroded his reason. Could it be that in some unfathomable way the distinction between life and death had so blurred for him that pretending to maintain it struck him as profoundly absurd? "Before yer was born," he went on. "Long before." He chewed contemplatively on a grass stalk. The funeral pyre glowed but Ulrich's body did not seem to be contorted or disfigured by the advancing flames; it merely grew increasingly transparent. "Young fella like yerself I was. Come along from Cantware, thinking I knew my way, could get along on my own, didn't need no help from man nor beast. Out to see the world. Come along the road at dusk, just this time of day. Down the road there halfway to the village, four big fellas come up to me, lit into me. Laughin', they was. Cudgels. Broke both legs, both arms, did somethin' funny in my head." He laughed again. "Just sport it was to them, for I had nothin' to rob. They woulda killed me, yer know, yes, sir, they woulda. Kill me as easy as squash a bug and think no more of it than that. But Ulrich come along. Come by accident. Drove 'em off." Hodge chortled with delight, rubbing his arms and legs, remembering Ulrich's triumph and the pain through which he had witnessed it. "Drove 'em off with fireballs—Bam! Bam!—snappin' at their heels like big dogs all the way down the road and outa sight. Then he brung me here, to Cragganmore, *floated* me back somehow, for I felt no more pain than that, and nursed me to health with his own hands, for he had that skill, although he were a lad scarcely older than myself. When I was well he says to me, 'Hodge, yer can go on yer journey, now, and I'll give yer a little somethin' to protect yourself agin the bullies of which the woods is full.' But I says to him, 'Ulrich, I owe yer my life, and it will be spent in yer service from this time forth.'" The old man gazed into the reflections of the flames on the water. Dusk was falling. Ulrich's body had vanished. "And so it has been, lad," he said. "And so it will be."

"But, Hodge, how can you serve a dead man?"

He laughed. "By keepin' alive his memory. By doin' the good he would have done, along the way. And then there are other ways, there are other ways." Hodge nodded, smiling mysteriously.

After dusk the last of the flames died away, and the embers winked out, cooled, fell to ash. They rose and stretched. Galen shouldered his knapsack and turned toward the road before he realized that Hodge was not with him but was hobbling in the opposite direction down the slope to the water's edge, pushing the little rowboat out into the darkening lake. "One more little errand," he called. "Shan't be long." The boat vanished in the darkness, and in a moment Galen heard it grounding on the shore of the islet. "Ashes!" came Hodge's distant mumbling voice, clear over the water. "Maybe a bone or two to make sure." He said something further in Latin, laughing more.

"Come on, Hodge!" Galen called. "There are things to do!" He had absentmindedly been fingering the amulet, and now he beckoned unthinkingly with the hand in which it was clenched. Instantly the boat skidded up at his feet, bearing a startled Hodge sprawled in its bottom.

"Don't *do* that!"

"Sorry, sorry . . . I didn't . . ."

"Think, lad! A sorcerer ye may be, but all the more reason to *take care!* Ye can't do just what you want, ye know. Got to think of other people." Awkwardly, the old man regained his feet and clambered out of the boat, folding a bulging leather packet as he did so. "Ulrich always said, he always said, 'Hodge, if yer a sorcerer, ye cannot cause hurt to them that does not deserve it.' That's me, Master Galen, and my backside! It does not need the hurt!" Grumbling still, he stuffed the leather packet in his knapsack. "Only one thing left to do."

"Wh . . . What's that, Hodge?"

"Why, destroy Cragganmore, lad! D'ye want to leave it to become a place of thieves and vandals, when it has harbored such as Ulrich?"

"Well, no."

"Then end it, lad. Cast a charm upon it." He waited confidently.

Hesitantly, Galen extended the amulet, waited until the moment felt correct, and gave the order: "Cragganmore! *Silva te celet!*" He felt the amulet twist in his palm, and in the last of the light he could see that his command was being obeyed. Vines swarmed up the walls, covering the battlements with leafy tendrils. Some grew thick trunks, and very quickly, for centuries were compressed into those moments. The walls crumbled, were overgrown, became a tranquil, wooded mound of earth. The Cragganmore that Hodge and Galen knew had vanished utterly.

"Good," Hodge grunted, shouldering his knapsack. "Come on now, lad. It's a long journey, where we're goin'."

They walked for several minutes through the silent darkness.

"Hodge?"

"Yes."

"I'm sorry. When I told you to hurry up, when you were in the boat, I really wasn't thinking." Galen stared down at the luminescence of the stone in his palm. "It won't happen again."

"Everybody makes mistakes," Hodge muttered. "Yer young."

Again there was silence, except for their footfalls in the darkness.

"Hodge?"

"Um."

"You know, I really miss Gringe. I wish he were going with us."

Suddenly a white form swooped low above their heads from behind, and a singularly abrasive voice said, "Hodgepodge!"

"There yer are *again!*" Hodge yanked off his cap and swatted his knee with it. "I wish yer'd *think* man! Now look what we're stuck with! Damn saucy bird!"

"Sorry, sorry," said Galen. But actually he was smiling in the darkness—smiling both at the astonishing glowing object in his hand and at the white spot that was Gringe hovering just ahead, showing them the path through the tunnel of trees.

It was after midnight when they came upon the camp. They saw the fire from a distance, glowing through the trees beside a little brook, and they halted, consulting in whispers, fearing that the campsite might be that of robbers. It was Gringe who scouted and came back saying "Ur . . . Ur . . ." So they proceeded, and soon saw that although some of the Urlanders were asleep in their sheepskin robes— Galen recognized the bulky figures of Xenophobius and Harald Wartooth—most were still up despite the lateness of the hour, and arguing.

". . . for a funeral!" Greil exclaimed. "All this way, while at home there are seeds unplanted and calves to be born! All because *you* said the chances would be good."

"And they *were* good," Valerian replied. In the firelight, Galen thought he looked extremely tired and frail.

Greil spat. "A major necromancer! Ha! A chaff-witted dottard who could protect not even himself!"

"Sit, Greil," Malkin said wearily. "We've been over it enough. Leave him alone. We agreed when we set out. Now that nothing can be done, let's at least have peace."

Greil scuffed the turf with his heel. "I know. But every time I lie down, every time I look up at the heavens and see the tail of the Great Bear pointing east . . ." He suddenly put a hand to his face.

"It's the equinox for all of us, Greil," Mavour said.

"*You* haven't all lost a daughter."

"That's true."

"Still, we can be quiet and hope that the gods will help whoever's daughter perished tonight."

Galen and Hodge emerged from the forest and into the ring of firelight, the humus cushioning their steps. "Hello."

The Urlanders' camp suddenly broke into action at the strange voice. Men rolled away from the fire and into the bushes, fumbling for their weapons; in a moment someone stood behind Galen, ready to strike. Valerian, however, had seemed to recognize his voice and had stood up slowly, smiling, a hand shielding his eyes against the fire.

"Who are you?" Greil demanded. "What d'ye mean, creeping up on us?"

"Oh for heaven's sake, Greil, can't you see who it is?"

"Ha! Now I can. What do you want, youngster?"

"I want to help you."

"How can you help us?"

"I can . . . I can slay Vermithrax." For a moment the words hung, as if they had been written in fire against the blackness. No one was more surprised than Galen himself, for although they had issued from his mouth, in his voice, he had not really intended to say them, had not intended to commit himself. But neither had he expected the incredulous and bitter laughter of the Urlanders.

"*You can, can you?*" Greil spoke with such vehemence that a strand of spittle fell across his chin. "What makes you *think* you can?"

"Because I hold the key to Ulrich's Craft. I am his heir. I have inherited his . . . power."

Again the bitter laughter. "And what good is that? What good was that to the old man himself?"

"It's different! I have something he did not have when he died! I have the . . ." He had wanted to say amulet but could not; nor could he open the hand that contained the stone. He felt a sudden surge of terror, a prisoner within a body which suddenly was no longer his. It was like the dread a small animal must feel when the net falls. But then, as quickly as it had come, the feeling passed.

When Greil said, raising his dagger, "In that case, you won't mind submitting to the same little test," he felt almost serene, and had actually moved half a step toward the man, only distantly aware of Valerian's voice commanding: "There'll be no more of that, Greil! No more tests!"

"Will there not? And *why* not, you young snot-nose? Do you want to let him come bumbling into Urland? Enrage Vermithrax? Get us all killed? I say no! I say Tyrian has shown us the way! We have the tests here and now, and not when *our* lives depend on them." Greil glanced around the circle, and got grim nods of agreement.

"And I say," Valerian spoke quietly, "that there'll be no killing here, nor any attempt to kill."

Greil was beyond listening. His face contorted, he gripped the dagger with both hands and lunged at Galen. The blade never reached its destination. Moving with remarkable speed and agility, Valerian chopped a stick of firewood across Greil's wrist and, as the dagger went spinning and the big man doubled in agony, delivered a kick to his stomach that sent him collapsing backwards.

"Now come to your senses, all of you!" Valerian still had the club, although after a moment he tossed it into the fire. "What kind of way is this to treat friends who want to share our troubles and to help if possible. Offer food!"

Grudgingly at first, embarrassed, the Urlanders drew Hodge and Galen close to their fire and scraped

out the last of the evening's gruel. Soon even Greil
came over to them and, rubbing his wrist, apologized.
"It's a kind of madness," he said. "A kind of sickness.
We all have it in Urland. You'll see. It comes because
there's no way of fighting back."

Gradually the camp settled. The talk grew desul-
tory, and one by one, men drifted back to their
sleeping-robes, leaving only a yawning Henery on
watch a little distance from the fire. Surreptitiously
Galen tucked the amulet inside his shirt, drew his
sheepskin over himself, and fell asleep watching the
last of the embers. He had never in his life been so
tired, or so full of anticipation.

Hodge fell asleep chuckling, one hand on the
leather packet into which he had gathered the ashes
from the island crematorium.

Valerian was the last to go to bed and the last to
sleep. Frightening images, images of spreading wings,
rose out of the fire. Nor did they cease when
Valerian's eyes closed and sleep approached; indeed,
they grew more intense and more terrifying. As bad
as the awful waking dreams themselves was the
knowledge that for some unfortunate woman of Urland, these images had been, that very afternoon, no
mere nightmare but a terrible, final horror. Despite all
generous intentions, Valerian uttered a small prayer to
Weird, god of fate and labyrinthine circumstance, that
the victim may have come from one of the northern
villages of Urland, from Turnratchit, or Verymere,
or Nudd, and that she was not from Swanscombe, not
someone that Valerian knew and loved. And yet, even
as Valerian slipped into a troubled sleep, it was the
villagers of Swanscombe, sickened by shame and loss,
who sat beside their hearths that night.

CHAPTER FIVE

The Chosen

WHEN HER MOTHER ASKED HER, CRYING PITEOUSLY, whether she had had a happy life, Melissa Plowman could not reply. She supposed that she had been happy. Like all other girls in Swanscombe village, she had been allowed to play much more than she had been made to work, and she recalled a childhood wrapped in love and laughter. Even the labor of harvesting, or thatching, or milking, or tending to the bees, or gathering the eggs, or any of the various tasks around the homestead, even those were not onerous, for she had learned early the chants and songs and games and gossiping that helped work time to pass quickly. So she supposed, remembering all the fun, that she had been happy.

But she knew from travelers—who never tarried long in Urland—and from some of the hushed stories told by the fire, that children lived differently elsewhere. In not every village were the equinoxes greeted with such dread and passed with such mourning. In not every village did girls weep on their thirteenth birthday, or did fathers lie and pathetically attempt to forge and alter documents that clearly showed their daughters had come of age, or to bribe the dark-clad officials who kept the roles. In not every village were there twice as many boys as girls. And in not every village was one's whole childhood overshadowed by the passing of gigantic wings, wings whose approach brought such a hush of fear to the village that no one screamed, no one even breathed, and work and play ceased altogether. Although the presence in the hillside cave in the Blight was one that she had grown up with, accepted as a fact of life as inexorable as nightfall or moonrise, still she knew that her life could have been lived without it, had she been born elsewhere, and she knew she would have been happier then.

So, even while attempting to comfort her mother by saying that, yes, she had had a wonderful seventeen years, she understood completely that such things all were relative.

The question was more complex even than that; for, looking at the matter very calmly as she now did, alone in the sleeping loft, surprising even herself with her lack of fear, she recognized that there were pleasures, and that happiness contained the grains of sorrow which in turn—the world evolving ironically as it did—ultimately overwhelmed that which had engendered them.

The Lottery, for example.

She had hated and dreaded the Lottery for over four years—eight lotteries—with a fear that she shared with all the other women, a fear that was a stolid part of Urland womanhood, a fear that would begin to creep over her like a palpable, cold creature as the fated days drew near, until at last she felt as if her legs would not move, and she had to be half carried, walking stick-legged, to the Gathering where the lots were cast. And yet, she was not perverse but she had long since admitted to herself that within the terror was a delight, a delight that grew and grew during the swooning moments of the draw until, when the name on the lot was read, it burst into joy that found expression in a cry of the purest relief and ecstasy. Almost immediately, with thought and sympathy, the cry would be mingled with sorrow for the other creature, the friend, who would now die and die most horribly for the land. But the fact that the first reaction in the midst of that horror had been joy caused Melissa, an intelligent child, to think. The other girls must have felt very much the same—a fact that she quickly confirmed with friends when they talked as girls do, late into the night. She confirmed also that that surge of joy was the single most powerful emotion which any of her friends had ever felt; and, since that was the case, she wondered to herself —never asking, for the thought really was unspeakable: How much of the dragon-centered activity *was designed to provide that surge?* Could it be that the dragon, finally, was only a device? Could it be that on some profound level the residents of Urland, despite their protestations to the contrary, did not *really* wish to rid themselves of Vermithrax?

She did not know. It was a mystery. Certainly her mother's tears, and the tears of her friends, were real enough.

Certainly the distant creaking of the tumbril, which caused her father to wrap pathetically helpless arms about her, was real enough. She shuddered, but she remained extraordinarily calm; she had been calm ever since that morning . . .

Ever since she had shared with all the others of the town the great hush as King Casiodorus mounted the stone dais, as she had seen him do eight times before, and looked upon his subjects with a gaze of profound sorrow and pity. Old Horsrick, Chamberlain *Res Dracorum,* had mounted the dais with the king, as usual, and had raised his right arm so that the loose sleeve fell away from it down to the shoulder, and then slowly had lowered the bared arm into the bowl, closing his eyes as he did so. This time, however, had been different. Melissa had felt no purging swirl of relief as the name was read, for she knew even before Horsrick drew out the chosen shard and turned it over that the name was hers.

"Melissa Plowman!"

She had neither screamed nor fainted as others had done. The fear had drained away to be replaced by a pale relief that at last it was over, all the suspense and the waiting; the day for which she had been unconsciously trained since infancy had arrived. She stood very still, aware of being surrounded by the cries she knew so well, and she felt as if she had no body at all. Then, incredibly, she laughed. It was a thing no one ever did in the presence of the king, and that no one had ever done before at a Gathering; and although she would be forgiven under the circumstances, nevertheless those nearby joined her parents in striving to calm her and silence her. She would not be silenced, for in that instant she had glimpsed a profound absurdity, of which Weird himself was only a tiny part. . . .

There were hands touching her, guiding her, soothing, calming her. And at length, calm, she was taken home for her last hours, those hours she had always wondered about, so awful she thought they must have been for the other Chosen she had known—like being with guests who had overstayed their welcome, when there was nothing left to say. Of course, her mother wept uncontrollably and Melissa soothed her, but it seemed to her that the sorrow and frustration of her father were even more pitiful—the impotence of a strong man in the grip of powers beyond his comprehension, wandering along the household paths that he knew well, touching the tools that had grown from long use to the shape of his hands. He was a carpenter; he had made all the furnishings in their dwelling and in half the dwellings of the village. A tree he understood. Grains and grooves, dowels, bevels and tenons, all these he understood and fashioned with an honest craftsman's eyes and hands; but what was happening to his daughter he did not understand and had never understood. He roamed bewildered, groaning, and Melissa finally had to fetch him from the window of the workshop and draw him down on the settle beside her, so that they could sit for a time as they had done during the firelit evenings of her childhood. This time, however, she told the stories. She told all the amusing and wonderful stories that she could recall from her childhood. She spoke for over an hour, and several times they laughed together before they lapsed into silence and left each alone with private thoughts and memories, staring into the fire.

"Shall I . . . shall I fetch Brother Jacopus?" her father asked at last.

"Why?"

"Why, to bring the Christians' message. Perhaps if you believed, even now . . ."

"That death is not death? That it is possible to live forever? Do *you* believe that, Father?"

"Well, no, but there is a comfort in it."

"A childish comfort, to be sure. No, let us keep our dignity and let us call things by their names. It will be easier to do that. Leave the illusions to those who need them."

"I keep hoping," her mother said, "that the men— Valerian and Greil and Malkin and the others—will come back in time, and that they will have found the great necromancer, and that he will destroy the creature before . . . or that the Thing has died in its cave since the autumn equinox." Melissa did not reply. She had resigned herself so totally to the Giving that her resignation had almost become resolve, and she had been able to refuse the traditional, calming potion that the apothecary, Offa, had mixed for her. But her mother's mention of Valerian had sent her off on a reverie of her own. Valerian had been the one love of her life. She had known many boys, of course, and grown with them, romping and intimate, through the anarchic turbulence of childhood; but Valerian she grew to admire more than all the others. Speed, grace, and a watchful animal reserve had set Valerian apart. Together they had grown, shared hopes and fears, success and disappointment, and in all their adventures Valerian had been the leader. It was Valerian who proposed that they climb the great oak outside the wall of Morgenthorme, in order to catch a glimpse of the Princess Elspeth—who was never allowed to mix with the other children—playing with her white pony and her white rabbits in the garden. It was Valerian who proposed, although they were only nine at the time and forbidden by the *Codex Dracorum* from witnessing a Lottery, that they observe the ritual by hiding among the boulders in the hills. And it was Valerian who had led her, although she had been weak with terror, across the Blight and up the very slope that led to the mouth of the cave, charred by dragon's breath and acrid with the stink of dragon. Just as Valerian had promised, each of them had found what they had come for—a perfect dragon scale wedged amidst the rocks and washed and bleached clean by countless rains and suns. Valerian had whispered that these were magical and would give magic protection from Vermithrax, since each of them now controlled that much of the dragon itself; but when Melissa had proudly taken her scale home, her mother had screamed in terror, her father had blanched and drawn back, and together they had insisted that it be destroyed. They had thrown it into the fire but it had not burned; instead, it had fed the flames in a strange and baneful way, causing them to curve up and out from its edges in a hissing cauldron in which all had watched visions, horrible and fascinating, until the scale suddenly and without any warning had evanesced, and the unearthly radiance had vanished. Later, Melissa learned that Valerian's father, Simon, had taken Valerian's scale in his blacksmith's tongs and had hurled it as far as he could into the Swanscombe River that flowed beside the forge, and that it had exploded on contact with the water, like the substance she had once seen a one-armed traveling necromancer use, leaving a dome-topped cloud of spray and smoke. So both of the scales, treated violently, had responded in kind, although Melissa had thought it strange that, when she had actually held the object—like the wing of a giant fly, it was—she had sensed neither good nor evil emanating from it, but only profound antiquity. It was the same sensation she had felt once as a very small child when, while playing on the riverbank, she had kicked out a curiously shaped piece of stone which her father had told her had been made by people who had lived at the village site so long before, so long even before the Britons whom Melissa's Saxon forebears had driven away, that no one knew who they had been.

Valerian. Melissa smiled. Valerian had been so central in her life for so long, at once so important and so distant in Valerian's own curious way, and she had always felt so protected by Valerian's decisiveness and ebullient optimism, that she had grown to share her parents' assumption that their friendship would develop into marriage. She had assumed this, quite without reason and, she realized in retrospect, quite without any indications from Valerian. When she had discovered Valerian's secret, less than a year ago, by chance, swimming in the pool beneath the falls, she had been both horrified and fascinated. Gradually, with the passing months, she had learned to see the absurdity and the pathòs in the situation and she had grown up enough to laugh, for she had realized that despite all Valerian's bravado, it was she, Melissa, who had finally been the braver of the two. And yet, after everything, there had been between her and Valerian more than friendship, of that she was certain; and she would carry Valerian's secret to . . .

"There won't even be a grave!" her mother wailed suddenly. "There won't be a place to put flowers! There won't be . . . anything!"

"But there *will*," Melissa said quickly. "There *always* will be. I'll always be here. In everything. In the wind, and the water, and the flowers themselves. And . . . and in the children. Remember! Please!"

The creaking of the tumbril had been drawing closer; as Melissa finished speaking, it stopped outside the doorway. Melissa's father started up from his seat wide-eyed as if, now that the ominous sound had ceased, he heard it for the first time. A horse stamped and snorted beyond the door. Someone knocked gently. "Time," a voice said.

"Horsrick!" Plowman looked wildly around, as if for a weapon, but Melissa embraced first him then her mother. "It's all right," she said. "Don't come." She opened the door.

Horsrick, Chamberlain *Res Dracorum* of Urland, awaited her. He seemed at first glance a twin of Tyrian—the same black-dyed woolen jerkin, the same black-tanned leather doublet, studded helm, and greaves. On his breast flamed the same crimson dragon. The cut of his moustache and beard mimicked Tyrian's. But there was an essential difference between them—Horsrick was clearly a man whose heart was not in his work, at least this part of it. His demeanor, his posture, his gestures—all were apologetic. All said more plainly than any possible words, "I'm dreadfully sorry that we're both mixed up in this, that it has to be this way. I wish there were something I could do, but, you see, I'm a victim too."

"Step in, please," he said, indicating the little cart.

"I think I'd rather walk, Horsrick."

Concern spread on the man's face. "Oh, but you can't, Miss Melissa. It's never been done, you see. It's always been that the tumbril cart took the Chosen at her door, and left her only in the Blight—beg pardon, Melissa—and that her foot never touched ground between that place and this. It's in the laws and the *Codex Dracorum,* and neither you nor I can change it, don't you see?"

"All right." She stepped in and, when Horsrick came shuffling toward her, unwinding a strip of rawhide, held out her crossed wrists. "And I suppose I must be tied, too?"

"Oh yes, Miss. It's there plain as can be in the records and in the *Codex:* '. . . to be bound with rawhide three feet in length, as it was at the beginning, and wound three times in either direction, cruciform . . .'" He fumbled at the lacings. "Not too tight, is it?"

"Repent!" The reedy voice arose some distance behind her, and for the first time Melissa was aware of the silent crowd following. She had known, of course, that the villagers would come—they always did—but she simply had not noticed. "Repent your sins, Melissa, and be saved! It is not too late!" A fist rose up from the back, and Melissa glimpsed a sparse head of sandy hair.

"Be quiet, Jacopus!" Horsrick paused in his work and glowered at the man who had called out. "Get down. Scandalous!" he muttered to Melissa. "The way these Christians behave! Presumptuous! No respect for tradition and proper ritual, none at all! Well, there we are. Giddup, Nerf!"

Prodded, the old piebald mare jerked into motion, and the creaking of the tumbril recommenced. The procession moved forward with a single, long slough- ing sigh, like the breath from a dying creature. Here and there in the tail of people behind the cart there appeared brightly painted placards bearing dragon in- signia, and banners, and when the procession had reached the rise at the village's edge, a child's dragon- shaped kite struggled upwards. The whole affair had a festive atmosphere. Had it not been for the scraggly figure of Jacopus, who had detached himself from the rest of the crowd and was scampering along the hill- side, shouting something about setting a candle to the Devil, it would have seemed like the Celebration of the May. Someone had even woven a little garland of wildflowers for Melissa, and she wore it like a trailing crown.

The low road which they followed crossed Swans- combe bridge and wound northeastward about half a league to the edge of the Blight. As they approached the place from which people watched the Givings, Me- lissa saw that the king's party had preceded them. Un- like his father and his grandfather before him, Casiodorus always attended the Givings, although no one could tell what he thought or whether he knew anything about the Chosen. He was an aloof ruler, unlike his father, who had been fond of the village girls, and his grandfather, who had been fond both of the girls and the Swanscombe mead. A stark white and golden figure, Casiodorus stood with his retinue at the edge of the greensward, watching the procession approach. With him were his rather simpleminded new queen, Nevera, whom he had found among the hillfolk somewhere behind the mountains and who smilingly applauded everyone and everything—in fact, she was already applauding, Melissa could see— and the stunningly beautiful but rather absentminded Princess Elspeth, who would play with nothing except white animals. Also with the king were several re- tainers, advisers and functionaries, although not—to Melissa's relief for she hated the man—Tyrian. As the procession wound past the knoll on which the royal party stood, Casiodorus joined the rest in bowing deeply to her. Melissa was on the point of returning the bow from long habit when she was halted by Horsrick's whisper: "No, no, you must not, according to the ritual! The first Chosen did not bow, nor must you! It is written in the *Codex*: '. . . the Chosen is the queen of Uroborus, the Great and Perfect Worm, and raised above all earthly rulers; and the Chosen is the savior of her people, and honored over all . . .' "

"I forgot," Melissa said. She looked at the bowed king, his feebly applauding wife, and the trembling graybeards that surrounded him, and she was flooded with a sudden compassion. The irony of the situation amused her. Frivolously, smiling, she blew them a kiss from her bound hands, and was delighted to see that the gesture caused gasps and ripples of consternation among the crowd and the royal party. Would that, she wondered, become part of the ritual? Would another Horsrick, in another time, with another Chosen, stand at exactly this place and say, "It is written in the *Codex Dracorum Novus* that you must now blow across the palm of your left hand while I halt the tumbril . . ."?

Ahead lay the Blight.

It was a fan-shaped area perhaps a league wide, directly in front of the dragon's cave, and it was distinguished by its blackened rocks and its utter lack of life. The dragon breathed here. The dragon emerged onto the ledge in front of the opening and exhaled gouts of flame that rolled in liquid balls across the Blight, until they exhausted themselves and drained away amidst the pebbles. From the whole region arose a stench like scorched vomit. In the center stood a charred oaken stake.

At the edge of the Blight, where the lush green of the June foliage gave way to stunted and flame-scarred stumps and boulders, the procession stopped. Here occurred the last of the ceremonies, the Touching, when each of the villagers, crowding around the cart, brushed Melissa's garment, so that she would bear away with her into the Blight and into oblivion, all the six-month accumulations on their souls. The

Touching was most clearly an expression of their shared guilt, shame, and impotence, and most came forward with downcast eyes, either silent or muttering something incomprehensible. "You must touch their heads," Horsrick whispered hoarsely. "Forgive them!" So Melissa did this; and as she did, she began to feel that she had transcended herself and had magically joined all the others who, for longer than the memory of Swanscombe, had stood condemned in this spot and conducted these ceremonies.

Casiodorus looked on from the green knoll.

A bulging sphere in the west, the sun touched the horizon.

The earth trembled. A few pebbles shook loose from the hillside and bounded down in little metallic percussions. The crowd gasped and then exhaled in a low, grieving, and anticipatory moan. The horse shuddered.

"I'll walk from here," Melissa said.

Horsrick stiffened. "It's never been done. No, the Chamberlain and the cart must go with you as far as the post. That's the way it's *always* been. That's the way it's written!"

"I know, in the *Codex*. Well, let's get on with it, then." Melissa gripped the front of the cart and peered forward, across the Blight and up the hillside to the cave's mouth. She thought for a moment that she saw a whiff of smoke. She was far past fear, and had entered a state of euphoric curiosity and anticipation.

Horsrick tugged reluctantly at the bridle. "Come on, Nerf! Giddup, Nerf." Although the horse balked at first, it yielded and began to pick its way down the slope. The sun was now a half-circle on the edge of earth; the ground shook again, and this time there was an unmistakable jet of smoke from the opening. The old nag whinnied piteously and braced its front legs, but Horsrick hauled on the reins, and again it proceeded down the remainder of the slope and across the flat to the place where the charred post stood.

"Don't tie me," Melissa said. "Please." She was

staring mesmerized at the cave mouth, relying on Horsrick's arm to guide her out of the tumbril.

"Sorry, Miss, but I must, you know. *And* read the proclamation." Horsrick glanced nervously up the hillside while he fumbled with yet another length of rawhide and tied it loosely around the post. "You never know, if everything is not done exactly as it ought to be done, what the Thing will do." A rumble heavier than the others shook the earth and the horse skittered backwards. "Whoa! Hold on, there!" One foot on the reins, fumbling inside his jerkin, Horsrick found a creased parchment, drew it out, unfolded it, and began to read: "Now be it known throughout the kingdom that this woman, having lawfully been chosen by the lot of fortune and of destiny, shall hereby give up her life for the good of Urland . . ."

His voice, made into a thin wail by distance and by tension, scarcely reached the crowd at the edge of the green. For them, the figures of Horsrick and Melissa were reduced to insignificance by the enormity of the Blight, and by the fact that their perspective allowed them to see, as the last crescent of sun vanished, the emerging head of Vermithrax.

". . . and by this act shall be satisfied the Powers that dwell underground and all spirits that attend thereon. And in gratitude for this sacrifice, His Majesty has declared the family Plowman free of obligations, taxations, levies and imposts for a period of five years . . ."

Vermithrax's head rose above the ledge. The dragon did not look down at first; rather, it looked across the Blight and out to the distant hills whose tops were lit by the last of the sun, and to the horizon beyond. The great scaled head, like nothing else on earth, turned slowly as it searched that darkening line of horizon, searched for gliding shapes. Only when it had done this did it look down beneath the edge of the great bowl that lay before it, down over the little clusters of spectators to the horse, to the cringing figure of Horsrick gaping over the unrolled parchment, to the white-clad girl.

Whinnying piteously, the horse bolted and ran, the

tumbril bounding across the boulders behind it. And
Horsrick, despite his long experience with this dragon
and despite his commitment to proper ritual, raced
through the remainder of the proclamation: ". . . or-
dained and signed this day, etc., Casiodorus, in his
glory the monarch of the realm, etc., etc., his seal, his
mark, and duly read etc., etc., . . ." Then he turned
and fled to the verge of the Blight.

Melissa was alone. She stood quite still, her head
raised, meeting the glance of the dragon. She felt quite
bodiless; nothing hampered the immense curiosity that
had enveloped her.

But it was not Melissa that drew Vermithrax's first
attention; it was the horse. Poor, frenzied Nerf had
been halted in its flight by the jamming of the cart
between two immense boulders, and now it struggled
pathetically between hopelessly twisted shafts. For
several moments Vermithrax observed this struggle,
and then, very slowly, and with what in another time
and place might have been dignity, it drew itself to the
edge of the ledge and pushed off, plunging a hundred
feet before the great wings completed their unfolding
and the counterbalancing tail straightened; veering, it
began its glide toward the horse.

Urlanders would disagree on what happened next.
Some said later that the dragon passed only low
enough above the horse to absorb its scent, and would
have passed on, had not the maddened shrieking of
the creature drawn it back. Others claimed that it circled above the horse for several moments before finally dropping upon it like a gigantic hawk. Still
others insisted that the glide path never varied, but
led directly to the unfortunate animal, and that the
dollop of flame which ended the horse's life was a
mere extension of the creature which, a moment later,
fell upon the still-smoking corpse. However they may
have disagreed on the details, none of the witnesses
doubted that the old draft horse was incinerated and
consumed and that some time, therefore, passed before the dragon's attention turned to the motionless
woman. Dusk had fallen; some said that the dragon
took flight and glided, low, the half-league to the

woman. Others said that it ran, moving with uncanny
speed on its ill-adapted legs . . .

There was still enough light for Melissa to watch
the approach. From far away the dragon's eyes trans-
fixed her. She saw nothing else; whatever remained of
her will, her intelligence, and her individuality was
drawn relentlessly into the twin vortexes of those eyes,
and it seemed to her when she looked into them that
she was staring across the horizons of time itself, infinitely profound, and at the same time into equally unfathomable pools of pain and loss. She entered a
dimension utterly new and different. Simultaneously
she was all that she would never be—child and old
woman, mother and matriarch, queen and singing
peasant. Intensely she was all of these and none, nothing, vapor and dreams, wishes and yearnings as old as
blood. Never till that moment had she felt that she
was beautiful, had been so sure of her radiance; yet
she knew that, no matter what she was or might have
been, she would never satisfy the need she saw there,
a bottomless need. And when she spoke, it was for
both the dragon and herself, united then in an atmosphere their own, and bound forever: "Poor thing."

Vermithrax moved forward around its eyes.

"Poor thing," she said again.

And then a great, torn wing lifted in the last of the
light, and enfolded her.

CHAPTER SIX

The Forest Pool

VALERIAN HAD NOT SLEPT WELL. IN DREAMS, THE dragon moved. In dreams, with terrible clarity, a torn dragon wing had lifted above Melissa while Valerian stood paralyzed, powerless to help. The question that was always present, but present most insistently after the equinox, hung as if painted across the heavens: *Have I done this? Is this my fault?* In fact, swimming up into consciousness, Valerian realized that the words had actually been spoken, although no one else seemed to have heard. All were snoring in their robes.

Sweltering, Valerian rose and followed the river to a little upstream pool at the foot of a small rapid, and there, without ceremony, undressed and slipped into the cool and soothing water.

Beside the dead fire, Galen had also been dreaming. He had dreamed of Ulrich, and in his dream the old man was vibrantly alive, turning from the conjuring table with a question; yet, the voice that spoke that question was not Ulrich's but a much, much younger one: "Is this *my* fault?" Galen rose gently up and broke the surface of consciousness. He opened his eyes but did not move. Two feet in front of him was a praying mantis, stationary; its folded wings bedecked with dew. For a crazed second between dream and wakening, Galen thought it was the insect that had spoken. "No," he said very softly, laughing "It cer-

tainly isn't *your* fault." And he blew gently, causing the
iridescent wings to spread.

From behind came a sound: a movement, a sigh, a
rustle of clothes on sheepskin. Someone was getting up.
Galen lay still until the soft footfalls had receded, then
looked up to see Valerian's retreating back. "Hey," he
called softly, not wanting to waken anyone else, "wait
for me!" But Valerian was already out of earshot.
Galen pulled himself out of his robe, checked to see
that the amulet was still safely suspended around his
neck, and pulled on his boots. The forest was alive
with birds; to the west the mountaintops glistened. A
frog leaped into the river at his approach, and a sala-
mander on a mossy rock lifted the membrane of its eye
and stared blankly. "It's all right," Galen said. "I'm
not going to hurt *you*." He felt magnificent; he felt
pure, and powerful, and absolutely certain of what he
had to do. He felt—he hesitated to admit this even to
himself—but he felt *heroic*.

When he reached the pool, Valerian was already in
the water and stroking toward the sunlit center in a
steady crawl. "Hey!" Galen called, beginning to strip.
"Great!"

"What?" Valerian threshed around, momentarily
bewildered, then located him.

"I said that's a *great* idea!"

"Swimming? No! It's not! For one thing, the water's very cold. And for another thing there are . . .
there are . . . snakes. Yes, snakes!"

"Snakes?" Galen shrugged, pulling off his shirt and
trousers. "Snakes are all right. They don't bother you
if you don't bother them." Naked, gasping a little, for
the water was indeed very cold, he negotiated the slippery stones and plunged. Once in, he luxuriated. He
had always loved the water and, whenever the weather
and his studies with Ulrich had permitted, he had gone
swimming in the river below Cragganmore, sometimes
drifting and dreaming for a lazy mile in the currents
before coming to his senses and jogging back naked
along the river path. Now the crisp tingling of this
spring-fed stream matched and sharpened his mood
perfectly, causing him to whoop joyously, to slap the

surface, and then to execute a perfect duck-dive, feeling the surface slip inch by inch down his raised legs as he sank into the green and shadowy underworld.

He was aware that Valerian had shouted as he submerged and had begun to swim away from him, but he had not caught the words. And now, having reached the stony bottom about six feet down, he saw Valerian only as a distant, bubble-swathed white shape above him. With long and easy frog-kicks, Galen set in pursuit, the stone brushing his ribs and belly, the amulet beating a soft tattoo on his chest. He gained quickly, certain in the first moments that Valerian was no swimmer, and beginning to estimate the upward glide that would allow him to seize one of those flailing ankles. For a moment he enjoyed this chase; but as he drew closer he glimpsed something that disturbed him profoundly, something that he could not be fully certain of, in the shifting shadows and curtain of bubbles. What he believed he had seen spun him back into early childhood. Once he had opened a door unexpectedly on his older sister, Apulia, and discovered that there were differences of which he had known nothing, but of which he was part. Then later, again in water, when one day he had been borne farther from Cragganmore than he had ever ventured on the river currents, suddenly rounding a bend near to the bank, he had chanced upon four girls from the village and heard them laughing in the water at the same instant as he saw their clothes littering the bank . . . So now, in the seconds before he seized Valerian's ankle, he was overwhelmed by the same exhilarating sense of difference which spiraled through his stomach like a scaly tail, and was at once both a dread and a joy.

The next instant they had both surfaced and Valerian, sputtering, was paddling away from him. "Well," she said. "Now you know."

"Sorry!"

Her upflung hands broke the surface. "Why sorry? It's not your fault." She rolled over and began a leisurely crawl toward shore. Treading water, Galen watched fascinated as she drew herself out of the stream, wearing nothing but a glinting band of silver around her neck, and began to dress. After a moment he followed her; she waited on the bank. "So," she said, defiantly, hands on her hips. "What are you going to do?"

"Wha—what do you mean . . . do?"

"Well, are you going to tell?" Her wide-spaced eyes held him steadily and he could not look away. He noticed for the first time that they were green. She shrugged. "I don't mind if you do. As a matter of fact, it would be a relief. It's been a strain all this time, having to pretend, especially the last year or two, since . . ." She gestured toward her chest, tightly constrained inside the leather jerkin. ". . . Well, you know. I used to be able to *feel* like a boy but I can't anymore." She picked up a stick, switched the ground with it, and tossed it into the current. "So go ahead. Tell. If you don't, I probably will anyway."

"But . . . but why?"

"Why the disguise?" She laughed harshly and then caught herself. "Sorry. I forgot you're not from Urland and haven't grown up with a dragon and with the same stupid traditions."

"Girls," Galen said, punching his palm. "Of course! The Lottery!"

"Exactly. If you live in Urland, and if you have the misfortune to have been born a woman, and if you are over thirteen, then the law says, or Casiodorus says, or *tradition* says—" She glanced heavenward. "—that you must take part in the Lottery."

"No exceptions?"

She shook her head. "None. There are only three ways out: First, if you're so sick that you're obviously dying—and don't think that people *haven't* tried to get out by poisoning themselves; second, if you have a very rich father who can cross palms with gold and see to it that your name never goes on a lot; or, third, if you have poor parents who do something else, like—" She shrugged. "—like disguising you as a boy when you're born."

"But that's awful!"

Again she shrugged. "It's only awful because it's

new to you. When you've thought about it long enough it'll just become a fact. A fact of life."

"But . . . but it *twists* everything."

"Yes. That's what fear does when it's been around for a long time. It perverts everything and everyone. Believe me, I know. That's why I *hate* it." She pounded her knee. "That's why I organized this expedition."

"*You* organized . . ."

"Of course. Who did you think organized it—Greil? Malkin? Oh, I see. You're surprised because I'm a woman, not just because I'm young. Well, it shouldn't surprise you, that fact. After all, I've pretended to be a man all these years, and isn't that what men do, go around organizing things, keeping order, being efficient?"

Galen did not reply. He laced his boots.

"Sorry," she said, after a moment.

"What for?"

"For being rude. It's hard, you know, when you're afraid all the time. Sometimes you just . . . strike out."

"I know."

"How would you know? How could you know what it's like, twice a year, seeing another woman die?" She stood up suddenly. "Anyway, let's get back. We should be moving. Besides, you have news to tell."

Galen shook his head, also standing. "Not me."

"But . . ."

"Look, Valerian, I'm just a simple magician. I *have* something special, something that might help with the dragon. As a matter of fact, I'm pretty sure that it *will* help with the dragon; it's just something I have for a little while, something I can use. But after this is all over I'm going away. Maybe to the Western Isles. Maybe even farther." He waved his hands in a stay-off motion. "So I don't want to get involved. I don't care if you're a woman. I don't even want to *know*."

Valerian laughed abruptly, incredulously. "But you already *do* know. So what are you going to do about it?"

"Nothing. It's not my responsibility, it's *yours*. You've pretended that you're something you aren't, and nobody else can put it right. Don't ask *me* to do it. I'm just along to deal with the dragon. Maybe." They were both standing. Valerian stared at him for a long minute, and it seemed to Galen, looking into those odd, wide-spaced green eyes, that he had passed a test that had nothing to do with the fact that she was a woman, or whether he would tell. She was looking at him as if she had just discovered him, and as if he had pleased her. Then she turned, and in the mannish walk that she had perfected over the years, followed the path back toward their camp.

"No man, woman," said a reedy voice in a fir tree just above Galen's head.

"And don't *you* tell, either."

"Warn! Warn!" said Gringe, launching himself softly off the branch and gliding through the tunnel path. "Tee-*riam!*"

"What?"

"Hodge! Warn!"

"Hodge!" A dreadful vision had suddenly flickered with the sunlight on the rippling surface of the pool, and Galen had seen it clearly: There was Hodge, rising stiffly from his night's sleep, muttering to himself, reaching back into his robe and withdrawing very gently the pouch of ashes that he had brought from Ulrich's pyre; there he was, beginning to open it, to ensure the safety of its contents; and at the same moment, elevated slightly—Galen could not tell how far distant because the vision was dreamlike—there was Tyrian, a black radiance in the sun, notching a war arrow into his great yew longbow, drawing it with terrifying ease, and bringing it down as he sighted along the shaft, until . . .

"Hodge!" Stumbling and slipping on the mossy rocks, Galen broke into a full run along the path toward the camp. In a few moments he was there; for an instant as he burst into the clearing, he thought that he had no cause for alarm, that the vision in the water had been false. Everything seemed calm. Two or three men squatted at the fire, others were dressing, others just beginning to pull themselves from their sleeping robes, and Valerian stood in the center, near the fire.

Old Hodge, one hand raised in greeting, was beginning to move toward him across the clearing. Everything seemed to be in order—except that those in the clearing were frozen in their various postures, and the air was filled with the sudden whinnying of startled horses; except that on a knoll fifty yards behind the camp stood Tyrian, his bow a diagonal slash across his body and his right hand beside his ear; except that Hodge's arm was not raised in greeting, nor was he looking at Galen. He was looking in astonishment at a glistening arrowhead protruding three inches out of his chest.

"Hodge! No!"

He fell before Galen could reach him. At the same moment the camp broke into frenzied activity, a mêlée of shouting men and crying horses. Tyrian notched another arrow into his bowstring and, with a jerk of his head, signaled his men to do the same. His voice rang clearly above the tumult. "No nonsense there! All that's happened is that another fake sorcerer has failed to pass his test."

"But the old man wasn't . . ." Greil began, before Valerian's foot on his instep silenced him.

Gradually the uproar subsided, the horses calmed. Very slowly, as it became obvious that there would be no protest nor resistance from the cowed Urlanders. Tyrian lowered his bow and replaced the second arrow in his quiver. Then he and his men began to move forward, leading their horses the fifty yards toward the corpse.

Hodge was not yet dead. When Galen reached him, he was breathing through a froth of blood. With great difficulty, he raised himself on one elbow, fumbled inside his jacket, and pressed the leather pouch of ashes into Galen's hands. "Lake . . . of fire . . ." he said. "Don't . . . for . . . forget. You . . . Hodge . . . just mes . . . *messengers!*" This last word he uttered with a particular urgency, staring fixedly into Galen's eyes even as the life left him and his head slumped against Galen's supporting arm.

"No! Hodge! You can't die! Not you, too! You can't!" Desperately, gripping the amulet at his throat,

Galen ransacked his repertoire of charms. *"Excede mors! Reveni vita!"* But it was no use. Hodge had passed beyond the reach of any charm, and the amulet, in a warning that the impossible and unnatural was being asked of it, burned Galen's hand. He dropped it and gripped the pouch of ashes.

"Little treasure there? Let's have a look at it!" The shadows of Tyrian and his men fell across Galen and the corpse; their horses snorted. Galen lowered the old retainer to the ground and stood up, clutching the pouch to his chest. His face was wet with tears and he was trembling violently. He was so frightened and so furious that he choked when he tried to speak. "You'll get no . . . nothing from me! You're not a wa—warrior; you're a *killer!* You ki—kill old men and wo—women!"

Tyrian's hand dropped on the hilt of his great sword, and Galen was close enough to read the engraving on its hilt: *Cave! Tendrun sum!* I am Tendrun. Beware! "Yes," Tyrian said, his mouth unmoving, "and impertinent boys if need be, for I do what is necessary to keep the peace in Urland. The bag!"

Galen retreated, but only half a pace, for the point of a dagger had pierced the skin at the base of his skull and he felt a trickle of blood on his neck.

"Make no mistake," Tyrian warned. "Jerbul will kill you where you stand. He would like nothing better."

Guttural laughter sounded behind Galen, and he was enveloped by the stench of rotting teeth and rotting meat, palpable as fur.

"For the last time," Tyrian said. "The bag."

Eyes shut tight, Galen yielded, held the bag out, felt it taken.

"What's this—ashes? Bits of . . . bone?" Tyrian laughed harshly. "If *that's* what the old fellow was going to use on Vermithrax I *have* made a mistake. Why, that's what he'd *be*. Here you are, lad. Take the keepsake if you must."

"No kill him?"

"No, Jerbul. Not now. Back off, now! What is your

name?" There was a moment's pause, and then the tip of the polished yew bow probed under Galen's chin and lifted his head. "I'm speaking to *you,* boy."

"Galen."

"Well, Galen, since you seem bound for Urland with these citizens, let me tell you what they already know very well. In Urland, King Casiodorus's word is law, and I am the executor of that law. I do what I must to keep the peace, and to keep Vermithrax at peace." He indicated the corpse of Hodge. "Sometimes I am wrong. I thought I was killing a sorcerer, a man dangerous to Urland, but I have killed an old fool. But I *act,* and I am alive. It is those who would have opposed me and opposed my duty who are dead. Now listen well, young Galen." Again the tip of the bow hovered at the boy's throat inches from the amulet, and Galen felt, through his pain, and anger, an increased heat from the stone. It seemed to be responding to the red dragon emblem on Tyrian's chest. "When you enter Urland, you enter a land that has made its accommodations with its fate. We are realists. Occasionally we have troublemakers from outside who disrupt our arrangements, arguing from principle. Usually they are young, like yourself, and usually they do not . . . stay long. See that you are not one of them and you will be welcome enough; trouble the peace and you shall have me and my men to reckon with. Do you understand? *Do* you?" The bowtip probed upward.

"Yes."

"Good. I trust in that case that we shall not meet again." Still watching Galen, Tyrian mounted his horse, a magnificent black stallion gleaming with sweat. His men also mounted, and he gestured the way forward with his bow, saying nothing more. Jerbul was the last to mount and leave, and he looked back with distinct regret, not sheathing his dagger until he was well down the road.

Clustered around the body of Hodge, the Urlanders watched them go. "I'm sorry, lad," Greil said, laying a hand on Galen's shoulder. "The old man didn't have to die. It was just a stupid wilful action. It's the way Tyrian is. Such things happen all the time."

"Brutish," Malkin said.

"I hate him!" Valerian said with such vehemence that a strand of spittle fell across her chin. She wiped it off with a sleeve. "I hate him and his rotten little army, and the rotten king that pays him!"

"Shh, careful, lad," Malkin said softly, glancing fearfully around at the others. "Word might get back."

"I don't care! You all know that what I say is true. Casiodorus is no fit king to keep on traditions that make no more sense, and to let the land sicken and die. You *know* that, and you hate him too, as much as I, and silly Elspeth too! Do you think *her* name goes on those lots? Ha! Not bloody likely! I hate them all!" She spat and would have gone on had she not at that moment caught sight of Galen watching her. He was massaging his bloodied neck where Jerbul's knife point had pricked him, and the look she caught from the corner of his eye as he turned away said, *No, her name does not go on the lots, nor yours either!* She flushed and then, to cover her embarrassment, said gruffly, "Well, let's go to work. Thanks to Tyrian and his louts, we have a burial to do before we move on."

They dug a grave for Hodge on the slope of the grassy knoll above the camp, and wrapped him well in his old sheepskin robe. One eye they could not close; it remained fixed in death, staring, it seemed to Galen, directly at him wherever he moved and causing Hodge's last words to keep running through his mind: *Remember, the lake of fire . . .* Valerian drew a corner of the robe across his face, and the Urlanders lowered the body of the old man into the earth and covered it. Gringe watched silently from a dead elm on the hillside and he remained unmoving there after the little procession had taken to the road. Xenophobius the muleteer left last, casting dark glances at Galen's back, and muttering about strangers and ill luck. Long after the rumps of the mules had vanished, Gringe rose from his tree and, circling once over the new grave, glided toward the dark mountains which were the great barrier between Urland and the rest of the world.

Valerian and Galen had been walking some distance ahead of the others.

"Well," Valerian was saying as the raven caught up and passed over them, "looks as if you don't have anyone now."

Galen nodded. "I have a mother and father. At least, I think so. I haven't seen them for years. The fact is that I guess I was a nuisance to them and they sort of . . . well, *sold* me to Ulrich when I was just a kid. I don't remember them too well. They went away somewhere."

"*Sold* you! What did you do?"

Galen flushed and shrugged. "I don't know. It was a long time ago. They just wanted to get rid of me, you know. They always wanted to travel." He shrugged again, anxious to get this conversation away from himself. "How about you? Any folks?"

"Just a father. My mother died soon after I was born."

"Too bad. What's your father do?"

"He's a blacksmith. And a silversmith too. The best. See?" She opened her shirt at the throat to reveal the cunning band that Galen had glimpsed in the forest pool. Looking at it closely now, he gasped at its beauty. It was elaborately fashioned of several twisted cords of silver, each made of interwoven smaller strands, and fastened at the ends by small, silver reptilian heads, which strained toward each other at Valerian's throat but which remained separated by the width of a finger. "It's called a torque. My father says that neckpieces like this were worn by the warriors of the Old People, who were here long, long before even the Romans, and that sometimes they would go into battle wearing nothing else." She paused, and smiled. "My father solved the mystery of how to fasten them around the neck. He wouldn't let me watch while he placed this on me. He said that it will bring me luck. He said that if nothing else it would make stronger my disguise, because no woman was ever allowed to wear a torque. But he made *this* for me, too." She held out her right hand. Circling the little finger was an exquisite silver ring, a tiny, perfect copy of the torque. So fine were the strands of silver, and so intricately were they interwoven, that Galen could hardly trace their convolutions. He could not imagine how the blunt fingers of a blacksmith could have fashioned something so delicate. "And he made one exactly the same for my best friend, Melissa." Valerian laughed and shook her head. "You know, I think when he did that he had pretended for so long that he actually thought of me as a boy. He actually believed that I might marry Melissa, and he saw the rings as a kind of . . . a kind of betrothal."

"Does she wear her ring, too?"

"Always. Even after . . . well, never mind."

They walked for a while in silence. Gringe glided ahead through the forest, flitting from tree to tree like errant snow from the looming mountains ahead.

"Is that where your name comes from, too?"

"From the Old People?" She laughed. "No, Valerian is a wine. A Roman wine."

"What's wine?"

Again she laughed. "A drink. Like mead, only it's made from grapes."

Galen shrugged. He had never drunk mead, and he didn't have the slightest idea what grapes were.

"Well, anyway," Valerian went on, "the Romans loved wine, and they brought a lot of it here and stored it. I guess it gets better the older it is. They stored a lot of it in big jugs in caves where it was cool and dark. Some of them must have left in a hurry when the Saxons came, because the day I was born my father and some other men were in the hills, looking for lost sheep, and they came to the old Roman fortress behind Swanscombe. The oldest man with them could remember his grandfather telling how he had fought a battle there with Romans and Britons. Anyway, they went even farther—they could hear the sheep in the hills—and they came to a cave where the Romans had stored wine. Father said there were one hundred big jugs, and he said the wine was delicious. It had just gotten better and better all those years.

They took some back to the village then and more later, and before two years had passed they had drunk it all at feasts. But when he came back the first time, after discovering the wine, I had been born, and he and my mother drank my health in old, old Roman wine. He said it was the happiest day of his life."

They walked a long time in silence. Galen mused over the story the girl had just told him, and the insight it gave into the life of a family. Never, in all his life, had anyone wanted him just for himself. What he had been had apparently been so annoying to his parents that they had got rid of him as soon as possible, and Ulrich had always wanted to mold him into a sorcerer. "What's it like?" he asked.

"What? What's *what* like?"

"To have someone—your father—who wants to keep you just for what you are?"

"I don't know. I've never known anything else. I thought you were asking what it's like to pretend for all these years. That's awful. Terrifying."

"Terrifying?"

She nodded. "Because if you pretend to be something long enough, you actually become that thing. After a while it's no longer an act. You're *it!* And the fact is that I don't *want* to forget I'm a . . . a woman."

"So, what are you going to do when you get home?"

"I don't know yet, but I think probably I'll tell what I am—before the next Lottery—and make some sort of recompense." They trod several minutes in silence. The great mountains, closer now, loomed over them. "I wonder," she said, "if guilt and pretending always go together. Do you think they do?"

CHAPTER SEVEN

Swanscombe

SATED, VERMITHRAX LAY INERT. THE SUN GLEAMED
on its length, steaming away the last vestiges of earthy
damp and warming the bare and shredded places
where torn scales had not regenerated. The sun felt
wonderful, and Vermithrax released a lazy, fiery exhalation of contentment, which snaked thirty feet
among broken stones and briefly ignited nondescript
bits of matter. On the hillside at the edge of the
Blight, the two parties of spectators—villagers and
courtiers—had begun to leave silently. Vermithrax
watched with a baleful eye until the last figure had
vanished, making sure that no hero, glinting like ice
in his armor, was going to come forward and, posturing ridiculously, offer battle. It had happened two
or three times, many years before, that the basking
and replete Vermithrax had had to rouse itself to deal
with that sort of presumption, and had then gone on
to vent its wrath on the countryside at large, incinerating villages, crofts, and forests indiscriminately.
Now, however, it seemed that there was no longer
need for that sort of nonsense; there were no more
heroes.

When the ridge was clear of humans, Vermithrax
allowed its eyes to close contentedly. and for a
little while it dozed. It was quite alone. Nothing approached it save a few witless insects, drawn by the
scent of scraps, and a single dragonfly which rested

for a time on a nearby rock, contemplating the monster. The sun rose higher, got hotter, and the insect noises in the Blight grew more insistent.

Half a mile above, a gyrfalcon turned in lazy circles, also contemplating the dragon. It had witnessed the entire sacrificial scene—the arrival of the festive procession, the immolation of the horse, and the martyrdom of Melissa, and its rhythmic circlings had not changed. All of this bestial human activity was of little concern to the falcon, certainly of less concern than the cautious emergence of an otter's snout from its hole in a muddy bank of the Swanscombe River. The falcon circled and waited.

From that height it could see the entire southern end of Urland. Swanscombe village lay directly beneath. Immediately to the north was the Blight, its blackness relieved only by the shimmering pale green shape of the reposing Vermithrax, and farther to the northwest, hazy in the distance, stood the col of Morgenthorme, the fastness of Casiodorus, to which the royal procession was even now returning. Far to the north—the gyrfalcon knew this, for it had reconnoitered the previous day, although it could not now see them—were the northern Urland villages of Turnratchit, Verymere, and Nudd, each tucked into its surrounding hills. To the west, flowing northwestward to the distant sea, was the shallow Varn, the river that marked the western boundary of Urland, and to the east, beyond the dark lake that was part of the broad south-flowing River Ur, lay the mountains over which the falcon had passed the day before, after its release by Galen. On all its horizons, Urland faded gently through green hills and fields into mists so soft that it was impossible for even the falcon to tell where the land ended and the sky began. Ever since leaving Cragganmore the falcon had traveled westward, and it intended to continue in that direction the next day, or the next. For the moment it was concentrating completely on the cautiously emerging otter; yet there was something else, something undefinable, that urged it to stay in Urland, to stay for at least the summer.

The otter's head and shoulders were now exposed.

Twenty leagues to the east, Galen, Valerian, and the others were nearing the end of the last pass through the mountains. They had traveled swiftly since that morning, for they were very cold. In fact, several of the Urlanders wore their sleeping robes draped around their shoulders for extra warmth, so that they looked like shaggy, bulbous beasts. From the top of the pass, before clouds hid the sun, they were given a westward view of Urland which was almost the same as the falcon's, except that the Lake of Passages lay a mile ahead at their feet, and the beautiful green and undulating landscape that was Urland was laced with long shadows of the gathering clouds. Valerian strained to see the Blight, to point it out to Galen, but she was unable to do so, for it was indistinguishable from the shadows of the great clouds. They stopped only briefly; then, led by Xenophobius the muleteer, the most anxious of all to set foot once again on his native land, they began to descend the serpentine stretch of path toward the Lake of Passages.

The cool shadows of the clouds touched Vermithrax. The dragon groaned—a hollow reverberating sound among the boulders—and awakened. The dogged pain had returned with the vanishing of the sun, and with it a vague unease that the dragon could not at first identify. Yet it was familiar, a premonition, a foreboding. Scarcely moving its head, Vermithrax glanced around. No, there was no immediate threat, but threat there indeed was, approaching. Threat and fate. A deep part of the dragon, far beneath memories and decrepitude, exulted. Something beyond all ordinary senses, a sense of perfect, circular time, caused Vermithrax to stir, to raise its head, and to summon its dignity. It knew that it was being watched, that there must be no hint of weakness or decay. It began to move, wings spread and neck magnificently arched, back up the slope toward the opening of its lair. When it reached the ledge in front of the cave, it turned and looked once more out over the brooding valley of the Blight, and to the ridge of hills beyond. Then, because it knew instinctively that when the

challenge came it would come from the east, it looked
to the mountains far across the Lake of Passages. But
nothing moved in the milky distance; no unfamiliar
scent drifted on the breeze. As the first of the rain began, Vermithrax entered the cave and began to wind
its way through tortuous passageways down to the
lake where fire played, and where the three dragonets
hissed and postured and tested their prowess against
each other. Vermithrax found its way to the ledge
above the lake and settled there, simultaneously
soothed and troubled by the shapes moving in the
dark waters.

Far above, the falcon had hung patiently in the turbulences and crosswinds that heralded the coming
storm. It now decided its moment had come. The otter
had just emerged from its earth and was gliding warily
toward the river. With a graceful movement, the falcon tipped forward and folded its wings. Down it hurtled, implacable, guiding its plunge with infinitesimal
adjustments of its tail. Its talons entered the otter's
heart just as the first rain struck. Another instant and
it was airborne again with its dangling prey and, when
the thunderbolts rolled across the Blight, it was feeding comfortably among the crags, protected by a bee-
tling overhang like its own dark brow.

Galen and the returning Urlanders were in the middle of the Lake of Passages when the storm began.
They had hoped to get across ahead of it and so had
hurried the launching and rigging of their boat and
the unfurling of its linen lateen sail; but they were
only partway over when the aroused lake began to
roll, and the shifting winds, glancing off the mountains
behind and the cliffs at the north end of the lake,
swung the fragile sail wildly. With considerable difficulty in the lashing rain, they managed to lower the
sail and gather it inboard. Then they took to the oars,
holding the cumbersome vessel steady while the storm
raged and the reeling mules brayed out their fear. Violent, the storm was also short, and soon the wind
abated and the rain thinned. Through the shifting curtains, Galen glimpsed the far shore; stroking in time
to Malkin's commands, the oarsmen soon brought

them to it. Xenophobius was the first out and he immediately fell to his knees and kissed a large rock. "Urland."

"A bit extravagant, isn't it?" Malkin asked, heaving on the painter to steady the boat in the swell.

"You know what these hillmen are like," Greil said, coming to his aid. "All emotion."

"Well, it's my country, dragon or not!" Xenophobius exclaimed, glowering at Galen. "And I'm not leaving it any more! No more fool's errands!"

So they returned, and so Galen had his first sight of Urland. The storm passed as they turned inland, but the sky remained overcast and mists drifted through the drenched countryside. In two hours they came to a juncture in the road, a juncture presided over by a strange, ancient piece of Celtic statuary, so chalky and eroded that Galen could not tell whether it was a bird or a bat. Here they turned left. "Morgenthorme that way," Valerian said. "Swanscombe this way. Not much farther now. We should be there for supper." But Galen noticed that the pace had begun to quicken despite everyone's fatigue, and he at first attributed this fact to the nearness of home; then he saw that the Urlanders had gathered into small bunches and were whispering among themselves and that they had begun to descend into a region of, at first, sparse vegetation, and then, very soon, of no vegetation at all.

"What *is* this place?" he asked and then had to ask again, for Valerian appeared not to have heard him.

"It's the Blight," she said. "It's where . . . well, it's the lair of the dragon." Involuntarily she glanced up at the mist-shrouded hillside. "There's nothing to worry about; that is, not right now. We just have to keep moving. Come on!"

"Where?" Galen had stopped and was squinting up. The mists cleared briefly. "There? Is that it? That cave?"

Valerian nodded. She was walking backward and, although she also had glanced up quickly at the foreboding opening, she was looking now at Galen and gesturing urgently. "Come on. There's no point staying here. Really. I know you want to see . . . it, but it won't be there. It'll be asleep. It always sleeps after, . . . Galen, come on!"

But he was beyond hearing her. He had jogged off the path and begun to climb the hillside, slipping and stumbling in the loose scree, toward the cave's opening, half a league distant. Valerian was shouting after him: "Don't be a fool! You haven't seen what it can do!" He kept going. She stamped her foot, shook her fists, and called to the retreating Urlanders, whose pace had quickened even more: "Henery? Malkin?" They too were beyond hearing. She was alone on the road. She hesitated only a moment, stamping in fear and exasperation, and then she began to scramble after Galen.

Very quickly Galen learned what the dragon could do. The first evidence lay in the larger boulders, most of them split and ominously flattened on the side facing the cave, eroded or melted by unearthly heat. And then, a few rods farther, there was even more grisly evidence—bits of bone protruding here and there from among the crevasses. He was contemplating these when Valerian caught up with him. "Those are human," he said.

"Of *course* they're human! What do you think . . . we've been trying to tell you . . . this is where . . . the sacrifices are made!" She was bending over, laboring for breath after the uphill sprint. Like Galen's, her eyes were watering from the stench of dragon.

"There's a thigh bone, shoulder bone . . ."

"Galen, let's get out of here! Please!" But he had started up the slope again, undeterred by the smoldering bits of wood, charred bits of an oaken axle, and by two grotesquely twisted wheel-rims lying beside it. Valerian, however, now saw these for the first time and recognized them. "The tumbril cart!" And she recognized also, although she refused at first to believe the evidence of her eyes, the ring lying on a flat-topped rock close to the charred axle. She sank slowly to her knees and reached out for it. "Melissa," she said.

The ring was unmistakable. The mate was on her own finger, and she recalled, in a rush that brought tears, all the times of the ring. She remembered Melissa taking Valerian's hand in her own the first day the ring had been there, and saying very softly that it was almost too beautiful to wear; and Simon, Valerian's father, smiling in that way he had that was both pleasure and sadness, and the next week giving Valerian a second ring for her friend, identical, and Melissa crying when Valerian gave it to her on the equinox eve of their first Lottery and saying that it was for luck . . .

Melissa . . .

Valerian went no farther. Holding Melissa's ring, she watched dumbly as Galen toiled the last few feet to the dragon's lair. She was suddenly overwhelmed by the conviction that the world was mad and incapable of producing any curative sanity, and that Galen labored doggedly toward his death, as did everyone, and that there was nothing whatever that could be done to stop him.

Far below, from the greensward at the western edge of the Blight, Greil, Malkin, and others had paused. They had missed Valerian and Galen in the Blight, but had been too frightened to go back; there had been no volunteers. Now they watched while Galen, a tiny insect, climbed the last slope to the cave's mouth. They knew well what became of young adventurers who went too close to the earth of Vermithrax; sometimes they came back with dragon scales and sometimes they did not come back at all. They knew also that Vermithrax would probably not emerge so soon after the feast of the equinox, unless direly provoked, and they wondered, curious and watching, whether this young would-be hero, maybe sorcerer, intended to enter the dragon's cave in pursuit of it.

Galen had no such intention. But then, he had no real *intention* of climbing where he did in the first place. What had drawn him was no concise thought but rather an urge, a profound urge which seemed to center in the middle of his chest, right under the amulet. Indeed, twice as he climbed he touched his chest to ensure that the treasure was safe, and both times he felt—he was sure that this was so, despite his sweat

and the ardor of his curiosity—the emanation of unusual heat.

He slipped and fell several times. When he looked
at his hands he found that they and the rocks were
coated with a gelatinous slime, gleaming like mother-
of-pearl in the declining sun, and that it was from this
substance that arose the evil dragon odor. The stench
had grown stronger as he came closer to the cave.
Scattered amidst the scree were dozens of belly-scales
and, although Galen had no way of knowing this, unfamiliar as he was with the physiology of dragons, it
was from the holes left by the scales that the slimy
substance issued and would continue to issue until the
torn places crusted over. The suppurations left a
gleaming trail down through the caverns into the
bowels of the earth. With the substance ebbed Vermithrax's life, for although it was not blood, it nevertheless transported energies through that wracked
frame, and the semicomatose state into which the
dragon had sunk when it had returned to the depths
and the lake of fire was in part a sleep of enervation.

Galen knew none of this. He knew only that the
vomit odor as he approached the mouth of the cave
became overpowering, and that he had involuntarily
clenched his sleeve across his mouth and nostrils. He
was distantly aware that Valerian had dropped behind and that the other travelers had also paused—
but far below—and were watching the last stages of
his climb. Only Gringe, a clucking, disapproving presence, had stayed with him.

The last few yards up to the ledge were the most
difficult, for not only was the incline precipitous, but
any possible footholds were made treacherous by loose
and slippery rock. It was clear that no one had made
this climb for many, many years. Slowly and cautiously, by scraping away the scree as he proceeded
and finding small supporting ledges for his fingers and
toes, Galen ascended at last to the ledge at the cave's
very mouth. Unlike the area below, this ledge was
brushed clean of dirt and pebbles, polished by the
scuffling of leathery wings and scaled belly, and it
sloped gently down into the mouth of the cave. Pant-

ing after his climb, Galen for a moment was seized with vertigo, with a panicky fear that if he did not grasp the granite wall and shut his eyes, he would plummet into either the void behind him or the pit in front. In a moment, however, he had steadied himself, and when he opened his eyes he found that he was staring into a cavern which to his surprise was not completely dark; although he could not see how the light entered, there was, glimmering through other apertures in the porous rock, enough of it for him to see some distance down the abysmal corridor, past the spiky protuberances that stuck out like growths on a monster's gullet, to the place where the corridor turned. Yet, even at that point, it seemed to Galen that the eerie light did not diminish, although it subtly changed its nature, becoming warmer, and flickering. . . .

Nor was the tunnel silent. Once, as a child, Galen had wandered farther south from Cragganmore than he had ever gone, entranced by the magic of that time of spring when the songs of the blackbirds are richest among the marshes and when a green haze of swelling buds hangs in the forests. Enticed by this day, he had wandered away from both Cragganmore and the village and soon found himself deep among the hills, walking on ancient paths. He was neither lost nor frightened; rather, he was curious about one particular path that was so little used that it was almost completely overgrown. Pushing on, he soon arrived at what appeared to be a shallow depression among the hills, a place, perhaps, where a prehistoric river had eddied behind an ice dam ten thousand years before. In fact, this may have been what at first caused the depression, but as Galen drew close, he saw that its grassy slopes had been carved into rudimentary earthen seats, and that the center of the bowl had been slightly raised. Not until he had entered the circle and stood on this earthen podium did he understand that he had entered a theatre, a theatre so old that no one in the village any longer knew or cared what it had been. But Galen knew, for Ulrich had described to him how three hundred years before, the

Romans had built such places, and how on summer afternoons people had gathered in them and conspired to create another world, a world in which they dwelt for a little time, and from which they emerged larger in all ways, more heroic, more forgiving, more human.

A theatre! The boy had turned in awe, gazing up at seats that filled slowly with ghosts, now laughing, now listening with rapt attention, now weeping. As he turned, he grew aware of a whispering which was not the breeze, for no breeze stirred; nor was it an animal or another human, for there was no one and nothing else in that still place; it was the sound of his own sandals moving in the grass, wonderfully amplified. When he realized this, he laughed, and his laughter was perfectly returned to him from all around. He had raised his arms then, and when the theatre stilled, he had spoken one word—his own name. Instantly it returned, not distorted, but large and perfect, *GA-LEN*. In awe of the magic of that charmed spot he had not repeated it but had stood receiving spectral applause, applause that was not for him alone but also for his namesake, the great healer who had attended Marcus Aurelius himself and, perhaps, some who had traveled from Rome to civilize this wild land. Galen. He had never forgotten how his name had sounded in that tiny, perfect amphitheatre. . . .

So now, peering into the mouth of the dragon's cave, and again more curious than afraid, he detected sounds that he could not at first identify, although he thought them to be small sounds swollen unnaturally large—a flat droning that shifted suddenly and repeatedly in pitch, as if it had been turned sideways— an insect! But beneath that, far beneath that sound were others echoing up through the serpentine corridors with a blessed faintness—for they were terrible, like the shrieks of demented children and the howls of tortured beasts. It was in answer to these that Galen spoke another name, *Vermithrax!* He heard it swallowed by the corridor for a long moment, and then given back, still in a whisper but a whisper magnified to enormity: VERMMMMMITHRAXXXX. Instinctively he recoiled. Nothing followed the name but echoes and diminishing reverberations, and then the reverberations dwindled to whispers and the whispers, finally, to unintelligible rustlings.

Carefully, clutching the amulet, Galen turned and descended from the ledge. He had decided on a plan of attack, and for the first time he was frightened—frightened lest the task be beyond him. His heart thumped wildly. Skidding and slipping, he returned to where Valerian knelt, clasping something and frowning slightly, abstractedly, as if someone had just asked her directions and she did not know the way. Here he turned, and into his right hand he took the amulet, feeling it pulse like a living thing against his palm. With his raised fist he blotted from sight the entrance to the cave, and he addressed an enormous boulder posed just above the cave's mouth. Speaking with utter authority and confidence, certain even of the Latin, he said in a voice that was uncannily like Ulrich's, "Now, great stone, hear my command: *Tu saxum saxorum, in adversum monteur—operam da! Nunc te demitte in super latibulum inquinatum draconis!*"

The amulet shuddered in his hand, but did not burn him. In that swooning moment he felt that everything he was, and had been, and would ever be, was concentrated in the tiny stone and then released, and that he himself, pure force, hurtled toward the boulder. But when he opened his eyes he was still standing beside Valerian, who had risen to her feet, saying in an awestricken little voice, "It . . . it's *falling!*" Indeed, the huge boulder had tipped forward and, with a crash that shook the hillside and the valley, tumbled to the ledge in front of the cave, sealing the entrance completely. "You *did* it," Valerian shouted, gripping his arm, her grief forgotten.

Galen nodded slowly, openmouthed.

He had in fact done more than he intended, for the impact of that gigantic rock loosened others on the hillside above, and they in turn released others; before the dust of the first fall had settled, another had begun—more terrifying because it swiftly became an avalanche.

"Galen! Run! Come *on!*"

And run they did, in giant staggering, downhill strides until they reached the footpath along the valley floor. Even there they were pelted by ricocheting shards and pebbles. They had thrown themselves flat behind the boulders at the bottom, and they stayed there, coughing and choking, until the dust had settled. They were still there, still trembling with their arms around each other, when the Urlanders found them.

"You *do* have it," Greil said reverently. "You *do* have the Talent."

"Dangerous," said a reedy voice not far away. "Power like that! Could kill people!"

"Xenophobius, you fool," said Malkin, shaking violently, "can't you see what he's done? He's sealed the cave! He's killed Vermithrax!" And gaping in mingled awe and fear, he edged forward to touch the sleeve of Galen's cloak.

Xenophobius grunted, "Maybe," he said, but he too was shaken by the violence of the event. The others ignored him. The realization that the cave was shut fast and the dragon was imprisoned slowly dawned on them.

They crowded about Galen but, except for Malkin, no one touched him. A magical circle formed around him, a space that not even Valerian penetrated, and in the center of it Galen was led, triumphant and isolated, to Swanscombe.

Comfortably full of otter, the falcon had observed the whole incident from its ledge, and although it had recognized Galen and Gringe, it had only the most fleeting desire to glide down and greet them. Already other, primal urges had begun to assert themselves. Already it had begun to yearn for the freedom of the moors, and for another to share that freedom. Already, also, it had begun to sense that it would be best to be away from this place, and very soon. Replete though it was, the gyrfalcon longed to glide off the ledge, to rise inconspicuously on the first updraft, and to drift to the northwest, far away from Swanscombe and the Blight. It was restive to be gone; yet it stayed.

It stayed, shifting uneasily from foot to foot. There was something yet to be done. . . .

Almost exactly midway between the south-flowing Ur and the north-flowing Varn, Swanscombe village nestled on the south bank of Urland's smallest river. It had been built at a little rapid, to take advantage of the waterpower there, and a waterwheel worked a primitive mill that ground the village wheat to flour. Like that of all other buildings in Swanscombe, the roof of the mill was thatched, and its walls were mud and wattle. The village was not large, perhaps thirty-five residences in all, scattered around a central granary, but the adjoining fields and gardens were generously spaced and, with various outbuildings, Swanscombe covered perhaps twenty acres.

It was, and had always been, the heart of Urland. No one knew really why this was so. It was not merely because of its happy location—happy, that is, until the arrival of Vermithrax—or because it was situated on the main road through the south of the country. Over the years, Swanscombe had initiated many popular movements that had affected all of Urland, and had produced more than its share of leaders. In fact, in the century and a half before Casiodorus's taking power and his malignant pact with the dragon, the majority of Urland's leader-kings had come from Swanscombe. Even now, on all matters except those having to do with the pacification of the dragon, as Swanscombe decided, so decided the northern towns. And like it or not, the king often had little choice but to follow.

The travelers paused only very briefly on the little rise overlooking Swanscombe before starting down, their pace quickening as they descended, until at last young Henery actually burst into a run, jogging ahead, waving his arms, shouting. "Everybody! Everybody! Come on out! He did it! Galen did it! He killed Vermithrax! Vermithrax is dead!" But there came no response except for the squawks of angry chickens scampering out of his way and a sudden hoarse rousing of dogs from where they had been sleeping in sun-

Galen wakes Ulrich from trance

Galen, Valerian and Ulrich examining dragon scales

Tyrian prepares to stab Ulrich

On the road to Urland,
Galen performs tricks with Hodge's pack

First young maiden being led to her doom

The maiden is menaced by dragon's claw

King discovers Galen's source of power—the amulet

Galen at the mouth of the lair

Baby dragon nuzzles the dead princess

Galen looks up at dragon on Lake of Fire

Galen crouches on Lake of Fire

Galen stabs Vermithrax

warmed doorways. Some returned snorting in disgust to the village ahead of the troupe; others wriggled in ecstasy at rediscovered masters. But there were no humans to be seen in the street, and no response came to Valerian's call for her father at the doorway of the forge, Simonburgh, which sat a little apart from the village. Valerian came out shrugging and looking around anxiously.

It was Greil who silenced them with an upraised hand. "Shh! A voice," he said. "From the Granary."

There was indeed an insistent and querulous voice as if someone were complaining about damaged goods or a sterile sheep, a voice none of them at first recognized. Yet it drew them.

The Granary was the center of the village and the traditional place of sharing. Here the village meetings were held, informal ones as well as formal, for much of the village's business was accomplished incidentally while wheat was being flailed, corn and maize were being shucked, or grain was being stored. The Granary was an imposing half-timbered barn about two rods from the village well, with doors at both ends. It was roofed, like all other buildings in Swanscombe, with closely woven thatch. It was large enough to accommodate all the villagers, and here, indeed, they were all to be found, crowding out through the doorways at both ends, rapt by something happening in the center of the building.

"What is it? What's going on?" The travelers asked.

"Shh!" those on the edges replied. "He's going to do it *again*."

And at that moment the crowd parted to let out two drenched figures, a man and a woman, incongruously garbed in what appeared to be linen nightshirts. Their bare feet made small slapping sounds on the packed earth, and they left two watery trails. "Damn," the man was muttering, "damn, damn, damn! That water was *cold!*"

"Oh, stop complaining," his wife said. "It's a small enough thing to put up with to be saved, isn't it?"

"Saved from what, I'd like to know."

"Saved from monsters! Saved from dragons! Didn't you hear what . . ."

The rest of their conversation was lost to Galen and Valerian, for they had squeezed into the space left by the departing pair and found themselves inside the hall, able to distinguish the voice they had heard from outside. ". . . Saved from sins, born again, purified in spirit, into the fellowship of Jesus Christ, and so protected against all evil and all enormity, even that of Leviathan incarnate—the dragon on yon hillside!"

They could see the speaker also. He was a tall, scrawny man clad in a grimy brown cassock cinched with a rope at his waist. When he spoke of Vermithrax his thin arm probed upwards out of a looping sleeve. A tonsure of unkempt red hair circled his skull and was cut off square above his eyes, one of which turned outward. He seemed to have lost all but two of his teeth, and he was incredibly dirty, from the frayed and manure-caked hem of his garment to his dusty neck.

"Jacopus!" Valerian whispered. No one paid any attention. They were all intent on the priest, who was summoning another convert to the baptismal tub. This was a plump and warty woman of indeterminate age.

"Are you sure it doesn't hurt?" she asked.

"Hurt? Hurt?" Jacopus cried incredulously. "The balm of our Lord? How can you speak of hurt? Think on the torments of Hell!"

"Still, it can't be good for a body to get wet like that. Not all over!"

"It's once in a lifetime, woman. Think of your soul!"

"Well, have you done it yourself?"

"Of course. Three years ago, before I became a priest of the Church."

"Look out, Ingrid! Look what it did to him!" said a heckler near the back, and a ripple of nervous laughter ran through the crowd, laughter silenced by a baleful but curiously amused glance from Jacopus's walled eye. *Laugh!* the eye said. *I feed on laughter!*

"Well, all right." Eyes tight shut, the woman stepped into the tub and Jacopus began the sacrament.

"Jacopus," Valerian whispered again. "He came here two weeks ago from the Western Isles, talking about Palladius, and St. Patrick, and Columba, and a lot of other Christians that nobody had ever heard of. Odd duck, isn't he? Funny thing is, he's been making converts ever since, one or two at a time. But he's never managed to bring the whole village together before. Not like this."

Jacopus had meanwhile completed the baptism of Ingrid, and had raised his arms for silence, his glance darting around the Granary. The audience fell silent, and he savored the silence before he began to speak. "You have a monster," he said, and his strange roaming glance isolated each listener and spoke to him or to her alone. "A monster that you think of as a dragon, and with which you have come to certain unspeakable *accommodations*. To it you sacrifice young women. But I am come to tell you that it is the heavy darkness of superstition that has obscured your vision and your comprehension, and that it is no dragon that you have in your presence, for it is well known to the scholars of the Church that there is no such creature nor ever has been, save only in the sickened imaginations of the sinful. This that you call a dragon is in fact Leviathan himself, the first creature of the depths and of godlessness. Further, I am come to save you from your superstition and from your fear, for I shall exorcise this Thing, this Devil from your midst through the power of the Holy Ghost, as it has been given me to do." He again glanced abstractedly around at the assembly. "This is my mission!"

"Too late," said Galen.

"What? What? Who spoke back there?"

"I did." Galen waved an arm above the thronged heads.

"You want to be baptized?" Jacopus's eye blazed. "Come forward, my son!"

"No! No, not that at all. I just wanted to tell you that the job's done. The dragon's finished. Locked up. Dead."

At this, a great commotion arose in the Granary,

and to Galen's surprise its tone was more aggrieved and alarmed than jubilant.

"Who *are* you? What sort of news is this? Come forward, and speak!" Simon the blacksmith, Valerian's father, had stepped into the cleared circle, and Jacopus gave way before him. Simon was a huge redheaded man with a broad forehead, a turbulent red beard, and wide-spaced intelligent eyes. Galen would have known from his proud bearing and from a wry and knowing expression around his mouth that he was Valerian's father, even if he had not smiled broadly when he saw Valerian.

A way opened, and Galen went forward and entered the circle. Around him the Swanscombe villagers pressed forward and a hush fell. In the silence, he was aware of the bawling of a distant sheep. The touch of the amulet upon his chest comforted him. In all his life he had never felt so assured. "My name is Galen. I am the apprentice of the Magister Ulrich, the great sorcerer, whom your delegation was sent to seek."

"We had no delegation," a strong voice said.

"We sent *no one*," said another.

"They went on their own . . . no authority."

Galen raised his arms for silence. "All right. No matter. The fact is that Ulrich was slain—murdered —by your official, Tyrian . . ."

". . . strong words . . ."

". . . best be careful, lad . . ."

"Murdered by Tyrian. I have inherited all the remnants of his power, and I have used this power to destroy the dragon, Vermithrax!"

"Heresy," Jacopus shrieked, hopping forward like an immense praying mantis. "Hubris! Impiety! Blasphemy! With *what* have you destroyed the dragon? With your chants? With your charms and incantations? With your superstitious mumbo jumbo? Nonsense! There is only one Power to equal that of Vermithrax, and I, Jacopus, am Its instrument!" So saying, he seized the formidable wooden cross that swung at the front of his cassock and raised it toward Galen as if he confronted the Antichrist himself and would bludgeon him to death. His expostulations had left froth on his lips.

"Easy. Easy," Simon said.

"Answer!" Jacopus again brandished the cross, and began to move threateningly toward Galen. "With *what* do you claim to have destroyed the dragon?"

"With this," Galen said, raising his hand. *"Nihil supra mysterium!"* He gestured briskly toward Jacopus's toes and a lightning ball the size of a man's head cracked there and spun long enough for all in the Granary to see it clearly and to smell its sulphurous odor. The effect was galvanizing. The crowd drew its breath in a low, whispering moan, and Jacopus reeled back, his threatening stance suddenly protective.

Galen was as surprised as anyone. He had not intended to this effect; he had not, in fact, intended anything. He had simply been annoyed by Jacopus's gibes and challenge, and had reacted instinctively, in one of those swelling moments when he was certain that there was in him, that there *surrounded* him, a power infinitely larger than himself, larger even than the amulet secreted within his jerkin. It was a power in which he sensed the presence of generation upon generation, layer upon layer of time, like the striated riverbanks he had often wonderingly examined as a child. He had felt this power, knew instinctively that it was correct and good, and would respond to his invocation. In all his few years, he had never felt more on the side of life than he did when summoning this lightning ball.

"The Old Magic!" shrieked Jacopus. "A heretic, an unbeliever, a wielder of the black arts!"

Angry now, Galen caused a second lightning ball to leap around the priest's ankles, sizzling and stinging like a glob of water on a hot skillet, until Jacopus flung up pleading hands. "I have told you that my power comes from Ulrich, Magister Ipissimus, murdered by Tyrian. I have used that power today against the dragon. If you do not believe me, then send a delegation. Take Jacopus and go to the Blight, and you will see that there is a rock at the mouth of Vermithrax's cave, and no sign of life behind it."

"Believe him," Malkin said solemnly, from near the back.

"It's true," Greil said.

"I saw it with my own eyes," said Henery, pointing a spindly finger as he relived his experience. "He was a bird! A white bird! And he soared from the valley to the ledge before the cave, and brought down the boulder, and soared back to us where we stood on the edge of the greensward! And at the same time there was a sound like the heralds make on Casiodorus's court days and . . ."

"Enough!" Malkin whispered hoarsely, elbowing him.

"It's dead," Galen said. "Truly. Go have a look."

"All right, son," said Simon after a moment. "I think we will."

Several of the assembly quickly organized themselves, and in the setting sun a small and solemn procession wound out along the serpentine road from Swanscombe toward the Blight. At dusk they arrived at the edge where, despite the deepening shadows, they could clearly see the blocked entrance to the cave. They stood very quietly for a long time. At last Simon said, "Can it really be? Is this possible?"

The others did not reply but stood in awe.

And then there arose from the throat of one of the younger men, a lad betrothed to a young woman who had so far escaped the fate of the Lottery, a cry so eerie and so jubilant that none had heard anything like it before. It was a keen and wailing cry, half joy and half lament, a sound that hung like a line of icicles in the cold air. Soon it was taken up by the others in different forms—laughter, and sobbing, and half-hysterical ululations that drifted over the Blight in a shrill cacophony. The change in their lives made by that shifted boulder was so vast that it was beyond expression in words; it required primal sounds. To be dragonless; to be without the threat of Lottery and ritual bereavement—that was, for the moment, almost incomprehensible. And so they wailed incredulously, like beasts, and fell to slapping each other like children. Eventually, soberer and quieter, they took the news back to the village. "It's true," they said when they arrived. "There is an enormous boulder . . . much, much bigger than the dragon . . ." And they were received with the same sounds of fearful belief and hopeful incredulity.

"Friends," said Simon, wiping away tears and holding up his arms when things had quietened, "it has been many years since we in Swanscombe have had cause for celebration. But tonight we have such cause. And I propose a feast and a dance in honor of Galen, who has freed us from the dragon peril."

"Yes! Yes!" they all shouted. "For Galen!"

Some of the men had already broken open casks in the rear of the Granary, and were raising dripping tankards. "To Galen!" And some of the girls had crowded close, reaching out to touch him. "Galen, will you dance with me? Will you dance with me, Galen?"

He was nodding, anxious not to give offence, but searching over the heads for Valerian. He could not find her. Only Simon was there, saying, "I'd be honored to have you as my guest. For as long as you stay in Swanscombe. You are welcome here."

Galen was still nodding, still looking. "Your dau . . ." he began, and caught himself barely in time, warned by the sudden horror in Simon's eyes. "Your son. Where is Valerian? He was here earlier."

"At Simonburgh. Come. We'll go there now."

Valerian was in fact already in her sleeping loft, filled with a new emotion which she knew was jealousy. She had watched the girls fawning on Galen and she had been angry. At that moment she had made a decision and hurried back to Simonburgh to act upon it. In the warmth of the loft above the drowsing cattle, she stripped and turned to look in the mirror of polished bronze that her father had fashioned for her when she was very young. She saw a boyish frame, sinewy and small-breasted still, but a body yearning toward womanhood. It was absurd to conceal it, foolish to pretend further. She washed, using the conduit of warm water that Simon had cunningly devised, leading from the forge, and then she opened a fragrant, cedar-lined chest at the foot of her bed, and she began to dress.

Later, when Simon and Galen arrived, she was still dressing; even after Galen had washed and Simon had attended to the needs of his cattle and oxen, she was still not ready. "You go ahead," she called down, in answer to Simon's query. "I'll catch up later."

And so Simon and Galen walked out together toward the Granary. It was a perfect summer night. The storm had passed completely and a new moon hung among clouds of stars on the eastern horizon. The air was soft and still; there was an odor of freshly washed blossoms, and from the edges of the village came the gentle lowing of cattle.

In the Granary, the party was beginning. From all over the village people were congregating boisterously, bearing food for the feast—huge tureens of steaming soup, piglets and lambs still on the spit, trays of hot bread, and huge wooden bowls of roasted seeds and vegetables. No one had spared anything, for an ugly past had fallen behind that day, and a new era was about to begin, an era that must be generously greeted to bear its promised bounty. One after the other, mead kegs were trundled from the stone cellars, rumbling along the ramps with a sound like gigantic laughter, and as quickly as one was emptied another was raised in its place. If the common village supply had ever been depleted, men would have slipped quietly away to raise trap doors in their own wooden floors and to draw out a keg put down for a happier day; for if ever that time were to come, it was now, the day of the death of Vermithrax.

In the loft at one end of the Granary a group of musicians had formed, and instruments not publicly played for as long as the oldest resident could remember now made their appearance. It was clear from the adeptness with which these were handled—flutes and lutes and tambourines—that the old skills had not been lost, but had passed from father to son in the evening seclusion of Swanscombe homes, quietly, the inherent yearning of their chords muted and tentative, lest Vermithrax magically overhear, or lest Casiodorus's troops object. It was clear also that the years of suppression had not lessened their art but had deepened and enriched it, for beneath the jubilance of the moment lay strains of bereavement, and grief, and suffering, and impotent rage. But joy was uppermost now. The instruments sang with a pulsing beauty and richness that far surpassed the sum of their parts and that several times caused the dancers to pause in the middle of their rounds, to listen openmouthed to an artistry they had not heard for years.

The mead flowed, the music grew in grace and variety, the tables bent beneath the weight of food. Tapers and torches lit the Granary and spilled light into the square, just as the music and the dancers themselves spilled into the cool night air.

As Galen and Simon approached the square, excited by the light and the sounds of merriment, they were startled by a figure that detached itself from the shadows and scuttled toward them.

"Jacopus!" Simon exclaimed.

The priest blocked their way, pointing, a huge insect. "Sinners!"

"Oh for heaven's sake, man!" Simon would have walked on, but Jacopus seized his arm.

"Unbelievers!" He was not declaiming now, but speaking quietly, and with a terrible vehemence. "Heathen! You believe this creature Vermithrax is mortal, to be slain like any other. You believe that it *has* been slain by this . . . this sorcerer. Credulous fools! I tell you that this is not a dragon, but the Prince of Darkness, and that it is not dead but sleeping. No human can slay it, for it is not mortal. It can be faced only by the power of the Holy Ghost, and driven deep underground or deep into the souls of men." Jacopus reeled slightly. He was very tired, and hungry, and deeply shaken by the events of the day. His teeth protruded, and he was pitifully pale.

Simon sighed and put a hand on his shoulder. "My friend, perhaps what you say is true. Perhaps it is given to you to see deeper into these matters than do we. But for now, for this evening, it seems to us that we are at peace. It seems to us that Weird, or Fate, or

God, has granted us a reprieve, and that we are safe. You say our safety is for the moment only; well, perhaps it is. Perhaps you are right, but it is real nevertheless and to be enjoyed. Come! Go with us to the Granary. Share our feast. Drink our mead. You are a man like us, and with the yearnings and appetites of a man. For tonight, enjoy. Tomorrow will be soon enough to think stern thoughts and to speak of the dragons of the soul."

Galen nodded agreement. This was a direct and manly speech, quite in keeping with the character of Simon, whose only fault, so far as Galen knew, had been to guard his daughter. But Jacopus shrank from the other man's touch, and his outstretched hand wavered between bestowing a blessing and leveling a curse; in that state of agonized indecision, an indecision reflected in his face and in his inarticulate growl, he drew back into the shadows from which he had emerged, and vanished.

Simon sighed. "Poor Jacopus. It would have meant so much to him to have killed that dragon."

"Probably," Galen said, "it takes courage to be Jacopus." The remark surprised him, for it was something Ulrich might have said. Evidently it also surprised Simon, for he was looking at his young companion in a fresh way, as if he had just passed a test, and he touched him on the shoulder before they entered the Granary.

As they went in a hush fell. The conversations stopped, the music trailed away, the dancers ceased their circling. For a moment, all was so still that Galen heard distinctly the dripping from a loose tap on the largest mead cask, and the soft call of an owl on the roof peak. Then Simon accepted the flagon of mead that someone handed to him and, turning slightly, raised it toward his companion. "To Galen," he said. "Dragonslayer!"

"To Galen!" The villagers cried, lifting their flagons. "Dragonslayer!" And in the applause that followed, Galen was drawn down into their midst, and thumped on the back, and shaken so fervently by the hand that the torches and the smiling faces became a dizzying blur. The musicians, bowing toward him, struck up a lively dance tune in his honor. Someone pressed a brimming flagon of mead into his hand. He had no idea how many men shook his hand, how many attractive girls edged close to speak to him. He forgot utterly his fatigue and the terrifying events of the day and began to enjoy himself.

After a time, however, the music trailed away and the revelers in the Granary again fell silent. The girl to whom Galen was talking was staring at the door, gaping in astonishment. He turned.

Valerian had entered. She was stunning. She was to the other girls as a rare and elegant bird is to the common run of sparrows and stolid robins. Over her long white dress she wore a cloak of rich blue, and both garments accentuated the curves of her young body. A simple white cap enclosed her short hair, and supple calfskin sandals her feet. The torchlight glinted on the torque at her throat, on the magnificent silver and enamel clasp holding her cloak at her breast, on the wrist bands, and on the low-drooping silver belt buckle at her belly, all cunningly interwoven with serpentine designs. *She is magnificent,* Galen thought. *A princess!*

He was aware of a circulating whisper, at first incredulous: *Valerian?* Then astonished: *Valerian . . . Valerian!* He felt the crowd's mood slide through awe and confusion, to uncertainty, to understanding of what this transformation meant. Then came the inevitable anger. "A woman?" someone said aloud. "A *woman!* And while our daughters risked their lives and died, *she* stayed safe in the guise of a man!" Indignation quickly swept the hall, and soon even children too young to understand the comment were echoing it and pointing accusatory fingers.

Throughout, Valerian remained serenely aloof, utterly confident, waiting for the hubbub to subside. When at last it did, she said, "It is true we cheated in the Lottery, my father and I, and it is true that I have escaped the dragon when perhaps one of your daughters would have been spared instead. For that I shall make whatever amends the elders shall decree. But it is also true that it was I who urged the journey to

Cragganmore, home of the sorcerer Ulrich, a journey that brought Galen, and hence resulted in the crushing of Vermithrax." Her chin raised challengingly. "Had I, a mere woman, been sacrificed as the tradition demanded, you would not now be celebrating the defeat of the dragon, but would be skulking in your houses, counting the days to the next Lottery and the next victim." She paused, and in that silence they knew that it was true. "So, I yield myself to your mercy, certain that I am, as you are, the instrument of incomprehensible Fate that works all things, and, therefore, all things for the best."

In the silence after she had finished, the owl cried again, and one of the musicians in the loft nervously cleared his throat. Then a remarkable thing occurred. The oldest of the old women came forward from the shadows of the hall. She was a crone—so crippled and bent that even to walk was an affliction, and so hideously ugly that people looked away in pity. Yet her voice, high and piercing as a hawk's cry, held them. "She speaks the truth. Had she not survived, we would not be celebrating this night. Listen to me! I have lived more years than I can count, and all of them in Swanscombe. I have known women, always, to take whatever defense they had against the Lottery. She is not the first. And some now here know whereof I speak." Her gaze swept the hall, and many of the women present dropped their eyes, and their expressions softened from outrage to shame and regret. "But *her* deception has brought us peace. So let us remember, and forgive."

Valerian had descended into the hall as she spoke, and people had already begun to crowd around her and Simon, to touch their arms, to take their hands. The big man could not control himself, and several times he had to turn away to dry his tears with a sleeve. As for Valerian, she met everyone's gaze directly, as she had always forced herself to do, facing down every suspicion and doubt before it was fully formed. Soon even the fathers of lost daughters were coming forward, even Greil, and little by little the festive mood returned. The musicians struck up the dance again. Several of the bolder young men asked Valerian to join them, but she looked so steadily at Galen that at last he could no longer ignore the invitation. "I can't dance," she whispered, as they joined the other circling couples on the floor.

"It doesn't matter," he said. "I can't either."

They danced. *This is what it is like,* Galen thought, *to be among friends.* And then: *This is how a hero feels!* But no sooner did he think that than he gasped in pain, doubled over, for a sudden heat from the amulet struck like a bee sting at his chest. He made excuses to Valerian. "My toe. Stubbed my toe on the loose board." After that he thought simpler and more modest thoughts. *I am a man. This is what it is like to be a man, to be alive.*

They danced into the night, until at last, when the moon had risen to its height above the Granary, they rested and turned their attention to the food on the great tables. Gradually they dispersed around the hall in smaller groups—men talking buoyantly, women laughing, pairs of lovers and shrieking flocks of children chasing each other in games of hide-and-seek. For the moment, for these people, Swanscombe was the world, and it was a world utterly safe.

When all had eaten, and when the mugs and flagons were being filled again, the musicians struck up a proud, sad rhythm which was not at all the rhythm of the dance. The music delved back through time itself, sinuous, querulous, searching, suggestive, circling upon itself so that the tail of the last movement was absorbed in the first notes of the one beginning. Conversation ceased. Most of those listening had never heard such music, at once frightening and entrancing, but the older people recognized it as the music of the Old Lays, the endless songs in which the history of the people was preserved, to be examined, and re-examined, and constantly elaborated and enriched. Then, into the open center of the Granary stepped the bard Benoc, the oldest of the men in Swanscombe and blind since birth, charmed for that reason, and gifted with an undistractable mind that had turned utterly to memory. Through all the vicissitudes of the years, through

blight, drought, skirmishes, and upheaval, Benoc had
endured, listening and recording, accumulating, sifting
the essential from the inconsequential, shaping and re-
shaping, so that each time he sang the Lays they were
the same as they had always been, yet different, more
sinuous and elaborate, like the intricate interwoven
designs on Valerian's silver brooches. Delighted, Valerian touched Galen's arm. Throughout her childhood
she had loved Benoc's songs and stories more than
anything else. She and her friends had spent hours
listening to him, this beatific and changeless old man,
roaming in a region of memory and imagination where
the differences of men and women did not matter, and
where she did not have to pretend.

Now in the hush, Benoc struck a soft chord on his
lute, a chord that was echoed by the musicians before
their melody receded behind Benoc's song. He sang
first, as was the custom, of the descent of the legend-
ary Saxon heroes. He sang of Saebehrt, Ethelbert,
Hengist, and Witta. He sang of Cerdic, Baeldaeg, and
Angenwit. He described their feats, their heroic
strength in battle against Romans, Britons, and unnatural beasts. His voice was perfectly pitched and limpid, not at all the voice of an old man, but rather of
someone eternally young and immortal. He sang of
the deeds of Beowulf, and of that hero's great fight
with the monster Grendel, and of his encounter with
Grendel's mother, and finally of his immolation by the
dragon. He told them of the arrival of Vermithrax at
Swanscombe, and somehow in a magical feat of tale-
telling, he swept all the Givings into one event, and all
the women who had sacrificed their lives into one
splendid heroine, immortalized; and in the telling he
included too the death of Vermithrax, but obliquely,
strangely, as one would speak of something imminent
rather than realized; and then to Galen's embarrassment he mentioned his name, turning toward him despite his sightlessness, and Galen shook his head and
said, "No, no, not Galen—*Ulrich!*" as if it were important that a record be put straight. But no one heard,
and it did not seem to matter, for the blind old man's

smile and the fluid structure of his tale included all of
that, all of Galen's concern and knowledge, and more,
infinitely more, so that the boy at once felt assured
again, ennobled by truths he had not perceived.

Benoc's song entered different times then and grew
elliptical and circular, so that the listeners were now
sure that they knew the subject, now equally sure that
they did not. It seemed sometimes to be the stuff of
myth and sometimes the ephemera of prediction, and
then both at once. It suggested that the evolution of all
the world traced a huge spiral, repeating again and
again the same events, yet each time subtly different,
even as identical twins grow apart with time and bear
the marks of separate experience. Such was the spiraling timelessness that underlay Benoc's song, although it
seemed to deal with the eternal themes of love and
honor, of duty and compassion, and of heroism.

The song did not take long—perhaps as long as a
lounging man would take to drain his flagon—but
magically it encompassed all of life in the listeners'
imaginations, all of existence. So rapt by it were they
that when Benoc had ceased to sing the images and
wonder continued on, and they all participated in that
magic and could not have said where the poet left off
and they themselves continued.

So it was that at the end of this perfect evening, far,
far away from the outside world and all its cares, they
were gradually brought back to a different rhythm, a
rhythm of distant hoofbeats. One by one they heard the
hooves, although some, those entranced the deepest,
did not hear them until they sounded on the cobbles immediately outside the Granary and were com-
bined with the blowing of winded horses and the creak
of saddlery as riders dismounted. Galen was one of
the last to return. He was aware of an intake of breath
around him and he turned dreamily to see Tyrian, his
hands on his hips, blocking the doorway. Behind him,
the despicable Jerbul lurked, grinning, fondling his
dagger.

"Celebrants," Tyrian sneered. "Celebrating a young
hero, are we?" His arm raised and he was pointing at

Galen. "You were warned! You disobeyed! You ignored that warning!"

"I have slain the dragon," Galen answered.

"Perhaps," Tyrian said. "We shall see. In any case—" And here he stabbed a warning finger at Galen. "—do not leave Urland!"

CHAPTER EIGHT

Morgenthorme

DESPITE TYRIAN'S WARNING, THE WEEKS THAT FOL-
lowed were the happiest Galen had ever known. He
never thought of leaving Swanscombe. For the first
time in his life, he felt at home. He accepted Simon's
invitation to move into Simonburgh and to learn the
working of silver and gold, a craft that seemed to Galen almost as splendid as sorcery. He helped with all
the summer labor of the village—the sowing and
planting, the cultivation and the reaping, the building
of new houses, and the tending of cattle and sheep on
the slopes. He took his place as a man that summer
among the Swanscombe villagers, and when he and
Valerian became lovers that too was accepted as nat-
urally as sunrise or the turning of the leaves in fall. To
mark the occasion, Simon crafted him a bold and
magnificent silver ring.

There were, of course, some wounds that did not
heal and would never heal. When Galen and Valerian
went to see Melissa's parents—something which she
felt she had to do—they found Melissa's mother hopelessly crazed, talking brightly to and about her daughter as if the girl were sitting with them; but when
Valerian gave her the ring that she had found in the
Blight on the day of their return, reality struck the
woman like a lash. For a moment she sat quietly holding the ring in the palm of her hand, and then she
stood up and flung it at Valerian, and spat, and ut-

tered such foul abuse that Melissa's father came shuffling from his workshop to restrain her. "Go, please,"
he said.

Nor was this incident the only cloud on Galen's horizon that summer. He was aware of Tyrian's surveil-
lance. Although he heard nothing further from either
the centurion or the king, several times when he
looked up from the task in hand he saw a dark horseman—a member of Tyrian's troop—on the horizon or
at the edge of the forest, and he knew that the watch
was being kept both on himself and on the brooding
lair of Vermithrax. One day, he and Valerian walked
west from Swanscombe. They intended to picnic in
the hills, but they grew so absorbed in their conversation that before they realized it they had passed the
Blight, descended the long slope into the valley of the
Varn, entered the woods oblivious to the clucking
warnings of Gringe, and emerged on the bank of the
River Varn itself. Through the shallows a large, gray
heron was stalking a frog sunning on a log. Something
about that heron, some familiar oddity in the way it
held its neck, caught Galen's attention. But it was not
the bird which jolted both him and Valerian back to
reality. A horseman was coming across the ford toward them. This was no ordinary traveler, of which
there had been several through Urland that summer;
this was one of Tyrian's cavalrymen and he was advancing at a brisk trot, lance lowered, horse's hooves
splashing in the sun. Furthermore, there were others
farther upstream, alerted by their colleague's sudden
activity. "All right!" Galen had shouted. "We're going
back! It was a mistake! We're going back!" And they
retreated up the road, shaken by the incident.

On the whole, however, the summer passed bliss-
fully, and Galen, who had no doubts that the dragon
was dead, was preparing to spend at least the immediate future in this agreeable village and this pleasant
land.

Then, one night late in August, when thunder rum-
bled in the distance, Simon suddenly raised his hand
for silence. They had been working and talking together in the forge, and at Simon's signal Galen

stopped midsentence, for he heard what Simon had heard—the faint but unmistakable fall of horses' hooves on Swanscombe bridge. It was too late for peaceful travelers to be on the road; it could only have been one of Tyrian's patrols. Unbreathing, they listened while the hoofbeats approached and stopped outside the doorway of the forge. Again there were guttural chucklings; again the saddlery creaked ominously; again a black-clad figure darkened the doorway—Tyrian himself. "You. Galen. Come with me. Casiodorus wants you."

"But . . ."

"Now!" said Tyrian. He was watching Simon.

Galen stood up. "I'll get my pack."

"As you are! Now."

"I'm going with him," Valerian said moving forward. "I'm going, too."

Tyrian blocked the doorway, smiling. "When we want you," he said, stabbing a finger at her, "we'll come for you!"

Then, as quickly as they had come, the horsemen had gone, and Galen with them, their hoofbeats again echoing distantly on Swanscombe bridge and away on the road to Morgenthorme.

Grimly, Simon reached out and took his shocked daughter into his arms.

His Majesty Casiodorus, King and Lord Protector of Urland, Dragon Tamer and Appeaser of Spirits, was not an imposing figure. He was pale and scrawny. He had been afflicted since childhood with an asthmatic condition which caused him to breathe through his mouth, lending him an unfortunate and perpetually simpleminded expression. His eyes, too, were somewhat rheumy, and he had developed the stoop of very tall men who are constantly bending to hear. He was over six and a half feet, a height sufficient to silence supplicants, or to withdraw from tedious conversations simply by straightening his back and staring through a window of Morgenthorme across the moors to the distant hills. He rarely did this, however; unlike Tyrian, he was at heart a kindly man. He loved small dogs and roses and he loved his distracted daughter, Elspeth, with a passionate protectiveness. Sometimes, wandering in his garden, or stroking a puppy, or watching Elspeth's childlike delight in one of her white animals, a surge of infantile joy would pass through Casiodorus so intense that he would straighten, suddenly grave, and say aloud, "I should never have been a king."

Indeed, he never should have been. Saxon kingship owed little to succession, much to ability and presence; and had it not been for the extraordinary circumstances prevailing in Urland at the time of his father's death, he never would have inherited the throne. He knew that fact well and would smile ironically, recalling it. But, of course, he meant something more human by the comment; he meant that there was in him a terrible softness incompatible with kingship. That very quality, which in other men might have been endearing, in a king was a weakness. Publicly, of course, he had sealed it over—or believed that he had. He had trained himself to make decisions quickly and to stand by them once made, right or wrong. He had also trained himself in the Steady Gaze, fixing courtiers and petitioners alike with a stare that was in stark contrast to the slack mouth beneath it. In many cases, this contrast in itself passed for intelligence or perspicuity. The most formidable protective device he had perfected, however, was his reliance on logic and directness.

He had always loved straight lines. The road leading to Morgenthorme was straight for the last half mile, the castle itself was a neat rectangle, and the corridors and staircases inside were as angular as possible. There were no turrets, no spiral staircases. The furniture, too, was rectangular and set squarely in its various rooms, each piece carefully aligned with the others.

Casiodorus had found that living among objects correctly placed, and in rooms correctly blocked off from one another, developed a sense of sequence, the key to clear thinking. Above all he prided himself on being a logical thinker. Reason—or if not reason, rationality

—was the foundation on which he had built his rule. This is not to say that he could not improvise; on the contrary, he had shown that he could be as flexible and pragmatic as any other king if need be, but no matter what vagaries occurred in his policy or strategy, he was careful to keep alive in his court and in himself the sense of reason underlying all. This, he liked to believe, he had inherited from his great-great-grandfather, together with the centurion's armor that he wore on ceremonial occasions, although it was slightly large for him and required felt pads on the shoulders. The Romans, he would remind Tyrian when that officer and his men had impulsively transgressed the bounds of decorum, were logical. Roman roads were straight; Roman battle plans predictable; Roman reasons for action sensible. They would not, for example, have shot an old man at random, only to discover later that he had been a powerless retainer, a flunky, and that the person who should have been apprehended was the boy. It would have been logical, he had pointed out, *to have made inquiries,* and he had dismissed Tyrian with a wave of his hand.

That incident had occurred six weeks earlier. For six weeks, he was torn by indecision and uncertainty. He had found it impossible to come to a logical decision. On the one hand, the boy Galen might simply have trifled with Vermithrax and annoyed it, in which case he should be seized and made an example of as soon as possible, in hopes that the dragon's anger might be somewhat appeased. Probably there ought to be an extraordinary Lottery, as was provided for in the *Codex Dracorum.* On the other hand, the boy was a hero not only in Swanscombe but through all of Urland, and to arrest him would be to risk an uprising. Besides, what if he *had* destroyed Vermithrax? What then? The entire balance of Urland power would be upset, and Casiodorus's very kingship would be placed in jeopardy unless, of course, he could somehow contrive to take credit for the dragon's death.

But how would he know? He waited for a sign. He had waited all summer for a sign.

Then, late in August, it came. He was in the treasury, deep under the foundations of Morgenthorme. It was a tiny bastion of a room, accessible only by a secret and labyrinthine stairway, which had been dug by the Romans when Morgenthorme itself was built. Here, by the light of guttering torches, Casiodorus watched closely as Knurl, the minter, prepared to pour small, easily transportable bars of gold. On the retort stand above the flame, the gold had melted and Knurl was reaching for the pot handle when Casiodorus stayed his hand. He had seen something in the molten gold, a trembling, and as he peered closely it came again, unmistakably.

Something deep in the earth had moved. Casiodorus hurried up the secret stairs and summoned Tyrian. "The boy Galen," he said when the officer appeared before him. "The young sorcerer. Bring him here at once. Do you know where he is?"

"In Swanscombe, Your Majesty."

"Bring him without delay. Even if you must ride all night. And Tyrian."

"Yes, Your Majesty?"

"Prepare for an extraordinary Lottery, the day after tomorrow."

"But . . . I don't know if we can do it that quickly, Your Majesty."

"Just *do* it! Furthermore, I want it to be held in Swanscombe!"

"Yes, sir. Very good, sir."

Now, waiting for Tyrian's return, Casiodorus's liver hurt as it always did in periods of stress and uncertainty. It was an inherited weakness; his father had died with a horrendously swollen liver, mumbling deliriously about Saxon ale and Roman plumbing, and at times Casiodorus did wonder about the purity of the lead-lined cisterns of Morgenthorme.

Pacing along the straight aisles from window to window, he drew deep breaths of morning air through his mouth, massaged his aching side, and awaited the arrival of the bumptious young sorcerer. No doubt he would be Saxon. They all were. Despite the fact that he had married a Saxon and often in the long evenings was paralyzed by memories of the gentleness

and humor of Elspeth's mother, Casiodorus had no
love for the race at all. They seemed a whimsical people, naïvely trusting and reliant on extraordinary coincidences and quirks of faith. Their prime attributes
were their childishness and resiliency. They lacked
fiber, control, discipline, direction. They were given to
sudden turbulences and exuberances. They . . .

Casiodorus halted at a window overlooking the
courtyard. There below, the Princess Elspeth was en-
tertaining her white animals. One by one they came
to her, the small white bear from the distant East, the
white dog, the white goat and pony, the white rabbit,
even a pair of white mice. She spoke to each in turn
and had a treat for each. *Freaks,* Casiodorus thought.
Colorless freaks that ought to be destroyed! Yet, in
the very instant of thinking this, he regretted it, for
there was his daughter among them, her blonde hair
the palest blonde, her skin like snow, her silken white
gown resplendent in the last of the light. The sheer
irrationality of his love for her dismayed him. She was
the center of as peaceful a scene as he could imagine,
a cloister sheltered by high, calm walls from the frac-
tious world beyond, a world in which dragons raged,
and simpering madmen roamed, and where even now
a plume of dust among the hills announced the approach of Tyrian's trotting horsemen. Nothing of that
other world had touched her; Casiodorus had seen to
that. And although she had attended the Lotteries
since the age of thirteen for the last ten equinoxes,
and the Offerings as well, she had never been at any
risk. Casiodorus had seen to that as well.

He was about to descend to the throne room where
he would receive Tyrian and his prisoner, when
Elspeth glanced up and saw him at the window. "Father," she called.

"Yes, my dear."

"See what has happened. A guest."

For a moment Casiodorus thought that she might
have intuited the sorcerer's arrival, for she had her
mother's Saxon prescience; but then he saw that she
was indicating a new creature among the others. A

white raven perched cockily on the knobby branch of the pear tree. "Ah," he said, "a new pet."

The raven said something rude. Casiodorus was sure his ears were not playing tricks; he had heard it quite clearly in the still of the cloister, spoken in a clear, reedy voice.

Elspeth laughed. "He talks," she said. "He says funny rhymes and riddles."

"So I see."

"He called me *Elves' bath.* Isn't that amusing? May I keep him, Father? Oh, say that I might."

Across the short distance, Casiodorus stared into the placid, baleful, mildly amused eye of Gringe. He was aware that the distant plume of dust had drawn closer and materialized into a mounted troop, approaching rapidly. "I have a feeling," he said, "that whether you keep him will depend on whether he wants to stay. But I must go, my dear. I have a meeting. We shall talk at dinner."

"Winner," said Gringe, and again the raven and Casiodorus exchanged a solemn and unblinking stare across the courtyard.

Tyrian was already waiting in the anteroom, drenched from a midnight rain, when Casiodorus entered the throne room through the secret passage. He rarely used this passage, for it was dank and full of effluvia from the nearby jakes, but he thought it expedient, although he could not say exactly why, to be found poring over affairs of state.

And so he was. Tyrian waited for him to look up; when he did not the centurion cleared his throat. When Casiodorus still did not look up, engrossed as he was, Tyrian spoke: "I have brought the boy, Galen, as you requested, Your Majesty."

Casiodorus raised his head then and looked into the eyes of Tyrian's prisoner, a wet and disheveled but defiant young man. "So," he said, "you are the sorcerer who brought down the boulder in the Blight."

"I caused a landslide," Galen said clearly. "I sealed the dragon's lair. I killed it." Pride shone through the fatigue of the night-long ride for an instant before

Tyrian's heavy gauntlet struck the side of his face and sent him reeling sideways.

"Your *Majesty!*" Tyrian said.

Galen said nothing. His eyes blazed. A *spirited boy,* Casiodorus thought nervously. *A boy to have with you, not against you.* Casiodorus regarded him from his great height. He was trying to recall what it had been like to be eighteen and to know that time and the world were unequivocally on your side. He could not remember. "You mean," he said at last, "that you sealed a fissure in the side of the hill."

"I sealed the entrance to the dragon's cave. I killed the dragon."

Casiodorus turned to look through the window again at Elspeth and her coterie of white creatures. "And do you think," he asked, gazing out over his threatened land, "that dragons do not lie somnolent for months, for years? And do you think that one puny boulder will impede Vermithrax when it chooses to move?" He turned back suddenly and was both gratified and saddened to see that Galen's face had fallen. "All that will happen is that it will be angered."

"But . . . but . . . The *villagers* believe . . ."

"Of course. They will believe what they want to believe. They will not think of the next equinox until it is near at hand. Why should they?"

Galen straightened his back. "The dragon is dead!"

"I assure you," Casiodorus said softly, descending the dais steps, "that the dragon is *not* dead. The dragon will burst out and rampage. *Then* what will you do, young hero?"

"I . . . I shall do battle with it, Your Majesty."

"With *what?* It is clear to me that one so young cannot have attained such knowledge and power on his own to bring down the boulder. It is clear to me that you have been given a gift."

Despite their watery enclosures, Casiodorus's eyes were remarkably penetrating, and Galen resisted the impulse to touch the amulet dangling inside his jerkin. "My teacher was Ulrich," he said. "I learned magic from him that would have no meaning to you." He lifted his chin. "The Threefold Transmutation for example, or the Seven Hierarchial Incantations, or the Exorcism of Edda, or the . . ."

"No, no," Casiodorus's eyes closed with patronizing weariness. "You are lying. You are a simple boy easily distracted, not a student. Why, you can scarcely pronounce these words, let alone invoke the powers behind them, whatever they may be. No, no. Clearly you are merely the messenger, the intermediary. Clearly, the power that shook the Blight comes not from what you *are* but from what you *have,* what you *carry.* Confess now. You are the keeper of a concentrate of power!"

Galen shook his head.

"You have a talisman secreted."

"No!"

"Where could it be? Where, among these rags?"

Galen shrank back, but Tyrian's iron grip restrained him. To his horror, Casiodorus's disturbingly long and feminine hand reached out, hovered, and touched with fearsome gentleness a spot at the center of his chest. "Here, I think!"

And there, of course, it was. With his free hand, Tyrian quickly frisked beneath Galen's jerkin and pulled out the amulet. The next moment, it lay exposed in Casiodorus's hand. Both he and Tyrian gasped at the sudden radiance of it, and even Galen, in the horror of his loss, saw that it was brighter than when he had last seen it. It glowed with a monitory intensity. "I warn you!" he said.

Casiodorus regarded him steadily. The hand that held the amulet stayed immobile and then closed. "You are hardly one to issue warnings, young man. You are a stranger. You have acted precipitously and presumptuously, and against the welfare of the state . . . You have *meddled!*"

"I wanted . . ." he began before Tyrian's gauntlet struck him into silence.

"You jeopardized," Casiodorus said slowly, "the welfare of Urland. You have never seen the dragon Vermithrax. You have never seen it enraged. You have never seen the horror that a furious dragon brings to the land—the death, the ruination. It is the very peace of Urland you have jeopardized. And your transgression is doubly serious, since you were warned by Tyrian, were you not?"

"Speak!" Tyrian said.

"Yes."

"Yes. And you blundered ahead in spite of that. Oh, no, you are not the one to issue warnings, my young friend. The fact is, you deserve to be imprisoned!"

A surge of fear swept through Galen. The very word, *prison*, made his flesh creep, but he did not flinch and he did not show his fear.

Casiodorus regarded him with sorrow, his eyes mournful, his lips puffing out slightly at each exhalation. "You have caused a disruption. A break in *order!*" The more Casiodorus thought about what had happened, the more vehement he became. Unlike his late brother, he had never been able to act on impulse; he had always fallen back on what he knew, on routines among which he felt safe. Again, the thought that assailed him at all such moments arose: *I should never have been a king.* On the other hand, unlike his gallant and impetuous brother, who had taken his sword and shield and had ridden against rampant Vermithrax seventeen years before, he was alive.

Tyrian cleared his throat. "If I could suggest, Your Majesty . . ."

"Yes, Tyrian."

"Imprisonment. In the dungeon. And then, if there is to be an extraordinary Lottery, perhaps our young *sorcerer* should accompany the Chosen into the Blight." Tyrian was grinning with anticipation. "I myself would be most happy to see that he arrives safely there."

"And what," Casiodorus suggested maliciously, caressing the amulet in his palm, "what if Vermithrax is really dead?"

"Your Majesty, with the greatest respect, that is unthinkable." Galen was surprised to see that Tyrian was shocked. He spoke with the same kind of hushed piety that Galen had heard before in Christians when they were not preaching. "You know, Your Majesty, the *Codex Dracorum* confirms that the dragons shall be immortal, that they shall live forever in Urland and in the lands beyond."

"And you know, Tyrian, that dragons are *not* immortal. Why, in your very lifetime *two* have been slain, one in Cantware and one in Anwick."

"There is anarchy in those places now. Chaos!"

"Yes, but the point is that *dragons die. Vermithrax* can die. It may even now be dead."

Tyrian's head shook almost imperceptibly on his thick neck. "Dragons perhaps, but with respect, Your Majesty, not the *last* dragon. That would make nonsense of the *Codex*."

Casiodorus regarded him balefully, envying the complacent simplicity of his reasoning. He wished that he himself could have such faith, such a blunt imagination that could not anticipate a transmutation of dragons back into the plasm from which they had emerged. He sighed. "In any case, Tyrian, I am certain now that Vermithrax is not dead."

Tyrian nodded. "You have had a sign, sir?"

"Yes."

"Good. I knew it would come."

"While we arrange the Lottery, lock this fellow up. Later we'll decide what to do with him."

"Yes, sir."

"Not in the dungeon, though, Tyrian. He'll get sick and die there. He is an . . . unusual boy. Keep him alive."

So Galen became a prisoner. He was not treated harshly; on the contrary, the room to which he was taken was more comfortable than his cell at Cragganmore. There was a chair with a back and arms, a washstand with a fresh jug of water, and a clever device by which some of that water could be warmed in a basin over a brazier. Here too was a tiny ground-level window into the courtyard.

For three days Galen saw no one but a skulking turnkey who brought him gruel and refused to answer all questions. He left food and went away. Galen ate nothing and paced until he was exhausted. On the first night, just as sleep was claiming him, the bed trembled! He could not have sworn that the trembling was sensed by his real body and not by the body in his beginning dream; but if he had been startled awake that instant he would have said yes, the bedframe had moved enough to cause its rawhide thongs to creak, and beneath the bedframe the floor had trembled, and beneath the floor the castle walls . . .

Several times that day it was repeated, each time more strongly, until, by dusk on the second night, the tremors had become sufficiently powerful to shake mortar from the crevasses of the walls.

"Let me out!" Galen shouted pounding the door. "It's an earthquake! Let me out!"

He clamored at the door and the window until he was hoarse, but no one came. He pried at the window bars until his knuckles were raw. He even tried to recall the Charm of the Second Degree of Transposition which he had once seen Ulrich use to soar through the wall of his conjuring chamber and land safely beyond the moat; but nothing happened, and Galen cursed himself that he had not learned better what the old sorcerer had tried to teach him.

With dusk, however, the tremors gradually subsided, and he drifted into a fitful sleep that was permeated by the odor of dragon and shot through with visions so ghastly that he awoke in the cool dawn bathed in sweat. "Vermithrax!" he said.

He leapt up and ran to the window just as a fresh tremor rocked the floor beneath him. He was about to shout out into the dawn when a remarkable sight stopped him. A girl clothed all in white had appeared in the garden. She was surrounded by white animals. Galen blinked. So still were they that he thought at first they were statues that for some bizarre ornamental reason had been placed there overnight, but then he noticed tiny movements—the flicking of a white donkey's tail, the slow, subtle arching of a cat's back, the turning, from the pear tree of a white bird's head toward him. Galen blinked again, and squinted. "Gringe? Gringe!"

The bird detached itself from the tree and in two lazy wing beats perched on the window ledge close enough that his wing brushed Galen's outstretched hand. "Gringe! Gringe, you've got to help me find a way out. You've got to help me escape."

The raven gave no sign that he had heard, except for a slight inclination of the head.

"Gringe, please! Can you get me out? Can you . . . steal a key?"

The raven slowly shook his head. Something very much like a child's laugh sounded in his throat.

"Well, can you get that lady to help me? *Please,* Gringe!"

The raven considered. Galen held his breath and then released it in a sigh of relief as the raven left the ledge and drifted back across the courtyard. In a moment, Elspeth stood and came toward the window of Galen's room. She was strikingly beautiful, tall and slim, moving with a sinuous grace. Her hair was pale blonde, swaying with the movement of her body, her white gown luminous. She kept her eyes cast down until she had knelt beside the window; when she looked up, he saw that her eyes were not the Saxon blue he had expected, but were brown, a strange, softer brown than any eyes he had ever seen, so soft that he thought she might have been blinded in a way that allowed anyone to look straight into the simplicity of her soul.

"I am Elspeth," she said.

"I am Galen. Are you . . . do you live here?"

She nodded. "I am Casiodorus's daughter." Again she waited, and there was a long moment during which they regarded one another placidly, like calm animals. And then another tremor came.

"Elspeth, your father put me here. Can you let me out? It's important. The dragon . . ."

"They hate my father," she said, frowning.

"Wh . . . who?"

"Everyone. All Urlanders. His subjects. Do you hate him?"

Galen shook his head. "No. I don't know him . . . And I'm not an Urlander. But Tyrian . . ."

"Tyrian!" Her eyes hardened. "Tyrian's different!"

"Yes. Well, anyway, he did have Tyrian lock me up."

"Why?" It was a child's innocent inquiry.

"Because I caused a landslide in the Blight. I blocked Vermithrax's cave. I . . . I thought I killed it."

"Did you? Did you kill it?"

Galen stared at her. Had she not felt the trembling? "I . . . I don't think so," he said.

"It would be wonderful if you did. It would end the Lottery. It would end all that grief and fear."

"You *know* about the Lottery?"

For the first time a spark of real life came into Elspeth's face. "Of course! How could I *not* know? We *all* suffer through them, all the women of my age."

Galen laughed doubtfully.

"What do you mean by *that?*" she asked.

"You? You're the *princess*. You're the king's *daughter.*"

"Yes." She waited innocently.

"Well, why should *you* take part in the Lottery?"

The flush began at her throat and rose to the roots of her resplendent hair. "My father," she said, after a long pause during which the flush vanished and her face took on a chalky pallor, "would not do anything like that."

"Privilege is privilege," Galen said, shrugging.

"He would not protect me and pretend otherwise. He would not."

Galen said nothing.

"And I think you're beastly to suggest it."

"Elspeth," he said after a moment, "forgive me. I'm not an Urlander. I don't know your ways. I don't really know your father, either. But I've lived in Urland all summer. I've listened to Urlanders speak. *They* don't believe the Lottery is equal for all. They don't believe that the daughters of nobles take their chances together with the commoners. They say that the preparation of the lots is always secret, always supervised by Tyrian and Horsrick, and that lots bearing some names are kept out."

Gradually the color returned to her cheeks. "Thank you," she said. She stood quite still. Behind her, the bevy of white animals was growing restive. She seemed, even as Galen watched her, to have become more regal. "I thank you," she said again, and she was gone.

Casiodorus, meanwhile, having dispatched couriers with news of the extraordinary Lottery, had spent the intervening two days cloistered with the amulet. It fascinated him. He found that he could not look at it directly. Whenever he tried, it stared back like a malevolent, unfocused eye. Frightened, the king had turned the stone over and contented himself with examining its intricate silver setting. The thing possessed enormous power—he could feel its radiance even while it lay on the table. Then, impulsively at dawn on the third day, he summoned Knurl, his minter, and ordered him to cart in from the midden chunks of lead pipe, drainage tiles abandoned since the Roman occupation, now almost lost under accumulated garbage. In fact, the first few pieces Knurl brought were dripping with offal. "Oh for goodness sakes, wash them *off*, man! Wash them off!" Soon there was a small pile of perhaps fifty pounds of wet lead in the center of the throne room floor.

"Now then," said Casiodorus, picking up the amulet.

"Sir . . ." Knurl was shrinking back.

"Yes? What is it?"

"With all due respect, Your Majesty, it's just that, well, many of these sorcerer's charms are known to have great power."

"Yes. Of course. Why do you think I have asked you to assemble all this lead? We are going to turn it into *gold,* Knurl. Do you have some objection to gold?"

"Well, no, sir . . ."

"I should think not." Casiodorus raised the amulet.

"Sir, he is right." Tyrian had joined them, unnoticed. "Some of these talismans—mind you, I'm not saying I believe it, only that it is said among the people—have not only power; but power that twists back upon those who abuse them, or who direct them toward ends for which they were not consecrated."

Casiodorus turned his rheumy gaze full on his centurion. "This is strange stuff from you, Tyrian."

"Yes, sir. I know, sir."

"Are you *afraid* of this stone?"

Tyrian stood silent. Never in his life had he admitted fear, not of pain, not of humiliation, not of battle, not even of Vermithrax. He had encountered all challenges with the fixed grin of the born warrior. He *was* afraid frequently, although he had never admitted it. Fear enraged him. But now he found himself nodding. "I have told you," he said, "that I killed the old man, Ulrich."

"Yes, yes. Go on. What are you suggesting?"

"Only that I am not sure I was truly the agent of his death. If this amulet was indeed his, I would advise you, sir, to treat it with the utmost respect."

"Not to get gold?"

Tyrian shook his head.

"Then we disagree."

Tyrian raised his chin. "With your permission, Your Highness, I will see to the horses."

"Go! Go! Get out." Casiodorus lifted the amulet as the centurion departed.

What happened next occurred so swiftly that Knurl was unsure of the sequence; but he believed that Casiodorus extended his arm toward the pile of lead, spoke in Latin, and was instantly enshrouded in a shimmering blue haze like ambient summer lightning. With a cry, the king dropped the amulet and fell back, his arm still extended. The talisman fell free, skittering across the flagstone floor. For a moment Casiodorus lay stiff, arm straight up, lips opened to utter another cry which never came. Edging close, gaping, Knurl feared that the king had been stricken dead. But then the eyes flickered.

"Your Majesty?"

"Up. Help me up, Knurl!"

With the old man's assistance, the king tottered to his feet, only to sink into a chair immediately.

"What . . . what happened, sir?"

"The stone *stung!* It felt like a score of bees."

"Leave it alone, sir! Destroy it!" Knurl stared apprehensively at the amulet. It had fallen under the table. It seemed inert, innocuous.

"Bring it to me."

Knurl found a stick and gingerly touched the thing. When there was no reaction, he tapped it out from underneath the table.

"It won't hurt *you*, Knurl. It won't do anything unless I give it an order. Then it will either comply or refuse. Give it to me."

Knurl picked it up with his fingertips and quickly dropped it into Casiodorus's outstretched hand.

"Now then," the king said, "we'll try one small piece of lead at a time. That one, Knurl! Pull it away from the rest!"

It was then, when Casiodorus was preparing to utter another command to the amulet, a command that Knurl was sure the thing would refuse with equal vehemence, that two things happened at once. First, a tremor shook the throne room; not a quake, but a gentle shudder sufficient to rattle the fragments of lead, and to send one tumbling onto the floor. Second, Elspeth entered.

"Father."

"Yes, my dear."

Again the tremor came. Elspeth stopped walking. "Father, why is the room trembling?"

"Because the dragon is not dead, my dear." Casiodorus sighed heavily. "The dragon has been slumbering only, and is now awakening, and is angered to find the stone at the cave's mouth. Very soon it will burst out through the rock our young conjurer put in front of it. Very soon it will be rampant again, wreaking vengeance for his affront."

"And then," Elspeth said after a moment, her head raised and her eyes curiously bright, "there will be an Extraordinary Lottery."

Casiodorus nodded. "Tyrian has orders to begin." He laid the amulet on the table.

Another, more violent tremor shook the room. Elspeth stood quite still while Knurl scuttled away; then she moved closer to her father. Her walk was stiff, her gaze fixed upon him. When she was quite close, she asked, "Father, this time may I put my own lot into the bowl for the Choosing?"

Casiodorus looked up quickly. "Horsrick would

never permit that," he said. "Nor would I. It would violate the *Codex*. Horsrick's men bring all the tiles to the bowl, in the collecting sacks. You know that."

"Then may I put my own lot into one of the sacks?"

The king shifted uneasily in his chair. "There's no need of that, my child. I have always done that for you."

She touched the side of his face and raised his head so that his gaze met hers. *"Have* you, Father?"

Casiodorus turned very pale. "What are you suggesting, Elspeth?"

She smiled sadly. "Only that you love me . . ."

"Yes, very much."

"And that you have protected me, as you protected my mother, from everything unseemly and threatening . . ."

Casiodorus said nothing. Very slowly, his head dropped forward; as it did so, the room trembled again, so violently that it seemed for a moment the wall of Morgenthorme might collapse. For a crazed instant, Casiodorus saw that event as appropriate, mirroring the collapse of all safety that for eighteen careful years he had built around her. He laughed abruptly. Then he wept.

Again the dragon shook them.

Elspeth crossed to her father and held his head against her breast. Her hair fell forward like a curtain around his face. "Dear Father," she said. "If I am not first a woman and prepared to take my place in this, this most important event in all our Urland, how can I be a princess?"

When Casiodorus had returned from the journey he had taken as his tears fell, a journey during which he had drifted over his daughter's years as a bird drifts over a green land, where it may never light again, she was gone. He was alone with the grotesquely twisted chunks of lead, with the alien and weirdly shimmering stone, and with a kingdom that had begun to crumble under him. For the first time in all the years of his reign he envied his dead brother, who had never sought to appease the dragon, but who had taken his lance and his best stallion and gone to battle it. Better to have died like that, in a hot white light, than to have lived all of one's life in shadows and uncertainties. He gripped the amulet once again and felt in it now a receptive and forgiving warmth into which he sank with profound gratitude.

When she left her father, Elspeth went straight to the room where Galen had been put and drew back the heavy bolt. The door creaked open, hitting the wall with a soft thud. "You were right," she said. The room shook as she spoke. "My father has been protecting me. I want to repay my debt, beginning now. Please go. Behind the arras at the end of the hall you will find a secret stair. It leads to the stables and the courtyard. Take a fast horse! Flee! Quickly, before Tyrian returns. He is certain to take vengeance on you. Go, for your life!"

Without waiting for an answer she hurried down the hall to her own apartment and then out into the courtyard. The spasms of the dragon's rage had become more violent, and chunks of masonry were now tumbling from the walls. The white animals cowered around her feet, wide-eyed with terror. Those that were tethered strained at their restraints. "Go," she said, freeing them one by one. "We must all find our own ways, now. There are no more protectors." She spoke with a cool decisiveness that the animals had not heard in her voice before, and it further bewildered them. In all their secluded lives, she had never sent them from her. They clustered pitifully closer. "Go. You are free. You must make your own way. Go now. Go!" She waved her arms and prodded them with her toe, and one by one they left her, fleeing through the crumbling walls or lifting above them toward an unknown wilderness. Gringe, the last to come to her, was also the last to leave; unlike the others, he did not fly to the safety of trees and crags, but continued to circle over Morgenthorme.

Galen, meanwhile, lost no time in making his escape. The hidden stairway was steep, narrow, smelly, and dark. Stumbling and falling, banging his head on the low ceiling, he emerged into the stable just as a particularly severe shock collapsed the archway and engulfed him in a cloud of dust. The corralled horses broke into snorting frenzy. Before he regained his feet, several of them had shattered their stalls and were leaping toward the door that had been knocked open by the tremor. Choking and gagging, Galen found his feet and flattened himself into an indentation in the wall while all but two thundered past; then, while those two were whinnying indecisively in their stalls, he staggered to the door and looked out.

In the courtyard that had been so peaceful and bucolic only an hour earlier, mayhem reigned. The white animals had vanished, replaced by a mêlée of running people, all glancing fearfully upward at the crumbling walls. Morgenthorme's gate was already open, and knights and retainers alike were dashing through it to the safety of the surrounding fields. Galen was on the point of running to join this exodus when he was stopped by a glimpse of a figure that was not running, a figure utterly still.

Tyrian.

Black against the pale wall, the centurion gazed over the heads of the scurrying peasants, searching. Galen shrank back, but he was not quick enough; Tyrian had seen him. The big man seemed in that instant to grow bigger. His back straightened, his shoulders swelled, his right arm dropped to the hilt of his great sword.

He advanced with the feline grace with which, Galen remembered all too clearly, he had descended after the slaying of Hodge; and as he came his blade, Tendrun, flashed from its sheath. Its magical amber and crystal pendants caught the pale sun. Tyrian carried it to the side, in the manner of a berserk warrior who, beyond himself, longed only to cut a swath through the insignificant foe. The stream of fleeing servants split, flowed around him. Galen could see the cold fury in his face, and could see too that he was speaking, although he heard nothing but the hubbub in front and the rising tumult of the two trapped horses behind. And then Tyrian was suddenly close enough to be heard: "Meddler!" he said with a horrible vehemence. "Little, meddling fool!"

Galen stood paralyzed with terror. He watched the sword rise, he watched Tyrian's left hand swing across to the hilt to strengthen the slashing blow at his neck. He ducked. He heard the blade sing above his head, heard its clangor on the stone doorframe, heard Tyrian's curse.

Several things happened then in swift succession. Off balance, Tyrian reeled backwards. At the same instant the earth trembled again, and this shock sent the remaining two horses racing frenziedly for the stable door. Still crouched, Galen heard them coming and he leaped back just in time to let the first one through. Tyrian was less lucky; the horse's shoulder dealt him a glancing blow on the chest and sent him sprawling in the manure heap. As the second animal crossed the threshold, Galen saw his chance. He grasped the bridle of the horse—Tyrian's own black stallion, still haltered from the night's ride—leaped and swung aboard. By the time Tyrian had sat up and found breath to shout to Jerbul, who was lurking near the gate, Galen was halfway across the courtyard. Jerbul reacted quickly, however. He seized a pike, a vicious barbed, hacking instrument on a long pole, and aimed it with lethal skill at the boy and the stallion lunging toward him. The horse slowed, hesitated, balked, reared. Jerbul took two grim steps forward and would, the next moment, have opened its belly with a single blow, just as he would cleave with the following blow the thrown and sprawling Galen, if a shrieking white shape had not plummeted down and attached itself to Jerbul's face.

"Gringe!"

Jerbul's cry joined the raven's, but what began as a shout of rage turned to agony as keen talons pierced his eyes. The next moment, the stallion's pawing forehooves had snapped Jerbul's neck and caved his chest, and Galen and the horse were across the drawbridge and on the open road to Swanscombe.

For only a moment, Galen's thoughts dwelt with gratitude on the raven before they rushed ahead to Swanscombe and Valerian. He assumed the bird was with him; but Gringe followed only briefly before

veering away and rising high enough to get a pano-
ramic view of several hectares of Urland. Directly below lay Morgenthorme, with its inhabitants still
milling out into the furrowed fields. Far to the southeast lay Swanscombe, its thatched roofs tranquil under
the noon sun. Between lay the Blight. Gringe looked
there last, for he sensed a direness far more grave
than the threat of Jerbul. From the Blight the earth-
shaking radiated, and in its center arose a plume of
smoke and furious steam. Even as Gringe watched,
the earth yawned in a ragged, fresh split, out of which
rose a wing, and then another, and then a screaming
head. Suddenly, the whole hillside surrounding the
dragon was molten, glowing with a radiance that ri-
valed the sun.

Gringe could not bear to watch. Fretting quietly, he
sank in a gentle spiral back to Morgenthorme and to
the white figure of Elspeth who had emerged from her
chambers and was crossing the ruined courtyard. . . .

Two hours down the road, Galen smelled smoke. It
was not the musky smoke of peat fires, nor the hot
clean smoke of a stick campfire. This smoke was thick
and heavy, laden with the odors of dry grass, and
smoldering timbers. As he rode, bits of ash and ember
fell at the roadside, threatening despite the rain of the
previous night to ignite the forest debris. But when he
reached the crossroads where a branch led east toward the Lake of Passages, and where the chalky figure of an old Celtic bird or bat rose balefully from the
forest, he saw the thick plume itself and knew what
must be burning. Another short, hard ride brought
him to the first of the hill hamlets in Swanscombe
Valley. The whole place was ablaze. Each flaming
building added its heat and smoke to the conflagration that swirled upward in massive billows. Cattle
screamed. People either stood on the hillside, too
shocked to move, or howled their outrage and fear
and lifted fists at something in the heavens Galen
could not see. The crops were burning, as were the
woods behind; and even as Galen watched, a copse
of oak beside him burst into flames. His horse shied,
twisting snakelike in tight circles of terror. He gave it

its head and was off again toward Swanscombe, choking, his eyes streaming and his belly full of dread.

The road lay straight and empty. No birds fluttered across his path, no rabbits bounded away, no squirrels ran chattering through the branches. For several leagues he and the horse were utterly alone.

Then, without being able to tell how, he was suddenly aware of another presence. His back felt cold and vulnerable, as if his shirt and jerkin had been ripped off by invisible hands, and his neck and the back of his head were also chilled, paralyzingly chilled, as if talons of ice had brushed them. He hunched over the horse's mane and glanced back, right, left, saw nothing—nothing but the flicker of a shadow on the road, and other shadows, hundreds, moving at various levels across the trees and bushes of the forest. Only after he had looked ahead again did the grim truth strike: *they were all the same shadow!* The same! An undulating, speeding blot on the forest. The horse, foam-flecked, had already sensed some approaching horror, and it was galloping in tremendous bounds, its neck flattened and straining against the reins, the bit clamped in its teeth, its breath welling up in wheezing gouts. All its efforts were futile, for the chilling shade crept relentlessly forward, edging up Galen's spine, across his shoulders, falling like a cowl over his head and onto the neck of the stallion. The terrified creature wheeled and reared, blindly flailing the air. Galen was almost thrown, but he flung his arms around the horse's neck and stayed on. In this position, dangling helplessly, he first saw Vermithrax.

The dragon came low, so low that when the tips of its black wings moved they almost touched the trees. And it was so slow that in a moment of surpassing panic Galen believed it was on a gliding descent toward him and would land with an obscene and gentle scraping on his face. He imagined himself smothered by the scaled underbelly of the creature. He screamed, and his cry blended with the wretched shrieking of the horse.

But the dragon did not land. Nor did it exhale flames. Vermithrax's rage had caused it to spew much fire in its rampage; at the moment when it chanced upon Galen, it was restoring that fire, building it for an onslaught on the next village, which it could already see ahead. Besides, it had sensed no threat from this fleeing man-thing, no latent force in or around him.

In Morgenthorme, on the other hand, it had sensed real challenge. It had been strangely drawn there after its emergence from the cave, and it had circled for several minutes above the castle, uncertain whether to descend for combat. Something lay there, something deep within the castle walls, that caused Vermithrax's inner eye to flicker with a vision from the lake of fire. But at last the dragon had glided off to the southeast, spewing gouts of defiance that exploded on the hillsides in fiery blooms.

Here there was nothing. Less than nothing. A screeching man-thing and a screeching horse. As it passed overhead, it released the high trumpeting of primordial dragon challenge.

The horse cowered. Its knees buckled and it collapsed, still facing the dragon and allowing Galen to clamp himself more firmly on its shuddering back. Gaping he watched the awesome body pass above, saw the slippage of scales as the skin undulated, saw the crusted places where scales had been torn away, saw the convulsions of the belly as the creature readied itself for another vomiting of fire. And then, just as the loathsome vent passed overhead, dripping indescribable offal, the most terrifying event in the whole incident occurred: the tail, moving as if it had its own life, dropped as the dragon itself lifted to clear a copse of oak, and its splayed tip trailed down so low that it actually touched the nose of the cringing horse, stroked its neck with obscene gentleness, draped like a heavy leaf on the top of Galen's head, slid down his back, down the horse's back, and was gone, leaving behind a hot dampness, an odor of rot and smoke.

Galen's scream again blended with the horse's. The top of his head was covered with threads of slime. It reeked horribly. Shaking, retching, he dismounted and cleaned the horse and himself as well as he could with roadside bracken before falling to his knees and vomiting into the ditch. By the time he was able to continue, the dragon was several leagues ahead, a ragged black dot beginning to descend in a shallow glide toward Swanscombe.

Galen remounted and dug his heels into the stallion's ribs. Still trembling, the horse had also found its legs and although it did not at first relish the prospect of moving in the same direction as the dragon, at last it did so under Galen's prodding.

In a few minutes they topped the rise that overlooked Swanscombe valley, and Galen's fear was confirmed—the village was in flames. The dragon had made two passes. The swaths of fire were cross shaped, with the Granary at the center. That building, the scene of Galen's triumph, was now engulfed by huge spasms of flame, as if, like a tortured and writhing animal, it yearned to consume itself. On all sides, barns and houses were burning and villagers were scrambling for water from the river. Most of their efforts were in vain. Even from his distance, Galen could see that the fired houses were doomed, and that there was only the slightest hope of saving the others. Again he prodded his mount, and the horse plunged downhill in a half-slide, half-canter. In a moment he had traversed the hay fields that were being ignited by random embers and was in the village.

Through flame and smoke he saw both heroism and horror. Men risked their lives to bring old women from blazing huts; men teetered on precarious ladders, hurling water; men and women formed ragged bucket lines stretching to the river. In some doorways lay the bodies of those overcome by smoke before they could escape, and in the streets lay the smoking carcasses of unfortunates caught outdoors by Vermithrax's scathing attacks. Stiff-legged animal corpses smoked in the stable yards. And everywhere there were crying children, some whole, some terribly burned, all turning toward Galen as soon as they saw him, the man on the horse, the man with power. It was not misery he was witnessing now; that would come later. That would come when the insulating, kindly shock wore off and agony began. Rather, what he saw on many faces, even some of the severely burned, was disbelief very like amusement, the fixed grin of incredulity: *It cannot happen here! We have taken all precautions! But it HAS happened here!*

Galen's vision blurred. Acrid smoke burned in his mouth and nostrils. *Have I done this?*

"You!" Greil limped toward him, his hunched shoulders heavy with menace. "You have a nerve to come back here after what you did!" He stooped for a cudgel, got a firm grip on it and continued his advance. Malkin and Xenophobius appeared behind him in the smoke, both picking up clubs when they saw Galen.

"Get out!" Malkin hissed. "Go!"

Galen turned the horse into the village.

Simonburgh was also on fire, although, because it was set apart from the rest of the village, it had escaped the full brunt of the dragon's attack, and only one corner was smoldering. There was no sign of either Valerian or her father. He wanted to dismount here, to dash inside; but he was aware that Greil and Malkin had blocked his path. He could not go back. Choking and blinded by the smoke, his eyes streaming, he rode upwind, splashed across the river and reined up in the meadow on the other side.

"Join the party!" The shrill voice struck him like a lash. He wheeled the horse, tensing for a stabbing attack from the side. But there was no one near. "Come to the party!" The voice was thin, bitterly mocking, cracking with outrage. It came from a figure on a little knoll to Galen's right, a figure brandishing a crooked staff. He was cowled and grotesquely thin.

"Jacopus!"

"Come! Celebrate! Isn't that what you told me to do? 'Come with us, Jacopus. Celebrate the death of the dragon!' Do you remember? That's what *you* said. That's what you *all* said! Well, *is this your party?*"

Galen could not answer. His mouth was dry. He was exhausted. His belly was lead. He gazed weeping through the shifting curtains of smoke upon the mayhem and pain across the river. His first impulse was to plead ignorance, to say that he had not known that this would be the effect of calling down the boulder. Then he recalled how proudly he had taken credit when it appeared that the dragon had been slain.

Crouched like a large insect, Jacopus was waiting for an answer.

It seemed to Galen that never had it been more important to tell the truth. "Yes," he said at last. "I have done this."

Jacopus bobbed with satisfaction. "You sought to do *good.*"

"Yes."

"And it *twisted* into horror, into Evil."

"Yes."

"Shall I tell you why?"

"Because," Galen said, so softly that Jacopus did not hear, "I'm no sorcerer. I'm not Ulrich."

"Because," Jacopus said, "you do not have Grace." He laughed abruptly. "Poor fool! How could you help anyone without the Faith, without the Word? You have done all you could have done—brought terror, and death, and burning children!"

"And your Faith, would it have stopped the children from being burned?"

"Yes!"

"Would it have stopped the terror?"

"Yes."

"Would it have killed the dragon?"

"Yes! Yes!"

In a transport of ecstasy and anger Jacopus again brandished his staff, waving it overhead.

At that instant, as if summoned, a shadow drifted over him. Jacopus and Galen looked slowly upward together. High, high, at an altitude where the plumes from many fires joined and became one with the clouds, they glimpsed a proud-headed and unmistakable silhouette.

Vermithrax was returning to the Blight.

CHAPTER NINE

Sicarius

MILES AROUND, THE COUNTRYSIDE WAS BLAZING. THE plumes from a hundred fires rose and mingled aloft. Soaring high among them Vermithrax was coming home. It paid scant attention to the figures near its lair. Its thoughts were far away, far to the west and north, where it was still possible that other dragons would see this grand havoc and, rejuvenated, come.

In this hope Vermithrax had soared much, much higher than usual; so it was that the shadow which fell across Jacopus was tiny and diffuse.

"Well," Galen said, looking back at the priest, "you're going to have your chance." He assumed that Jacopus would shrink from confrontation with the dragon, and that his declarations were mere posturing. But he was wrong. He saw that the other man's raised face was transformed. Jacopus *wanted* this. In fact, he had already begun to move like a euphoric sleepwalker toward the dragon's lair. The little crowd of villagers that had followed Galen to the river's edge halted, sensing what was about to occur.

With a fearsome dignity, Vermithrax descended. At one thousand feet, the dragon became aware of the smoking village, at five hundred feet, of the Blight and the altered entrance to the lake of fire; at three hundred feet, it passed above a horse and rider, and twinges of familiarity plucked at its innards; a bit farther on, very low, it passed over an oddly gesticulating

human thing moving toward its earth. A hero. Vermithrax grunted, and two tendrils of flame cascaded
earthward. With an instant of hovering, the dragon
settled at the entrance of its lair and turned.

Jacopus had meanwhile broken into a hopping run.
He had lost his sandals in his eagerness to reach the
Blight, and he limped and leaped as thorns and sharp
stones jabbed him. Awed and fascinated, Galen
prodded his horse and trotted along on a course parallel that of the priest. He was filled with premonition.
He wanted to call out to Jacopus: *Don't do it! You
will prove nothing! You have no real power! You will
die!* And yet, strangely, he felt in this crazy priest, this
filthy and scrawny outcast, power in the making. What
if there were a hundred Jacopuses, a thousand, all
with the same fervor, with the same wild eagerness to
sacrifice?

In the center of the Blight, unearthly and magnificent on its crag, Vermithrax perched immobile.
Floating blankets of smoke, spirals and gouts of windwhipped smoke, tortured the sun and sky into creatures alive and agonized.

Jacopus did not pause at the edge of the Blight but
plunged recklessly on up the scree. The paths converged there, and Galen was close enough to see that
the priest's feet were cut and bleeding, the lacerations
sufficient to have brought a less transported man to
his knees. And Galen could hear that the priest had
begun to mumble, to shout occasionally, emphasizing
these shouts with thrusts of his staff toward the
dragon. Galen faltered at the edge of the Blight. To go
farther, he knew, would be to associate himself with
Jacopus. The horse did not want to go. It balked,
grunting and skittering sideways. It had had enough
for one day. It could see and smell all too clearly the
looming shape on the crag, and its terror on the road,
when the great tail had slithered over them, had returned.

Yet Galen could not take his eyes off Jacopus, trotting, limping his painful way into the Blight. He was
at once pitifully human and transcendingly heroic, and
he drew Galen on a level below thought. The boy

prodded the horse forward despite himself, despite the cold terror that had laid hands on his belly and his back. He longed to be away, to be anywhere else, but he prodded the horse; the reluctant animal moved forward, and they were in the Blight.

Suddenly, so barren and still was the great bowl, he could hear echoing perfectly from the surrounding cliffs the shouts of Jacopus, which until then had been incoherent globs of sound. First, constantly repeated like a refrain, the dragon's name—*"Vermithrax!"*— as if Jacopus sought to hold the attention of the beast with that alone. But then, interspersed were other demands, other names, injunctions: "Worm! Cursed Thing! Devil flung from heaven! *Vermithrax!* Evil incarnate! I am coming! I am coming! . . . ."

Evil, said the cliffs . . . *coming* . . .

"Wait, Fiend! You will feel now the Power of the Lord God! You will shrink before it! I am the Light! Down, down into eternal Darkness."

Dark . . . nesss . . . the cliffs whispered back.

Vermithrax did not move. It seemed to Galen, who had halted at the foot of the last incline and dismounted to hold his horse, that the dragon had fallen comatose, or even—was it possible!—died there on its perch, so rocklike was the angular hunk of body, so fixed the basilisk eye. But in fact, Vermithrax was fully alert. Its gazing beyond the hills was a last vestige of hope—would another come before the last summoning smoke had trailed away? Flickers of anger swirled in its belly. It felt Jacopus's shouts and their echoes like blows glancing off its body, and its body ached. Its body ached in the raw joints where cushioning fiber had been ground away, and in cracked and eroded vertebrae. Sharper pains probed at its organs and fleshy tissues. It had begun to pay the price for its onslaught. So slowly and so slightly that the movement could not be seen from Galen's vantage point below, it opened its scaly lips and breathed a long, silent, falling cry of pain.

"Monster! Back whence you came! Back into the everlasting torments and fires of Hell!" Jacopus was drawing close. He was within two hundred yards. He had reached that portion of the ascent where the slope was so steep that he had to half crawl, his staff clattering on the stones, but he seemed totally indifferent to his own discomfort, to the bloody footprints that trailed his ascent. His eyes were fixed burningly on the dragon. He had formed no coherent plan. It is probable that if Vermithrax had allowed him to come close enough, he would simply have hurled himself on the dragon, beating and clawing, trusting utterly in the inspirations of Divine Power. Perhaps he would have groped for the eyes; perhaps he would have attempted to stab with his blunt staff through a pustulant spot left by a falling scale; perhaps he would have sought to be engulfed in the very jaws of the creature, kicking and screaming, jamming his staff crosswise in the great gullet.

But Vermithrax did not allow him to come closer. Body still immobile, the great head turned, and the creature's gaze enveloped Jacopus. The priest stopped scrabbling among the boulders. For a moment he remained on all fours, a graceless animal, and then he slowly straightened. "Fiend!" he said, but so softly this time that there was no echo. He had not known what he had expected in that gaze—perhaps the flickering malignancy of snakes and lizards, perhaps the bland indifference of aquatic creatures. Something, in any case, finally manageable and comprehensible. What he actually saw was quite different, and Vermithrax gave him full time to see it. It was a loss, a sorrow, a pain, and a hatred incommensurate to any human scale, as far beyond all notions of evil as eternity is beyond all notions of time. Profoundly shaken, Jacopus still had strength to perform an act of heroism that only Galen was close enough to see. He raised his staff in front of him, its Celtic cross turned fully toward the beast. He drew his last breath, knowing it to be his last and, a man on the final edge of being, he said clearly and loudly enough for the echoes to spill like splintered glass down the sides of the Blight, "Demon, get thee behind me!"

For just a second the little tableau remained so, intact. And then the horror for which Galen had pre-

pared himself came. The dragon squirted flame like a
man spitting carefully at some target in the gutter, and
the flame seemed magically to gather itself and fall
upon Jacopus all at once. There was only what he absorbed, no more. And when he had absorbed it, he
was no longer a human being; he was a charcoal crab
scrabbling amidst the rocks, uttering sounds horribly
amplified by the rock walls; he was a black pulp,
crumbling and shivering; he was a cinder with twisted
sticks protruding.

Somewhere, from the edge of the Blight, came the
long, keening wail of a woman, a woman bereft of all
illusion and all hope.

The dragon ignored Galen. Lizardlike now with
its wrinkled wings clasped at the body, Vermithrax
twisted and vanished into the tunnel. The tail tip went
last; and for an obscenely long time it lay drooped
over the edge of the incline, like a creature with a
separate life.

Only then did Galen mount his horse. Stupefied he
gave it its head, and the grateful animal hurried back
toward the greensward at a brisk trot. The knot of
villagers was still there, stunned by what they had
seen, this final horror in a day of horrors, and the
horse was almost upon them before they parted to let
it through.

Half a league down the road, the horse broke into
a canter, smelling the river grass and sensing solace.
And so Galen soon came back to Swanscombe. The
blazes had diminished. He found both Simon and Valerian, grimy with sweat and smoke, inspecting the
damage to their house. Miraculously, they had returned in time to put out the smoldering fire that
threatened Simonburgh.

They straightened as they saw Galen approaching and, when he had dismounted, they looked at
each other for several minutes wordlessly, the fire-
blackened father and daughter and the boy who
seemed to Valerian to have grown up overnight. Then
Galen shook his head and gestured futilely to the ravaged village. "I'm sorry," he said. "It's my fault. I'm
no sorcerer."

Simon stepped forward, and supported Galen with a strong arm around his shoulders. "Never mind," Simon said. "We can rebuild."

Valerian nodded. "They will rebuild," she said.

"I did all this!"

She shrugged. "We believed, too," she said. "We wanted you to try."

"Come," Simon drew him into the house. "We'll have soup. And there's meat. Later, we'll talk. Later we'll decide what's best to do."

And so they ate. They ate as the odors of the burning faded and a cool, full moon rose on the horizon. Galen had taken only a mouthful, however, before he began to fall asleep. He was still trembling from the horrors that he had witnessed that day, even as exhaustion claimed him, and he was clearly, both Simon and Valerian could see, not the cocky young magician who had come to Urland three months before. Guilt had replaced that confidence. Still, even as he stood up from the table to go to bed, reeling with fatigue, he said: "I shall need a weapon. Tomorrow." He was barely audible, but Simon heard him. Through the layers of his own exhaustion Simon looked keenly at this young man. He recognized that the Galen who spoke was deep inside.

"He said that he would need a lance," Simon said when Galen had gone.

"A weapon, yes," Valerian replied.

They sat quietly in the deepening dusk. The thought of lighting either lamp or fire was anathema to both. From outside came repeated calls, moans, bereft sobbing, gruff cursing. People were mourning. People were finding the new limits of their lives and building new defenses against a grotesque and encroaching fate.

"I want to tell you something," Simon said. Valerian could no longer see his face in the dusk. His head was bowed and he was inspecting his hands in the way of reminiscing old men. "When I was very young, oh ten, or maybe eleven, my father sent me away from home to apprentice. He wanted me to have a trade, you see, and not be a simple crofter like himself. He asked me what I wanted to be. I said that if I must be a craftsman, then let me be a smith. Like all children I was fascinated by the forge. I had watched for hours, watched the sparks, the red iron glowing, the crude metal changing into something else." Simon laughed. "The smith, he was a magician, you see. Well, my father made inquiries. He found the best smith in the land. He lived five days' journey to the north, beyond the northern villages. His name was Weland. I went, I stayed six years. By day I learned to be a blacksmith. I learned the qualities of metals, I learned to blend them, shape them. The old man talked little, but taught me everything. He showed me. At night, after the evening meal, he taught me the precious metals. I loved this best of all. Many, many nights, after I had learned to make my own buckle or brooch without his assistance, I would be startled by a hand on my shoulder. The old man was coming to get me, to send me to bed. I would have been working hours without noticing. I loved the gold and the silver. I loved the softness of it. I loved the way it could be curved in endless designs, like snakes. You know. I've shown you."

"Yes," Valerian said, touching the elaborate torque that lay, a talisman, around her neck.

"Then later I began to learn the weapons. First, the crude weapons—the pikes and halberds. Then the spearheads, the dartheads, the arrowheads. All the old Celtic lore, and Roman knowledge, too. Then finally the daggers and the swords, the seax and the scramasax, from which our race takes its name. Finally, for two years I did nothing else, I crafted swords. I named them, and traded them to warriors I saw once only. They began to come for my swords. I would waken, and there would be a large man, sometimes wounded, beside the hearth. I would open the chest in which I kept my weapons. He would choose one, pay me with never a question, and go away. I never saw these same men again. They had no further need to come. My swords did not break, no matter how violent the clash, and those who bore them bore them until they died. Even now it happens that sometimes a young man will ride through Swanscombe with a fine sword at his hip, one of my swords, and he will tell me that he inherited it from his father, or his grandfather."

Simon fell silent for so long that Valerian thought that perhaps the story had ended, or that fatigue had rolled across her father's thoughts like fog across the moors, obscuring what he had wanted to tell. Outside, the sounds had diminished and the hurt village was subsiding into a fitful sleep, its silence broken only by occasional cries and by the rustling of the last of the fires. Somewhere nearby, at lengthening intervals, a mother wept brokenly for her dead child.

"Only dragons," Simon said. "Only dragons broke my blades. I never saw it, but I heard. Sometimes boys in shining armor would come to me. Just boys, smiling. 'A sword!' they would say. 'Your best. And a shield, your best limewood, iron-bossed.' Oh, nothing was too good for them! I could always tell. I would ask, 'A dragon?' And they would nod eagerly, so pathetically full of pride, and name this or that creature that had been rampaging. Their retainers, older men, would wait in the background. Sometimes there would be banners. A festival. They would choose a sword and go, and then a few days afterwards one or two of those retainers would ride up, all blackened and blear-eyed and cursing, to tell me that the sword had been faulty, that in the moment of combat it had broken, and their young hero had died most horribly. Usually they blamed me. Sometimes they rode a day out of their way to blame me. Sometimes they threatened, sought vengeance, got violent. I learned to warn the young men. I would tell them, 'This sword is not dragon-proof. Do not take it for that. It will not work. Dragons are different. They are not vulnerable in the way of other creatures.' But they never listened. They scoffed. They died.

"Weland, my teacher, had observed all this, had observed it often and said nothing. Then there came a time when I had been beaten near to death after such an episode. He splinted the broken leg, bandaged the slashes, nursed me. When I was well enough to hear him clearly he said, 'You are at a crossroads. Either you must abandon the craft for which I have trained you and about which I can teach you no more, or you must take it further than it has gone before. You must forge a weapon that will slay dragons.'

"I told him bitterly that it was impossible and that, if this was my only choice, then I must abandon the craft, but he shook his head and said, 'There is a way, but there is also a price.' "

Again Simon fell silent. He leaned forward breathing heavily, his great hands gripped together. "I was young," he said suddenly, vehemently. "I was proud, skilled, ambitious. Of course I wanted to do something, to achieve something that no one had ever done before. Oh yes, he told me! 'Remember,' he said, 'that *every gain is a loss!*' But what was I to make of that? How could I have taken that seriously, or even understood it? I brushed aside his warnings, pretending I had considered them, asked him to tell me how I could make a weapon which would slay even dragons. He shook his head. He said that the knowledge would not come from him, that he had shown me all he could, that I had mastered the craft. He told me that what I required was beyond craft. Then I had an inkling. I knew even before he told me that when I had recovered he would send me to a sorcerer, a worker in the Old Magic. He did. I traveled alone many days, following the instructions he had given me, and I came at last to Cragganmore."

Valerian sat bolt upright. "Then you knew . . ."

"Yes. I knew Ulrich thirty years ago. You remember that it was *I* who sent you to him."

"But I thought you had only heard of him."

Simon shook his head. "I hoped that he might come himself. . . . I hoped even that he might use my weapon to battle Vermithrax."

"Your weapon! Then . . ."

"I made one, yes. Like Weland, Ulrich warned me. He listened to my request—oh, you see, I had a grand vision, that I could rid the world of the evil of dragons, once and for all—he listened and then he warned me. He said that it was the dream of all young men,

to confront dragons and to defeat them, but that there
came a point where compromises had to be made.
Deals had to be made. Did I want something badly
enough to give up something else?

"I told him I could not talk in generalities; that I
needed to know *what* things. But he refused. He said
that he did not know himself, but that the gods Grim
and Weird, who ruled the fates of men, would reveal
all things in time. But I must know, he said, that the
power I sought had its price, and that if I chose to
avail myself of it, then I would pay. Sooner or later
I would pay. I . . . I agreed.

"He mixed for me, then, a potion. It took two nights
and a day. I will not describe to you what went into it
—some things I do not know myself—but it contained
the very acids, fluids, and sinewy, tempering substances that, in the dragon's body, destroy a sword.
Where these came from I did not ask, but I know they
had been dearly bought. At certain times in its making, the potion seethed and shone with a green light.

"When it had cooled, he poured it into an earthen
jar that had been lined with crushed meerschaum and
semiprecious jewels. Nothing else, he said, would contain it. Then he gave it to me, with instructions for its
use. When I mentioned payment he looked at me pity-
ingly. 'But did you not understand?' he asked. 'You
shall pay, and so you *have paid* already. The pact is
sealed. Go, and make good use of it!'

"So I traveled home. I smelted the best iron, iron
almost without impurities, and in the last stage of the
smelting, following Ulrich's instructions, I added the
first half of the potion. Then I twisted the bars together and I beat them into not a sword but a lance.
A lance of my own design. I did my best. All my
years went into it. And what was strange . . ." Simon
faltered.

"Go on," Valerian said. "Strange?"

"There . . . there were no sparks! There was nothing wasted. It was as if, as I shaped it, the material itself—I can't explain it—as if it *sought* to be shaped.
And the color! It was like nothing I have seen. At its
hottest, when most metal would have glowed white,

this was green! An incredible green! Once, when I was a child, a traveler came. He was selling oddities and curios. He had a leathery thing, a pouch that he said was the skin of an unborn dragonet. When he held it against the light it shone green. It was the color of the lance as I tempered it."

"And so where is it?" Valerian asked. "What became of it?"

But her father continued as if he had not heard. "I chose a Roman name for it. Why? I am not sure, except that I saw a brave man slain once, a lone Roman and the last of his legion. He stood bleeding in the ruins of his hill fort, screaming at our horses, and his sword as he swung it whistled above the din. Perhaps I paid him a tribute. I called it *Sicarius Dracorum,* Dragonslayer. And I crafted a sheath for it, the finest tough boar hide, sinew-sewn, and I tooled it in long evenings and inlaid it with traces of silver and gold. Then I fashioned a box of the finest oak, a box with a secret lock, and I oiled and polished it until it shone. In it I laid the weapon."

"And then?"

"Then I waited. I waited. My reputation as an armorer had not diminished at all. Fighting men still came, Briton and Saxon, for my swords. But they were a mercenary lot, rich enough, able to pay, but interested only in rapine and plunder. From the day I made that lance to this, no brave young warrior has come to claim it. No earnest youngster with the gleam of selflessness in his eye."

"Until now. Galen."

"Yes," he said, nodding slowly. "Galen. I think so. In the morning we shall know."

"Where is it?"

"It is in a vault. Under my forge. I have not looked at it since I came to Swanscombe, a quarter century since."

Valerian sat speechless in wonder. It was full night now, but there was enough light from guttering buildings to see her father. He had leaned forward with his elbows on his knees, and his shoulders were moving in such an odd and unfamiliar way that it took Valerian a moment to realize that he was crying. He was crying soundlessly. She had never seen this before; she watched in awe. Throughout that terrible day, surrounded by pain and bereavement and horrors, her father had worked in a dogged and tearless way, and she wondered now at the force of the memory that had moved him so.

"There is something else you should know," he said after a moment. "It concerns the price of the weapon. It concerns the bargain made with Grim and Weird those years ago, when I was too young and foolish to think that it could ever be paid. It concerns your mother."

Valerian sat motionless. She had no memory of her mother. The word opened a quick little door on a dark and empty room.

"I told you," Simon said, "I have always told you that your mother died of disease. That she died fevered, but painlessly and, in her sleep. That is not true. I lied."

"The Lottery!"

Simon nodded. "You were just a babe. Not even a year. Casiodorus's father reigned. I knew, even before I saw the chamberlain's arm go down into the drawing-bowl. I knew. I said my wife's name aloud, *Lilla!* And then the man drew, and turned to look at me."

"My mother!"

"She was very beautiful. She was only a little older than you are now."

"And that's why, in the Granary last June, when I went in and everyone saw that I was a girl, there were so few cries for vengeance for punishment!"

He nodded. "Already many knew. There were midwives, wet nurses . . ."

"They . . . they pitied you."

"Yes. I owe them everything, you see. I owe them you." As he spoke, a sound came, a sound like distant drums. They both started to their feet. "The bridge!" Simon whispered.

"Horses crossing!"

Holding each other, father and daughter watched

through the opened window. At a slow walk, in single file, Tyrian's squad entered the village. The guttering firelight glistened on their faces, on their dragon emblems and accoutrements. There were ten. They bore no aid, no food, no solace. They moved in silence but for the footfalls of their stallions. Some distance behind, looking thoroughly miserable, came Horsrick, riding in a new and creaking tumbril cart drawn, precisely as the *Codex Dracorum* stipulated, by a piebald mare. . . .

Galen woke at dawn. He was aware of the thick movements of animals in their stables below. He was aware of the eerie silence of the village. He was aware, by the streams of sunlight spilling through cracks in the wattle, that it was going to be a very hot day.

For several minutes he did not open his eyes. He had been dreaming of Ulrich. In his dream the old man had been radiantly alive, busily and happily mixing potions, gratifying multitudes of supplicants. In his dream the old man had paused in his labors, noticing him for the first time, as if he had just entered, and earnestly giving him complex instructions which Galen could not hear. Ulrich was pointing to the liquid in his stone bowl; yet, the bowl was not a bowl but one edge of a rocky shore, and the liquid was not the water of the limpid pool that Galen could recall, but a saturnine lake, its surface flickering with baleful fire, its depths turning with incomprehensible shapes. Nor, as his dream evolved, was Ulrich any longer a man; he dwindled, first to a child, then to a dwarf, then, horrifyingly to a screeching and gesticulating tiny doll in Galen's outstretched hand, waving toward the lake. And his voice, the buzzing of a barn fly in the morning sun, repeated, "The lake of fire! The lake of fire!"

Even before he opened his eyes, Galen groped into his packsack, to the bottom of his meagre store of belongings, and found there, safe in the soft leather pouch where Hodge had gathered them, the ashes and charred bone bits that were all that remained of Ulrich. It was little enough, but it was some comfort in the midst of the disaster that had befallen him, and he held the pouch thoughtfully, regretfully. Ulrich had been dismally right about him, after all. Not only had he learned nothing but, when put to the test, he had failed. He had even lost the amulet. He was a disgrace.

"What's in that?"

Startled, he sat upright, stuffing the pouch back into his knapsack. "N-Nothing. Just a memento."

Valerian was sitting in the hay close to him, her legs drawn under her. "You looked as if you were having a nightmare."

"I was." He yawned, stretched, scratched a vague itch under his left arm.

"Me, too. At least, all the time I slept I had nightmares. About Lotteries."

Galen stopped scratching. "There's to be one, then?"

She nodded.

"When?"

"Today. Three hours before sunset."

"And you . . ."

Again she nodded. "Yes. I'll be in it. I'm glad." She was silent for a moment, and then she brushed a strand of hair back from her face. "Do you know what I hate most? The *indignity*. The way it debases us. But I want to be part of it, at last." She looked away, unable to meet his gaze.

Galen knelt in the hay, hastily gathering his belongings. "Is your father still here?"

"Yes." She rose as he rose. "Why?"

"I want to get a sword from him. His best." He was already climbing down the ladder from the sleeping loft. "I can't pay anything . . ."

"It doesn't matter," she said, but he was hurrying on, not listening.

". . . but if he gives me a weapon, I promise to make good use of it." He nodded grimly. "I can do no more than that."

"Vermithrax?"

"Yes."

"You're a fool. You'll die."

"Yes, but what should I do, run away?" He turned, and was surprised and puzzled to see that she was smiling.

"That's up to you. At least you'd be alive."

Again he shook his head. "I've failed once. If I fail again, if I fail as a man as well as a sorcerer, and if I live, then I'll *really* be dead." He was hurrying ahead of her through the shadows of the dwelling toward the forge, where Simon was already at work. Rather, Simon seemed to be at work, for he was pumping his great bellows, the reflected fire was shimmering on his face, and he was turning iron bars amidst the coals. In fact, he was only consoling himself with the habits of a lifetime. He had nothing to make that morning. No one in all of Swanscombe required anything from him. Later they would begin to build, but today they would be burying—burying and going to the Lottery.

The Lottery.

Late the previous night, after his men had encamped, Tyrian had come to see him. He had come alone, and so stealthily that Simon had not suspected anyone was there until he heard him speak beyond the shuttered window. "Smith! Do you hear me?" It was half a shout, half a whisper. "You will bring your daughter tomorrow, do you hear? You will bring her. She will take part in the Lottery. Do you hear me, smith?"

"I hear you," Simon had answered.

"She must participate!"

"I know that."

"The king has had mercy on you. But should you or she try to escape, there will be no mercy. *I* shall see to that. Do you understand, Simon?"

"Yes," he had said. *If I had courage to use the lance,* he thought. But he did not have the courage. He had never had the courage . . .

"You have a weapon?" He thought for an instant that Tyrian had returned, but this was a younger, clearer voice.

"Yes," he said, turning to Galen. "And it is yours for the taking, if you intend to use it as I believe. But you must help me get it. It is beneath the anvil."

Together, they heaved the anvil aside, revealing a trap door beneath. Simon bent and managed to pry it open. "It's been twenty-five years," he said. Below lay the oak casket, as fresh and gleaming as when he had put it in. He raised it. No rats had gnawed it, no worms bored in. Oh, but he had taken care! The little chamber was thoroughly brick-lined and mortared.

Gasping at its beauty, Galen reached out and lifted the casket, feeling the tough, masculine grain of its oak.

"Open it," Simon said.

"But I can't. I don't see how."

Smiling, Simon touched the secret place; as smoothly as if it had been made the day before, the lid swung up. Galen gasped again. He was astonished first at the cunning device; but then his gasp faded to openmouthed silence, for the weapon itself lay before him. Even Simon was surprised; he had forgotten how beautiful it was.

It was a slim lance head about eighteen inches long, gracefully proportioned. Unlike lesser blades it did not shine; rather, it stretched its dark length on the soft doeskin in which Simon had laid it those many years ago. Only its silver inlay stood out in intricate, swirling Saxon tracery along its spine and around the empty socket. Galen read the inscribed runes: *I am Sicarius Dracorum! Use me well!* Surrounding these runes was a magnificent configuration in pure silver: the head of a rampant dragon.

At a nod from Simon, Galen reached for it and picked it up. It was so light that it seemed made of some unearthly material. He reached to touch the edge, but Simon's hand restrained him: "Don't. We shall see this way how well it has kept its edge." From under his bench he picked up a dry oak leaf. Gesturing to Galen to hold the blade steady with only the slightest incline, he placed the leaf across the edge near the hilt. Gently it slipped downward; as it went, the blade bisected it, so that it fluttered in two halves past the point to the floor. "Very sharp," Simon said, smiling proudly. "Now the point." Once again he used an oak leaf, this time setting it carefully on the tip while Galen held the blade upright; and once again, with the slightest trembling of Galen's hand and the merest breaths of morning air through the windows, the leaf turned like a living creature, turned again, and impaled itself. Galen tipped the blade and let it slip off, looking from the weapon to Simon and back again with astonishment and delight.

Laughing, Simon took the blade from him and examined its socket. Then with care he selected from the corner of his workshop a stout oaken stave, and fitted it to the lancehead. When he had done this he handed the weapon back to Galen. "Now," he said. "Try the strength. Try the anvil."

"The anvil!"

Simon nodded. "Grip well."

For a moment Galen hesitated, but then, as Simon and Valerian moved back, he squared his feet to the anvil like a woodsman to a block of wood, swung the superbly balanced blade above his head, and with all his might brought it down on the center of the block of cold iron.

The anvil split. There was the slightest shudder through the lance, and the anvil opened, not with the crack of hardwood on a winter morning, but rather with the grudging resistance of cool butter to the knife.

"Still tough," Simon smiled. "A good blade. The best I can make."

Galen stared in amazement at the anvil. He leaned forward to touch the split place, but snatched his hand away. It was red hot! "With this," he said wonderingly, to himself, "or not at all."

"With that," Simon said, "or not by human means." They gripped hands, the blade a dark bond between them. "There is yet one more thing," Simon continued, bending and withdrawing a black canister from the crypt. "When I tempered the steel I used but half the potion. The instructions were that I should use the second half on the very day the blade was to be used, and in the presence of him who would use it." Opening the container, he gestured to Galen to lay the lance on its deerskin again. Over it he poured a pale green, viscous substance which caused the steel to tremble like a living thing and to emit an unearthly glow. He coated both sides. The trembling subsided; the glow vanished. The blade lay ready. "There," Simon said. "Take it up. I should have used it myself, years ago, but I lacked the courage. If you do not, then strike, strike for us all!"

"And I," said Valerian after a moment, very quietly, "I have something too. It is not as beautiful and terrible as my father's blade, but I made it for you. Last night. Because I knew that you would do this thing today and would have need of it." She drew back a blanket on the workbench. Beneath lay an object that Galen did not at first recognize, for it was crafted of interlocking and tightly wired disks, dragon scales, and it was only when he picked the object up, fitting his hand around the limewood grip inside the boss, that he realized what it was. "A shield!" It was not round like Saxon shields; it was a shape such as he had never seen—long and convex and so large that his entire body could lie hidden beneath it. "You'll need it," Valerian repeated. "There's nothing else immune to dragon's breath."

"There must be a hundred here," he said, touching the scales. "Over a hundred."

She shrugged, "I've gathered them. For a long time. There are a lot around, but you have to go, you know, up *there* to get them."

Simon, too, had been looking closely at the shield. Now he said, "But, you didn't have this many. You gathered more."

Again she shrugged.

"You gathered more *last night!*"

"Last ni . . ." Galen began.

"I only needed a few more, so I went up and got them. It was quiet, and I thought the Thing would be asleep. It was, I guess. At least, I didn't see it. Ah!" She raised a finger to Galen. "But what I *did* see was something you should know about." She shuddered as a cool wave of memory touched her, and she drew her arms around herself, pulling close an imaginary shawl. "Horrible! Ech!"

"What?"

"Well, the dragon isn't alone. There are at least two more of them. Little ones. Babies, I guess."

"Good Lord!" Simon exclaimed.

"Dragonets," said Galen. "They'll have to be killed, too."

"Funny," Valerian went on. "Funny that we never thought of it having young. But there they were. I almost stumbled on one in a shadow, out of the moonlight, and I *would* have if I hadn't seen the other one on a rock, silhouetted against the sky. When I stopped and stepped back the one on the rock hissed, *horrible,* like a wheezy old man laughing, and the other one answered it; it was right beside me. If I had taken another step or two . . ." Again she shuddered, and pressed her lips together. She pushed the hair out of her eyes. "Anyway, I didn't. So I'm here. And there's the shield. Maybe it will help you, maybe it won't."

"Thank you," Galen said. He was embarrassed and confused.

"When the time comes," Simon cautioned, "don't go out to watch the Lottery. Tyrian and his bunch will pick you up right away. Go up to the loft. Watch from there. Then, when everyone moves to the edge of the Blight, do what you have to do. You will have time enough, and it will be too late then for them to stop you. They dread the Blight; I don't think even Tyrian has ever gone into it. Good Luck."

They clasped hands.

Valerian embraced him and kissed him on the mouth. "I'll see you," she said. "Later." And it seemed to Galen that she was making both a wish and a promise—that it would be *she* whose name was drawn, she who would be saved by that dark blade.

"Yes," he said.

Later, he watched from Simon's loft as the Urlanders gathered for the Lottery. Since the first couriers had galloped out from Morgenthorme bearing Casiodorus's orders, parents had begun the grim journey with their daughters, and husbands, as the *Codex Dracorum* demanded, with eligible wives. The midnight roads thronged with travelers from the crofts, the hill-hamlets, and the northern villages.

Since dawn they had been arriving, gawking at the smoking ruins. Tyrian's men herded them into the central square, while a few patrolled the outskirts, watchful for any women who tried to slip away.

By the time Galen saw Casiodorus's party coming, resplendent in their white robes against the green, there were no more pilgrims on the road. All were gathered silently below, waiting. In the center was the platform constructed that morning, a platform dominated by carved dragons' heads on long poles. On the platform stood the great barrel that legend said had been used in the first Lottery. Always it was transported in Horsrick's tumbril and went back the same way to the cellars of Morgenthorme. It sat, a presence, awaiting the wooden lots which every woman had signed, and which Horsrick and his assistants had begun to gather, checking off each woman's name against the roll.

The royal party arrived and moved to the front seats reserved for them. Horsrick began the reading of the *Codex Dracorum,* as prescribed by custom, while his assistants collected the remaining lots. When he had finished, when the bowl had received all the lots, Horsrick raised his arms for silence. The Drawing was about to begin.

Galen found Valerian in the crowd. She was rigid with fear. A dreadful premonition began to form in the pit of Galen's stomach.

Horsrick's black cloak billowed in the breeze. Behind and above him, the carved dragons' heads nodded on their poles. The crowd hushed. Then a lone voice, the voice of an old, old woman said, "Stir the tiles!" The order was quickly taken up by others, "Stir the tiles! Stir the tiles!" Soon it was a whispered chorus, sweeping like a breeze. In response, Horsrick took the elmwood staff darkened by age and handling, inserted it into the bowl, and began to stir. A sigh of relief escaped the crowd at the sound of the tiles moving; for the moment they were satisfied and silent. But then the voice of another old woman, more impatient than the first, said, "Bare the arm!" And again the demand was hoarsely taken up in a thousand throats.

"Bare the arm! Bare the arm!" The chamberlain extended his right arm, and one of his assistants scurried forward, unsheathing his dagger. Clumsily, he jabbed at the fabric of Horsrick's jerkin just above the biceps and hacked around the arm so the entire sleeve of the garment fell away, leaving the chamberlain's left arm bare. The crowd exhaled softly, an animal sigh of relief and expectation. "Draw," they said. "Draw!"

Horsrick's bared arm sank into the bowl of wooden tiles, sank deep, to the bottom, stirred. "Draw!" His hand reappeared, gripping a single tile, and he began, his body stiff and his eyes upcast, the chant of the Chosen: "Hear me, my countrymen. Behold, for I am chosen. I shall die that you may live. I shall lay down my life for you and for your families. I shall go to the dragon for Urland, for my people, and for my king. I am the Chosen, and my name is . . ." Horsrick lowered his eyes to look at the tile, and the crowd held its breath.

"Valerian!" Galen whispered, numb with fear.

But Horsrick said no name. He said nothing. He gaped; he started back as if the tile had struck him; he glanced fearfully at Casiodorus and the royal party, and then wildly at the assembled Urlanders. "The name!" they demanded. "The name!" But still he did not speak, and for a ludicrous moment the chamberlain, who for that instant became simply a silly, cringing old man, actually tried to conceal the tile as if he had not drawn it, as if it were not gripped in his sweaty palm. "The name," the crowd screamed, in a bestial roar, a single, mindless animal, "The *NAME!*"

"The name of the Chosen," Horsrick stared wide-eyed at Casiodorus and spoke so softly that he could scarcely be heard, "is Elspeth, *Filia Regis. . . .*"

From his place in the loft, Galen did not hear the name, but he knew that something extraordinary had happened. The crowd was utterly stilled; Tyrian's men clutched their weapons in defensive, frozen positions, and for moments the only sound was the stamping of Tyrian's horse on the cobbles and the high, keening laughter of a distant bird.

Then Casiodorus was on his feet. "No! Impossible!"

"It is not impossible, my Lord," said a pale and shaken Horsrick. "It is the very name. See for yourself."

"There is some mistake!"

"There is no mistake, my Lord." And he dropped the tile into Casiodorus's outstretched hand.

Again the crowd held its breath, and in the instant they saw from Casiodorus's face that what Horsrick had said was true; Elspeth was indeed the Chosen. *"No!"* he shouted, no longer the king but only a father, "No!"

But the crowd responded in a vast fateful breath of relief and anticipation. "Yes!"

"You have misread it, Horsrick! Look, this is a mere scrawl. Unintelligible! Draw again!" And he flung the tile into the smoking ruins of one of the nearby buildings.

The crowd roared. Men shook their fists. Women, transformed into harpies by their grief, thrust indignant hands on hips and shouted out their protests. Among their voices, Galen could clearly hear Valerian's: "No! No! It was a fair draw! Let it stand!" Tyrian's men moved forward again, and a line of them appeared before the dais where Casiodorus stood, his dignity abandoned, his hair wild.

"Back!" he said, pushing Horsrick away from the bowl. "We will repeat this draw! The first was invalid!" And despite the roar of outrage surrounding him, he plunged his robed arm into the bowl and seized a second tile. "The name," he shouted above the uproar, "Thé name . . ." But he never said the name. He staggered back, stricken by what he had seen on the tile, incapable of speech. He gaped at his daughter as if she were a stranger.

And indeed, the Elspeth who rose now from her place at the front of the screaming throng and made her way onto the dais *was* a different woman. The old Elspeth had been wan; this one was flushed with new life and purpose. The old Elspeth had been reticent, even almost cowed at times; this one was calm, firm, self-controlled, and utterly assured. She lifted her arms, and in awe and respect the crowd fell silent.

Her voice was clear, like the cool song of a waterbird, and Galen could hear it perfectly in his hiding place. "The reason that my father will not tell you the name on the second tile," she said, "is that it also is mine. And so is this." She held up a third tile, then a fourth. "And this. The bowl contains as many tiles bearing my name as it does all of yours." She waited a moment for the significance of the statement to be understood. "Yes, there is a lot with my name for each of yours. Do you know why I have done this?" The crowd was spellbound, waiting. "To compensate. To balance all the Lotteries of other years when I have risked nothing, when my name was on no lots at all. It is correct that my name be chosen now. And so I go to meet the dragon, and to know what others before me have known." She spoke with a strange elation, before turning to Casiodorus, who was being supported by Horsrick. "As for my father, do not think ill of him. Forgive him. He has governed according to his lights. And if he has violated the *Codex,* he has not done so out of malice but out of love." She embraced the helpless Casiodorus in the long, last embrace of the unmarried daughter of her father. Then she summoned Horsrick and his cart. This time, there would be no delay between the Lottery and the Giving.

"No!" Casiodorus tottered forward, his eyes bulging, his hands outstretched. "No! I forbid it! Horsrick, do not bring the cart!"

The old chamberlain turned bewildered eyes on his king. "Sir," he whispered, "the Lottery has begun. The Chosen has been called. It is too late, Your Majesty!"

"Tyrian, stop this!"

Tyrian did not look at the king. He gazed out over the seething crowd to the horizon of the Blight. "The Lottery is more important than any one person," he said, "man or woman. What has been done is done. I cannot prevent this Giving."

Casiodorus sank into a chair that a retainer had placed behind him, and there he remained, staring without seeing, while the procession formed for the journey to the Blight. At last he allowed himself to be guided onto his horse.

As for the procession itself, for the first time in as long as any could remember, there was a kind of pride and even a triumph in it. Someone had found uncharred banners, and they fluttered in the breeze. Flowers had appeared to bedeck Elspeth and her cart, and several of the younger women had even run ahead to strew blossoms in her path. It did in fact seem much more the triumphal parade of a conqueror than of a sacrificial victim; but then, Galen thought, standing and picking up Sicarius for the coming combat, they believed that she *had* saved them, at least this once. Yes, that explained their exuberance; it was a triumph of hope.

Simon had gone with the rest. Only Valerian was left in the square. As the others departed, she climbed the platform and one after the other drew several tiles from the bowl. *Elspeth R., Elspeth R.,* Elspeth. . . . Thoughtfully she turned each lot over, before dropping it back. She stood a long time staring eastward, in the direction the princess had gone. And then, with a glance toward her own home, and up at the loft where she knew Galen was hiding, she hurried after the rest.

Now, Galen said to himself. *Now!* With Sicarius balanced in his right hand, bearing Valerian's shield that flickered with a thousand lights, he strode through Simon's dwelling and out into the sun. Valerian had shown him a high, fast path to the Blight.

He was eighteen.

He had never in his life used a warrior's weapon.

He was going to fight a dragon.

CHAPTER TEN

Battle

ELSPETH WAS BEING TIED TO THE STAKE WHEN GA-
len arrived. The forest path he had taken opened onto
the Blight above the main road, and he was able to
look down on Horsrick performing his duty, and on
the skittish horse. He looked down also on the gathered Urlanders, the distracted king among them, only
slightly removed with his court, at the edge of the
greensward.

The lair opened above him. Just outside and down
from it, wedged between two large boulders and pointing with one stick arm toward heaven still, lay the
charred corpse of Jacopus. Galen shuddered, remembering. There was no sign of movement yet in the
mouth of the lair; clearly, if Vermithrax was to be
engaged, it would have to be sought out. He remembered fleetingly Valerian's warning about the dragonets, but a careful inspection of the area in front of
the cave mouth revealed no sign of them. Could she
have been mistaken? Could she have imagined them?

His first step was to free the princess. It was uncon-
scionable that she should be tethered there like some
farm animal awaiting execution. He hoisted Sicarius,
and strode out into the last of the sunlight on the
blackened rubble of the Blight. In a few moments he
had reached Elspeth's side, and with one thrust, the
first stroke of Sicarius, he severed the thongs which
bound her to the post. "Thank you," she said. She
rubbed her wrists and glanced up the hillside.

In the distance, Galen heard the cries of protest from the throng on the hillside, and shouts of outrage from Horsrick who, having fulfilled all final obligations under the *Codex,* was now on his way out of the Blight.

But Galen did not *see* what was happening amidst the crowd. He did not see that Tyrian had mounted his horse and was coming at the brisk trot of a cavalryman down the road into the Blight. He did not see him push roughly past Horsrick, drawing Tendrun as he did so, and he did not see the horse increase its pace to a gallop over the last half league. In fact, not until Elspeth screamed a warning did he turn and find Tyrian almost upon him, sword raised, teeth bared in his mirthless grin. He ducked, and Tyrian's sword sang half an inch above his head. The stallion wheeled, but its footing on the rocky ground was uncertain and it balked at another charge. Tyrian dismounted. He was five yards away. He seemed enormous, his sword huge, his black clothing terrifying. The dragon emblem on his chest twisted with a life of its own, and Galen felt the lance yearning eerily toward it. The man moved in the coiled crouch of a skilled fighter, both hands gripping his weapon. He came slowly forward.

"Meddler," he said to Galen as he came. "I should have killed you at the start." As if in affirmation the ground quivered; Vermithrax was moving. "We will correct that, now," Tyrian said. "We will begin to make amends." He had come close, and he lunged.

Galen had also been crouching, his stance an imitation of Tyrian's. When the other man struck he raised Sicarius to parry, and felt the sharp shock of steel on steel. The pain of it shot through his wrists and into his shoulders, and the pain ignited him. Despite everything, he had meant no harm to Tyrian; his response to the warrior's charge had been defensive. He had wanted only to meet Vermithrax. But now the sharp pain reminded him that he was face to face with the man who had killed Ulrich, the man who had murdered old Hodge with a war arrow through the back, the man who had humiliated him, slapped him, treated him like a lackey. He was filled suddenly with an emotion he had never known—hatred. It was like a keen, white flame.

Tyrian laughed. His thick laughter echoed in the Blight like invisible boulders bounding on the slopes. It joined with the rumble of Vermithrax's movements, somewhere beneath. "Kill me? Is that what you are thinking? You little fool! Look at you! You can hardly lift that lance." And again, his laughter suddenly cut off, he lunged.

Galen was ready. He had never felt more alert or more intensely alive. He saw vividly, knew exactly what must be done. Again he parried Tyrian's stroke, and while the other man's sword glanced harmlessly away, his own weapon twisted back and down, like a scorpion's sinewed tail, and pierced Tyrian's shoulder just above the biceps. The centurion's thick body arched in pain and the arm flopped uselessly at his side. Blood splashed. He looked from the wound to Galen but there was no change in his expression, no sign of either astonishment or fear. His grin remained implacable. He said nothing. One arm seemed quite enough to wield the sword. Its point turned in tight circles at the level of Galen's eyes. He inched forward.

Galen's attention, meanwhile, had been distracted. In the flurry of Tyrian's onslaught he had forgotten about Elspeth, but now he saw that she was no longer beside the post. She was halfway up the slope, determinedly following the same fatal path that Jacopus had taken only the day before. "Don't!" he shouted. "Stay! You don't have to!" She gave no sign that she had heard.

Tyrian inched forward. There would be no dramatic lunges this time. Every move would count. He feinted, grinned as Galen dodged away, feinted again. Then he struck. The blow was fast as the flicker of a snake's tongue, a thrust to the heart.

Galen did not know how he avoided it. Had he been a hair's breadth slower he would have died pinned and squirming on Tyrian's sword. Instead he was alive, stretched tiptoe, twisting away like some pirouetting court juggler, and the side of Tyrian's neck, carried forward by the thrust, was exposed to him. Later, when he had time to reflect, he would wonder why he did not strike with all his force; why instead he allowed the edge of Sicarius merely to drift along that exposed neck between tunic and helm, and he would never be able to say truthfully whether his motives were kind or vicious. Was this the last of the warning? Or was there something of Tyrian even in him; was he toying with the man?

In any case, the second wound had no more effect on Tyrian than the first. He spun back to face Galen, shaking his head as if to fling away the new blood as a dog flings off water. Then he came forward again. He was breathing heavily. *You will regret that,* his eyes said. *You will regret that very dearly.*

Galen knew then with a cold certainty that one of them would die. He glanced up the hill again and caught sight of Elspeth just beginning the last, steep section of her climb to the lair's mouth. If he was to prevent her, there was no time to lose.

He moved to the attack. He felt magnificent. The lance rose singing in his hands and bore him up with it, up, up, until he seemed to be looking down at Tyrian from a great height, and in the instant before he struck, oblivious and impervious to the flailing of Tyrian's blade, he was filled with such mix of emotions—rage and pity and triumph—that he screamed from the brimming force of them, a dreadful warrior's scream that bounced and reverberated and took its mighty place among the echoes of the Blight.

Sicarius descended.

Driven exultantly, it pierced the post behind which Tyrian had taken refuge, the open dragon's mouth on Tyrian's breast, and the thick torso of the man behind it. Then, as swiftly as it had gone in, it was out, and Galen was backing away, holding it, watching Tyrian die. He was suddenly no longer a foe or a threat. He was simply a big man with a hurt arm and a crease of concern between his eyes, as if he had forgotten to keep some small promise, sagging to his knees, folding to conceal his mortal wound, then falling gently on his side.

The ground shook.

There was no other sound.

Galen turned and ran for the mouth of the lair. He did not feel triumphant or heroic. He felt breathless and nauseous. In fact he thought once that he would have to stop and vomit, but he controlled himself, swallowing hard, and in a few minutes had reached the foot of the last incline. He did not look at Jacopus's remains, shrivelled there, nor did he breathe when he passed that place of the pervading dragon-stench and the odor of roasted meat. Rather, he scrambled forward and up.

He saw no sign of Elspeth until he reached the ledge at the cave's mouth; there, amidst the loathsome excreta and detritus of the place where the dragon perched, lay a silken scarf. It was pure and white. It shone. Hers. Elspeth's. But why? Had it been accidentally dropped, or had she left it for some reason as she went forward to that darkness?

He did not pick it up. He might have done so had he not, peering ahead, seen something else white— too large to be another scarf—farther down the tunnel. Filled with a terrible premonition, he went forward, Sicarius held at the ready.

Again the appalling odor struck him. It was indescribably rank and putrid. It was a stench such as he could never have imagined, compounded of feces, decayed meat, abominable breath, and dank mold flourishing in crevasses. It was overwhelming. He gagged but forced himself onward. The formless patch of white shimmered ahead, now visible, now vanishing. He reeled toward it.

He sensed the walls closing behind.

The tunnel was like the gut of a great beast. Lime-laden water shimmered on the walls. Stalactites dropped in thin strands from the ceiling, and underfoot the passage was slippery with stagnant water and dragonslime. It was a maleficent and baleful tube, and it was lit both by strange sources deep within and by daylight angling crookedly through cracks to the surface of the earth. The light changed and shifted constantly, now waning daylight, now flickering, fading fire.

Galen descended. He was sickened to the heart, both by his surroundings and by what he was now sure he would find ahead, for the nearer he drew to the patch of white, the clearer it became that it was something horizontal, and that small dark shapes were moving on it. A few more steps into that stifling atmosphere, and he saw that it was, as he feared, the Princess Elspeth. Rather, it was the remains of the princess. She had never reached Vermithrax, never offered herself to the dragon. What had befallen her was even worse, was absurd and horrible: she was the prey of the little ones.

Dragonets, two of them, moved on her corpse. They clawed, gnawed. Her body was fast losing its shape, her dress had ceased to be white. They were the size of large, quick cats. From the ridge surmounting their eyes no horns had yet sprung, nor did they jet fire at Galen's approach. But in all other respects they were perfect copies of Vermithrax. Their teeth lined a harsh V of exposed gums; their fibrous wings arched out, claws threatening; their tails terminated in the loathsome spade that Galen had felt sliding across his skull.

They watched him with malignant red eyes. They were chewing with lazy relish, but their poised stances suggested that if he were to falter, or stumble, or show any weakness, they would be on him in an instant, teeth driven by muscular necks.

He did not falter. Sicarius drew him forward and determined what must be done. The first dragonet he beheaded before it could either move or cry out. Spurting fluids, its body scrabbled in ever-widening circles like a coiled spring let loose, while the jaws of the disembodied head opened and shut, opened and shut, helplessly yearning for Galen. The second was already airborne, leaping for him, as Sicarius slashed down upon it, missing the neck and catching it just behind the thorax. Abdomen and tail dropped earthward but—horrible!—the forepart of the body sailed on, borne on grim little wings, and actually grazed

Galen's shoulder before he managed to twist in the
narrow confines of the place and beat it down to the
earth. For a moment, beside himself with rage and
revulsion, he slashed and slashed until what had been
the dragonet was a pulped mass of tissue. And it was
only then, when he believed that he had beaten them,
and when his relief had welled up in a fit of retching,
that the third one sprang on him.

The third one had been late to the feast, had not
been part of the killing of Elspeth. It had lurked waiting in the shadows for the others to finish, and now,
with a baleful and exultant delight, saw that it would
have a feast of its own. Its embryonic wings unfolded
and fluttered. It drooled. Its muscular little legs contracted. It leapt, sailed, and fastened itself on Galen's
tunic. Its fangs cut. Its breath, though not flame, was
still hot enough to sear his neck. With a strangled cry
of horror Galen writhed and twisted. He struck the
thing with his shield. He tried to scrape it off against
the wall of the cavern but he could not. Only by an
extraordinary effort was he at last able to work the
point of Sicarius under its belly and stab upwards. The
lance went through. With a dreadful cry the thing
dropped away, its backbone severed. Even then, as it
lay thrashing in its death throes, it scrambled to seize
its killer's ankle. Galen stepped back and slashed,
again, again, again.

For a moment there was silence in the tunnel. Galen reeled back, sickened by the slaughter, twisting
lest the shadows be hiding yet another monstrous
thing. But there was nothing. He was alone with the
corpses.

The earth trembled.

Somewhere below, not far, Vermithrax was moving.
Galen took one last look back up the tunnel, back to
the twilit sky and the cool world of birds and flowing
streams, and to . . . Valerian. Then he hefted Sicarius,
swallowed hard, and headed down the tunnel in the
direction of the lair.

As he descended, the heat increased, and the oak
haft of the lance grew slippery with sweat. Sweat
beaded and then streamed on his face and neck.

Sweat flattened his hair, soaked his tunic. As if in sympathy, the walls also streamed, acrid and sulphurous, and strange white insects and lizard-shapes raised red eyes to watch him pass. Some hissed sibilant challenges; some scampered back into dingy recesses. The place seethed with reptilian life. And as the heat grew, so did the stench. It was oppressive beyond belief. No matter how he bent or twisted, he could not avoid it. It worked like acid, the odor of death and of inestimable age, into his very skin. He gagged, staggered, reeled onward, his vision bleared by sweat, and by stench, and by profound fatigue.

Soon the corridor began to broaden and the light infusing it grew more ambivalent. To his astonishment, he found that what he had assumed to be the pulsing of nerves in his hand and arm was actually the lance, throbbing with a steady, expectant rhythm, leading him on. The walls and ceiling all flickered now with a rosy sheen, and the passage opened suddenly into a vista of staggering immensity. Ahead lay an underground lake, a lake of fire, its surface covered with sheets and torn by blades of flame. Arching over it were granite vaults, broken at intervals by natural chimneys down which spilled the reflections of distant and fading daylight. No matter how intently he peered into the shifting gloom, he could not tell how large the lake was; it vanished into at least half-a-dozen side chambers, all of which could have been as large as this, could have led into others in an endless, echoing labyrinth. It was a maze of gigantic proportions, and somewhere inside was Vermithrax.

Galen remembered how he had stood at the mouth of the cave—had it been only three months before? It seemed a lifetime—and whispered the dragon's name in a challenge that was never answered. Now, with the throbbing lance telling him that the dragon was very close, although he could see only the flames and reflections of flames, and white, unnatural shapes moving under dark surfaces, he said the name again: "Vermithrax!" *Vermithrax . . . vermi . . . vermi . . . vermithrax . . . ithra . . . ithrax . . .* the walls said back, whispering among themselves into the farthest recesses of unknown chambers. He waited for the echoes to die down, and then he spoke the name again, not whispering, but imperiously, a firm challenge.

The dragon rose.

Events then happened so fast that Galen could not be sure of their sequence. In fact, he could not even be sure where Vermithrax came from, only that one moment he was looking into the flames of the lake, and the next he was gazing into the eyes of the dragon. So shocking was the suddenness of the beast's appearance that he did not have time to react before he had been fixed by its mesmerizing stare. Only the lance leaped and surged; the lance sang in his hand. Galen himself was lost by what he saw in the dragon's eyes and, immobilized, he watched those eyes. Slowly Vermithrax's haed tipped back, slowly its mouth opened. In the very last second before flame poured forth, Galen raised his shield.

The blast sent him reeling backwards. Flames cascaded around and over the edges of the shield, scorching his right hand, his lower legs, his hair. He shrieked with pain and terror, and the sound of his cry mingled with the high-pitched clamoring of the flames on the shield. Inside, the limewood handle smoldered against its boss. His knuckles burned on the scaled plating. He was driven helplessly back up the corridor, and still Vermithrax had not moved, had merely exhaled. Now it moved. Now it came toward him while he was still stunned and suffocated by the first assault, stepping with obscene precision on the flat stones along the edge of the lake. Galen watched horrified, watched too long, for another fiery blast engulfed him and sent him cowering behind the blessed shield, a helpless, quivering jelly of terror. Only the lance protruded. Only Sicarius took the full blast of the dragon's fire and shone white hot in it, as if that fire had given the final tempering. The blast was shorter this time. Vermithrax stepped, stepped again. Its head now hovered within twenty feet of its victim. A long inhalation hissed through the slits of its jowls; there would now, Galen knew, be an awful swallowing, and then the flash of fire.

He turned and ran. He ran as fast as his singed legs could carry him, around the corner and up the corridor, just out of range of the wash of fire, and up, up past the place where he had slain the dragonets, up past the corpse of Elspeth. All the way, the lance protested.

Vermithrax was not far behind. When it had recovered its breath, the dragon moved with remarkable speed, its snout projecting, its long neck stretched far forward to counterbalance the spade-tipped tail, wings fluttering, it ran on its claws and surprisingly nimble feet. It ran on familiar surfaces. But it ran for only a short distance before slowing, moving more cautiously around the corners. The human thing might be hurt, but it was not dead, and it was carrying a stick that had sung for Vermithrax's blood. The dragon had heard and felt that singing. The dragon had blown fire as much at the blade as at the cringing man and it had seen the lance glow white with the welcome heat.

So it moved more cautiously now that the man had scampered up the corridor and vanished. The important thing was to destroy not the man—for unarmed, the man was powerless—but the lance. Vermithrax slowed; its wings folded back, its plated feet slid, grating along the passage. Ahead was something unmoving—Vermithrax exhaled a squirt of flame to illuminate the corridor—something white, and around it, familiar shapes. The crusted neck stretched forward; the snout waved, sensing alarming odors on the cool evening breezes that drifted down from outside.

So it was that it came upon the corpses of its young. One by one it found them, and one by one it sniffed and nuzzled them. There was no replying shriek, no squirming, no small keen teeth to close on its nose or jaws. The bodies were stiff and motionless. They smelled of blood and other spilled liquids. With great care Vermithrax went from one to the other, Galen temporarily forgotten, leaning across Elspeth's mutilated body as it did so. And then, when it had satisfied itself that there was no life here, it did a curious and —to Galen, who was hiding, poised in a niche not fifteen feet away—a bewildering thing. It blew fire across the bodies. It was not the white-hot, incinerating fire that it had directed earlier at Galen, at Swanscombe, and at assorted challengers and earthworks over the centuries, but rather a pale shimmering bluish flame like the flickering of sheet lightning on a hot summer evening, like the pale fire Galen had watched shimmering among the battlements of Cragganmore one night long ago. It was as if Vermithrax had drawn from within itself the fragile essence of its life, pure dragon-spirit, and sought to breathe that back into the pitiful, hopelessly mutilated bodies. The blue fire flickered over them, a benediction, and faded.

Then Vermithrax slowly raised its head. And the flame it breathed was not benevolent, but a raw jet of liquid hatred that struck the earth and burst into spinning globules only a few feet from where Galen was concealed. The exhalation was accompanied by a sound that ran like ice along the inside of Galen's thighs and up his backbone, a keen and unrelenting whine of agony that could come only from a creature for whom sound was foreign, almost beyond its capacity. It was as if, for that one brief cry, Vermithrax had brought sound into being, and had poured into it a millenia of loss and losing. It was a cry for all that might have been and now would never be.

It was mercifully short. When it had died away, Vermithrax advanced with more grim determination than ever; in its haste, it passed unseeing by the niche where Galen stood frozen, Sicarius poised throbbing above his head. Galen watched the tip of the dragon's snout appear, the encrusted nostril surmounted by its fanglike horn, then the red eye couched in its membranous folds and pouches, and the great scabrous ridge that swept back and up into reptilian antlers. Behind the skull came the neck, the long, sinewy neck with its armored top and sides, with its thin, pulsing, and vulnerable scales. "Now!" Galen said to himself as he watched this neck glide by, knowing that in the next moment the heavily plated shoulder would heave into sight. "Strike now!" And with the roar of the pent-up warrior leaping at last from his ambush, he loosed Sicarius.

He was certain the lance would have gone to its destination with no guidance from himself. In fact, it might have been better had he hurled it, or simply released it; perhaps in gripping the hilt he deflected it from its predestined course, for it missed the throat and lodged deep between large scales on the upper neck.

The effect was cataclysmic. The dragon's neck writhed as if it were a separate creature, and its head lunged upward, horns raking the ceiling, sending showers of stalactites and broken rock cascading on its writhing back. Its claws gouged at the scree and slime, scouring out tons of debris. Its jaws yawned in pain; its intestines convulsed, loosing horrid effluvia into the already fetid air. Its tail lashed like an armored club.

Gripping Sicarius, Galen was lifted off his feet and flung against the walls of the enclosure; but he hung on, elated by the feel of the lance probing deep and deeper, searching for the mortal place. And then he fell. The dragon reared free above, the blade protruding from its neck. The oaken shaft had snapped.

Gripping the broken piece, Galen scrambled into his little cave, as deep as he could go, gasping as the dragon lunged backwards so that it could twist and peer into Galen's hole. It was far from dead. The red eye peered in. The cracked mouth emitted a preliminary wisp of flame that curled around the entrance and slipped up almost as far as Galen's feet. And then, as the head pivoted to deliver the *coup de grace,* the fire that would scour the chamber like a crucible and reduce its contents to white ash, Galen felt a breath of fresh air on his neck and, groping upward, discovered a chimney scarcely bigger than his body. The next instant he had scrambled up into it and the dragon's breath was roaring like a fiery sea beneath his feet. He hitched himself higher, gulping for the oxygen flowing down from above. Again Vermithrax sent gouts of flame searching the cavity, but Galen was well clear. Another minute and he hauled himself into open air.

Below, the earth trembled as Vermithrax twisted

around and retreated, hurt but far from slain, back to the lake of fire. . . .

Galen lay still for a long time. Never was an evening more beautiful. It was cool and windless, and somewhere nearby a nightbird sang. There was a full sky of stars, and above the eastern horizon hung the cradle of a moon. He had emerged into a little grassy area at the very edge of the Blight, and now he licked at the dew and felt it ease his parched lips and throat.

He lacked the strength to sit up. Despite the pain, he rolled over, gazed up at the stars that shone brilliantly through drifting clouds, and fell asleep.

So it was that Valerian found him.

She had stayed with Simon and the other Urlanders at the edge of the Blight, awed by the titanic struggle she could feel beneath her feet. She had stayed through the evening, long after the others had given up and had turned back in little groups towards their homes. She had resisted even the appeals of Simon and, as the night fell, she had gone into the Blight to search, calling Galen's name into the very mouth of the cave and then searching doggedly in ever-widening circles, right into the edge of the greensward where, she knew, small tunnels opened. At last her eye had been caught by something shining in the starlight—a length of oak staff. So she had found Galen. She did not waken him immediately. She did not want him to see that she had been crying, or that she was crying then. After awhile, when she had got control of herself, she touched his face. His eyes opened. "Hello," she said.

He could not smile. He could not move. He could not even lift his hand to touch her hair when she bent to kiss him.

CHAPTER ELEVEN

Heronsford

"I AM THE RESURRECTION AND THE LIFE, SAITH THE Lord."

A bell tolled.

"Whosoever believeth in Me shall not perish . . ."

Again the bell.

". . . but have everlasting Life."

The bell tolled and tolled. To Galen, it seemed that it was inside his very ear, and inside every one of his throbbing wounds. He pushed his hurt palms against his ears, but the bell penetrated with malignant insistence, and there were more guttural, earnest words as well. He rolled over, groaning, and with a great effort, opened his eyes. He was once again in Simon's loft, although he did not know how he had come there. He recalled the horror of the dragonfire beneath his feet, and for a moment he believed he was still in its midst, for the sun was streaming through chinks in the walls and spilling in undulating patterns on the golden hay.

The bell ceased its tolling. Voices now rolled up from below. He recognized Simon's and then another, the one that had been proclaiming, but he could not put a name to it until Simon did.

"Greil! Why, what's happened to you? What's all this about resurrection and everlasting life?"

"I saw him die, Simon!"

"Who?"

"Why, who else has sacrificed himself for Urland? Jacopus, of course."

"Yes," Simon said. "I saw that too. Awful!"

"Not awful! Marvelous!"

"Well, it all depends on your point of view."

"Marvelous! The man martyred himself! To save us!"

"Looked like suicide to me."

"Martyred himself! Such courage! Such selflessness! Didn't you see the way he climbed the hill? Didn't you see how he challenged the dragon?"

"I saw the way he died," Simon said. "Foolishly."

"No! No, not foolishly!" Greil's bell rattled discordantly as he waved his arms. "Magnificently! When you confront Evil it cannot be foolish, even if you perish. He is a martyr, Simon, another of those who has shown us the way."

"Greil . . ."

"Please, please. I know we have been friends all our lives, but please, now that I have been reborn, call me Gregorius."

"But . . . how do you know?"

"Know? I just do, Simon. It's a matter of faith."

"But as a man of reason. . . ."

"Reason?" Greil laughed, not unkindly. "Surely you do not believe that we are any of us, in any of the important things, reasonable men. Was it a reasonable man who walked those miles across the mountains to Cragganmore, with Harald Wartooth and Xenophobius the muleteer and the others, in hopes that we would find a magician to save us? Was it reasonable to have such blind hope? Such faith? And for your part, Simon, was it the action of a reasonable man to think that he could preserve his daughter by making her into a *boy?*" There was a peculiarly bitter emphasis on this last word that for Galen recalled Valerian's near chopping blow to Greil's knife-arm and her kick to the stomach that had sent him sprawling. *Boy* . . .

"No, not forever," Simon said, "only for a little while."

"Or," Greil continued, the bitterness vanished, "will you tell me that it was a reasonable man who all those years ago fashioned Sicarius—oh yes, I know all about that, and included in its tempering the spell from old Ulrich? Tell me, Simon, my old friend, was that the action of a reasonable man? Or of a man with *faith?*"

There was a long pause. "Perhaps," Simon said, "they are the same thing, after all."

"Perhaps. Yes," said Greil. "Think about it, my old friend, think about it. Come to see me." The bell began to ring again, rhythmically summoning converts from amidst the ruins, and Greil's voice faded as he proceeded along the road.

Painfully, Galen inched himself to the edge of the loft and descended the ladder. From the hearth came the delicious scent of cooking—soup and vegetables and seed-porridge—and it was obvious that Valerian was at work there. But he did not go in that direction; instead, he turned toward the forge where the voices had come from and where he knew he would find Simon. The big blacksmith was leaning against his doorpost in the sun, lost in thought. He was watching Greil's retreating back, and he was fingering the broken shaft of Sicarius. Galen stood at the entrance to the forge for several moments before Simon became aware of him; and then, when the older man turned toward him, Galen thought for a terrible moment that Simon was going to cry. "I'm sorry, lad," he said, slapping the broken stick against his thigh. "I really am."

"Why should *you* be sorry?"

"To send a boy on a man's errand and then not even to equip him properly! To give him damaged weapons! Bah!" He flung the haft into his forge.

"It wasn't your fault," Galen said.

"Fault? Well, it's never anyone's fault, is it? Just ... circumstances. We all tried our best, I guess."

Galen nodded doubtfully. Had he tried his best? He had done battle with Vermithrax; he had shown that he had courage enough when the time for conflict came. But he had also shown that courage was not enough. He remembered Ulrich's patient attempts to give him the power that might have destroyed Vermithrax, saved Swanscombe, and he remembered with regret his own indifference. He knew the disappointment Ulrich must have felt. *Someday you will need this charm. You must try harder, Galen!* And he had tried harder—or at least pretended to try; but the hills had been too green, the river too beguiling. The sorcery that would have taken him to the heart of life itself had seemed too remote, and he had preferred lazy afternoons and magic tricks. He had lost his chance, forever.

"Perhaps old Greil is right." Simon went on. "He's a posturing fool, but perhaps he's right. The Old Magic is dying out, Galen, isn't it?"

"Yes," Galen said weakly.

"Dying out," Simon said, looking at him with a strange intensity. "All over Urland. All over the world. The Old Magic and the magic places. Where are they now, Galen? Hmm? How long since you passed an oak grove interwoven with mistletoe and saw wreaths that the old priests left?"

"Only once," Galen said, "a long time ago."

"Or seen one of the stone circles that was not toppling and overgrown, but kept fresh and its altar used?"

Galen shook his head. "Not ever," he said.

"Or on a May evening, come upon a celebration to the horned god?"

"Never," Galen said.

"Dying out. All dying out. And do you know what is taking its place?" Simon gestured down the road, where a small group of villagers had gathered around Greil and his cross.

"Christianity?"

Simon nodded. "Greil may be right. If there are enough of them . . ."

"But . . ." Galen stammered, grappling with this new possibility. The image of Ulrich in all his majesty rose before him, infinitely preferable to the ragtag Christians who had passed by Cragganmore, preaching their strange tale. He could not believe that they would ever equal Ulrich, or that their faith could challenge the balanced powers of the elements. And yet, he recalled that Ulrich's magic had not saved even himself, that the old sorcerer was but a handful of ashes in a leather pouch. And he recalled too the odd respect he had felt for Jacopus at the moment of his death.

Far down the road, Greil's bell began to toll again; he was going forward, followed by the little shuffling crowd calling his simple message. "Yes," Simon said. "Gregorius is right. Perhaps if there are enough of us . . ." He was lost so deep in his reverie that he did not hear Galen leave.

"I can't believe it," Galen said to Valerian, back in the house. "It doesn't matter how many Christians there are, one thousand or ten thousand, they'll never kill that dragon. And if they can't kill Vermithrax, what hope?"

Valerian shook her head. "None," she said. "We can't kill it, the Christians can't kill it, and neither can you. That's why I've been thinking. Why should we put up with it anymore? What's the use in trying?"

"You mean . . . just . . . go away?"

She nodded. "Why not? Have you thought what life will be like anywhere close to Urland and the dragon? Have you thought what it would be like to live and work always frightened, always looking over your shoulder for either the dragon or Casiodorus's troops? To grow old in fear?" Valerian looked at her hands. "If we have a child, a girl, can you imagine the Lotteries?" She shuddered. "You haven't lived here. You have no idea of the shame and degradation . . ."

"Yes," he said, "I've seen it."

"Even if there is no child . . ."

"I know," he said. "It would be almost as bad." He fleetingly recalled his phantasies of only a few months before—how he would set bravely out for the west and for adventure—and he smiled bitterly. So, he had had his adventure and he would be going west, beaten, to escape. "Where shall we go?"

"Oh," she said, "*far* away! Even to the Western Isles."

Galen shrugged heavily. "All right. Now?"

"Yes."

They went to tell Simon, who was still where Galen had left him, his chin sunk morosely on his chest. "I shall be a very lonely old man," he said when Valerian had finished. "But of course it is what you should do." He straightened his shoulders and cleared his throat. "I think I shall go out now, and when I return it were best that you were gone. That is the way, I think. So. Let us say good-bye." Weeping, he embraced his daughter. "I have nothing to give you," he said, "Except what is yours already, and my love."

"Where are you going?" Valerian called after him.

"I am going to find Gregorius," he said, not turning back. Galen's ears may have tricked him in the emotion of the moment, but he thought that Simon laughed. "I am going to learn to pray."

Valerian wept after he had gone, and Galen held her.

Later, when they had packed, they left Simon's house and hiked up the road out of Swanscombe. Villagers were busy among the ruins; some had already started to rebuild. Most ignored them, either too busy or too shocked to be bothered with recriminations, but a few called blessings, and a few muttered curses. Wary dogs snarled and sniffed.

It was a cloudless, windless morning, a day brimming with sun. When they had passed the outskirts of the village and begun to climb the gentle sloping road to the west, their hands touched and held, although neither spoke; when they reached the top of the grade, they paused and turned back for a last look at Swanscombe and its valley. Even almost destroyed, the little village was still beautiful. The wheel of the gristmill, which had not been burnt, turned placidly, and in the nearby fields cattle browsed. Here and there through the lanes, horses trotted busily past, drawing carts and wagons. The business of building was proceeding, regardless of the dragon-threat. On some structures which had sprung back almost literally overnight, the thatch was already being replaced. And, all around, the green and tranquil hills lay like a benediction.

Galen glanced only briefly at the village and then continued trudging down the road to the west. He was exhausted and beaten. He wanted only to be gone from Urland forever.

To their right lay the Blight. Neither spoke as they passed. High in its hill, the dragon's crevasse gaped like a socket emptied of its eye. Even from that distance, Galen could see the tiny stick-dot that was Jacopus. He shuddered, remembering the lick of dragonfire on his legs, remembering the hypnotic dragon eyes into which he had stared, remembering his terror as the great jaws had opened to vent their flame . . .

"Don't look," Valerian said, holding her hand up like a blinker against his eye. "Don't remember. All of that's over, now."

But he could not help remembering long after they had passed the Blight and had begun to descend the serpentine path that led down into the valley of the River Varn. But then, as they descended, his spirits rose. They were, after all, going away from the Blight forever, and as Valerian pointed out, all of that horror was now behind them. Furthermore, it was a magnificent day, and the farther they went from the Blight the more birds sang in the surrounding trees, and the more abundant became the blossoms and the flowering bushes. Below, calm and silver in the sun, lay the Varn itself. The road led to the ford, the shallow gentle rapids that would be alive with fingerlings, leaping exuberantly in the sun and spray. Often during his summer stay, he had come down to fish for parent trout in the depths of nearby pools and he had spent many a lazy afternoon gazing across the ford, wondering what riches and adventures lay beyond in the far countries toward the sun. Now he was going himself.

He laughed. He had begun to feel in his stomach the kind of infantile exuberance he had not felt for years, not since the beginning of his study with Ulrich. He could recall that it was associated with animals, and with wishes that came true. He wished . . . he wished that time were back again and that without charms, incantations, amulets, or potions, but merely on the strength of his own innocence, he could conjure once again the animals of his fantasies . . .

"What are you thinking?"

He laughed. "I was thinking about when I was small," he said. "Before I went to Cragganmore. Sometime I'll tell you what I could do then. Sometime . . ." He stopped. He stood still, peering intently into the valley. Something had moved there, something that did not belong. It was white. It had appeared briefly above the tops of the trees, disappeared, appeared again farther to the left, and again vanished. He touched a finger of his free hand to his lips, as if silence would let him see better. Again the object appeared and vanished, a white shadow and then suddenly it had veered into the pathway itself and approached until it was clear that it was a bird, a white bird strangely shaped, a white . . .

"Gringe!"

The raven wheeled and returned in the direction they were going, making the summoning motions with its wingtips that Galen had come to know well.

"He wants us to follow. Come on!" He broke into a trot, pulling Valerian behind.

Gringe stayed just ahead, moving so slowly that he was scarcely airborne, occasionally glancing over his shoulder to ensure that they were coming. In a few minutes they had reached the flat portion of the old streambed and then, after passing through a short tunnel amidst the oaks and alders on the riverbank, they emerged at the edge of a gentle slope that led down to the river and to Heronsford. For a moment they were dazzled by the reflections of the sun on the bubbling water and on the glistening expanse of stones and pebbles; and then, when their eyes had adjusted to the new light, Valerian gasped in dismay and Galen's heart sank.

Between them and the river stretched a somber band of horsemen. In the center, his kingly garments resplendent in the sun, was Casiodorus.

For a moment no one moved. All were frozen in a stark tableau. Even Gringe seemed to hang midway between the groups. Then, as if ordering the play to begin, the raven emitted a single, raucous squawk. Casiodorus's horse moved forward.

In the seconds before the cavalry charged to hack them mercilessly into the earth, Galen remembered all that he had done since his arrival, all the disaster that he had brought to Urland, for which his death and Valerian's would now be retribution. He remembered Tyrian's warning after the death of Hodge, and the feel of Jerbul's dagger in the nape of his neck. He remembered his naïve presumption in calling down the landslide that had irked the dragon and stung it to fearful vengeance. He recalled the devastation of Swanscombe, and he imagined that horror repeated again and again through all of Urland. He remembered the feel of Sicarius leaping forward of its own volition and burying itself in the chest of Tyrian, and he remembered the warrior's look of astonishment. He remembered poor, flailing Jacopus on his futile climb to the dragon's lair. He remembered Elspeth's mutilated body, and the other bodies he had seen in the past days, on the roads, in the fields, amidst the ruins of dwellings—men, women, and children. And, remembering all of this, he was overcome by such a profound sorrow and guilt and humility that he actually sank to his knees. *Have I done this? All of this? What have I done?*

Casiodorus's horse moved forward. In horrible slow motion, Casiodorus's sword arm swept out and back, dropping toward the hilt of his weapon, and Galen knew that the charge would come now, the horses clattering across the gravel.

But the charge did not come. Casiodorus did not draw his sword, nor did his men follow him. His hand swept back in a holding gesture, and his horse came forward alone, very slowly, until it had covered about half the distance to where Galen and Valerian waited in the shadow of the forest. Then the king dismounted, dropped his reins, and approached on foot. Galen stood up.

"I have something of yours," Casiodorus said. His face was awful. He was a man who had passed beyond grief, beyond fear, beyond hope. His blanched skin was drawn tight over the bones. His voice was sepulchral, and his eyes, when they looked at Galen, did not seem to see him or, rather, saw him as an insignificant detail in eternity and space. Galen's stomach convulsed; he had seen that look once before, in the eye of the dragon. "Do not be alarmed," the king went on. "We shall not harm you nor prevent your leaving Urland, if you choose to go. But before you decide, there is something you should have." With his gloved hand he reached into a leather wallet and placed the amulet in Galen's extended palm. "It has brought me nothing but grief," Casiodorus said. "Do you see? Even now . . ." and he opened his hand so that Galen could see the holes burned through the fingertips and the palm of his glove. "Perhaps, had I not taken it from you, my daughter would be alive. Perhaps the dragon would not have come forth again. Since I took it, I have had no rest. I have had pain. I have had visions beyond anything I can describe to you. I have seen my land ravaged and my daughter swallowed by the earth. I wish this talisman had never befallen me."

"It . . . it is an ancient stone, Your Majesty," Galen said weakly. "I do not understand its power."

"But it does not assail *you*. See, how tranquilly it lies in your hand."

"I . . . I cannot explain that, Your Majesty."

"I can. You are innocent. You have not abused its power, or any power. You are a courier, although what you carry and to what end, I cannot tell. Do with it what you will; and go in peace." So saying, the king raised his right hand in an absentminded benediction, his thoughts already elsewhere. When he mounted, he gave the animal its head, and it turned back down the riverbed toward its stable in distant Morgenthorme. Its footfalls made small splashes at the edge of the stream. The other riders wheeled their mounts and fell in behind; two of them trotted a little ahead up the beach, between the king and the shadowy forest.

When they had gone, Valerian breathed a heavy sigh of relief. "Come on," she said. "Let's get across this river before he changes his mind."

"There's something . . ."

"Come *on*, Galen."

"No, wait. Wait. There's something . . . something I have to do." Galen had actually started forward with her, even before the last horseman was out of sight around the bend in the river, but he was stopped, puzzled by something he had seen in the rapids. A heron. The presence of the bird was not unusual; what *was* unusual was that it stood in the exact center of the rapids, quite undisturbed by the horsemen, and it was looking directly at Galen. It balanced on one foot in the predatory position, the other tucked into the gray feathers of its body. Its elongated neck was only slightly thicker than the leg. Its swordlike bill was a tiny triangle underneath keen, unblinking eyes. Its splendid wings, broader than Galen was tall, were fully outstretched. Nor was it only the heron's unusual stance, like a warning sentinel, that had arrested Galen; he *knew* this heron. "Wait . . ." he said again, sitting down slowly. Gringe had also perched and was waiting in a tree at the water's edge behind the heron and directly above it.

The amulet hummed in his cupped palms. He drew his feet up so that his hands rested on his ankles, and then he looked at the stone, looked *into* the stone, for his gaze was immediately drawn deeper than it had ever been drawn into Ulrich's conjuring bowl. In the center of the stone lay an immense cavern filled with an eerie, shimmering luminosity. There was a man kneeling there, clad in skins, and the man was watching something that amazed and frightened him, although Galen could not see what it was. There was fire and water. Galen had never seen such sinuous fire, fire that flowed from in front of the figure and gradually encircled him until Galen wanted to cry a warning. *Get out! Get out! It's a lake of fire! Run!* But then, just as the first wavelets of flame touched it, the figure changed and turned. His skin garments became flowing robes, the protruding jaw became a white beard, the horrified stare became a smile of triumph, and the supplicating arms rose in greeting.

"Ulrich!"

Ulrich it was, rising out of the lake of fire in a vision

so real that Galen actually thought for a moment that
the old sorcerer was alive again.

"But . . ." said Galen drawing back.

The vision vanished.

"But . . ." The birds remained; and above the
heron, above Gringe, a third had appeared, a falcon,
turning in small spirals. The three formed a perfectly
straight line above the ford.

"Ulrich you . . ."

*When all things converge, you will know beyond
doubt what must be done . . .*

Galen gaped at his knapsack, rummaged in it for
the pouch of ashes, and leapt to his feet. "He's here!"
he shouted. "He's pulled a trick! We're going back!"

Valerian shrank away from him, shaking her head.
"No," she said. "No."

"Listen to me! Please listen to me! I know what has
to be done. I'm the only one who can do it. I *must* do
it."

"Why? Why must you?"

"Because I'm a . . . For the Craft. For Ulrich."

"For *Ulrich?* For a dead man?" She was shaking
her head incredulously.

"But he's *not* dead! That's the point. At least, not
really dead."

"Galen, I *saw* him die. Tyrian stabbed him. He's
dead. He's burnt."

"Yes, but he's a sorcerer, don't you see? That's
what we've forgotten all this time. It's a matter of
faith. Of seeing."

"I know what *I* saw—a sword going in one side of
a man and out the other. Are you going to tell me
that that man is alive?"

"You'll see," Galen laughed strangely. "You'll see."

"You sounded like that crazy old man just then."

"Hodge! Yes! Hodge knew! That's why he gave me
. . . Oh, I should have *seen* it. I should have seen it!"
He seized her elbow. "Come on. We've got to hurry."

She reached to touch his face. She was crying.
"Please," she said. "We can still go away from all this.
Just you and I."

He shook his head. "Not yet," he said. "Come on."

At the same moment they both realized that while they had been talking the air had grown cooler, the sun less bright. The edge of a dark full moon had begun to blot out the sun, and an unnatural twilight descended upon the hills and downs. The birds cried out in soft alarm.

"Do you know what that means?" she asked, taking his hand and turning back with him toward the Blight.

"What?"

She replied matter-of-factly, drying her eyes on the back of her free hand. "It means," she said, "that someone is going to die."

CHAPTER TWELVE

The Lake of Fire

THE BIRDS FOLLOWED THEM. THE HERON ROSE WITH a sweep of its great wings and passed low above them, its head extended, its gaze fixed on a distance they could not see. For a time the falcon also circled overhead, its shrill and lonely calls falling like splinters of a shattered benediction. Then both passed on, and only Gringe was left to keep them company; Gringe, drifting softly amidst the trees, chuckling irritably while he waited for them to catch up.

The eclipse deepened.

They were breathless when they reached the crest of the hill, but they began to run down the eastern slope. The Blight became visible, a dark presence, behind the bushes on their left, and very soon they were in it. They left the tree line and began to climb the dark slope toward the dragon's lair. The last of the pale sunlight transformed the hillside. Always before Galen had viewed the Blight on overcast days, when the slopes had been dull with diffused light. But now, the weird sun threw individual boulders and crevasses into relief and brought their colors to baleful life. They were dark—browns and grays—and nothing lived among them except the occasional furtive lizard, flicking his tongue at the approach of the humans and vanishing instantly. The rock itself was earthen brown on the flanks, covered with a velvet coating which could be mistaken for fine moss, except that it was dragonslime, laid down over the years, gleaming now like pale film. Galen shuddered to feel his shoes slip on it. Still gripping Valerian's hand, he pulled her stumbling along over the uneven surface. Alternatively, he was convulsed with horror at the prospects of what lay ahead and exhilarated at what he knew might be, if only. . . .

The mouth of the cave gaped above. They clambered up the last incline, slipping in scree that rolled into little avalanches beneath their feet, grimacing as they passed the charred and fly-blown thing that had been Jacopus. Then they were on the ledge, peering into the gloom of the lair. This time Galen wasted no time calling the name of Vermithrax. The last thing he wanted was to let the dragon know of his approach if it were lurking below, and he raised a warning finger to his lips as Valerian started to speak to him. Quickly he dropped his pack, opened it, and pulled out the pouch of ashes. Then he went forward. He did not pause, not even long enough for his eyes to grow accustomed to the gloom, but hurried down into the foulness of the passage.

In fact, there was no need for silence and caution. Vermithrax was not below. Restive, nagged by its neck wound, lured out by the false twilight, the dragon had taken flight over the scorched land. It had met no opposition, encountered no challenge; yet it felt a deep unease, a threat that caused it to sweep in a broad circle as far west as Heronsford and to pass searching three times directly over the Blight itself, before lifting away toward the southeast. The first of these circling passes occurred moments after Galen and Valerian had entered the cave; indeed, had Galen hesitated instead of hurrying Valerian inside, the thin shadow of the dragon would have drifted over them. Even so, they were close enough for the dragon to sense them, to veer slightly, to resolve to make only a very short reconnaissance . . .

Inside, his eyes still unaccustomed to the gloom, Galen almost stumbled upon the bodies of Elspeth and the dragonets. He had forgotten to warn Valerian about this horror, and she barely suppressed a scream

when she saw it. Fists pressed into her mouth, wide-
eyed, she shrank away.

"Sorry," Galen whispered. "Yes, it's Elspeth. I
meant to tell you." The walls amplified his whisper.
I meant to tell you. "Come around this way." He
beckoned to her and then hurried on, down toward
the Lake of Fire. By the time Valerian had recovered
and edged past the corpses, he was out of sight.

"Galen! . . . Galen!" But there came no answer except the echoes, *Galen* . . . from both the passageways
that forked, right and left, ahead of her. The walls
glimmered. Something soft and wet scurried across
her instep. She thought, unable to rid her nostrils of
the stench of the place, that she would be violently
sick. She had determined to go with Galen wherever
this strange, last compulsion might lead him, into the
very teeth of Vermithrax if necessary; but now her
resolution faltered. She saw those teeth moving in the
shadows of the walls. Ahead, around the corner, she
heard the sibilance of leather wings. When something
else covered her foot, something heavy and cold and
pulsing, she cried out and fled back toward light and
air, toward the reassuring green of nature that lay
beyond the Blight. She arrived on the ledge sobbing
with relief.

The eclipse was almost total.

Above the dim land, three miles to the south, Vermithrax turned toward home.

Deep inside the tunnel, Galen was oblivious to her
absence. The pouch of ashes he bore like a grail in
both hands at chest level. Down he went, entranced,
past the niche from which he had lunged with Simon's
lance, past damp walls and the alert eyes of newts and
salamanders, down, down, toward the Lake of Fire
where pale shapes moved beneath the surface. Soon,
reflected flames summoned him. He rounded a corner, then another, and there it lay. Groups of flames
danced on the surface, now blending, now separating.
Under the vaults, other arms of the lake stretched
away to unknown and sepulchral regions. Ahead, the
stepping stones beckoned him. Under and around
them moved abysmal shapes. To do what must be

done, he would have to walk out on those stones and be as vulnerable again as he was when Vermithrax had come before. Where *was* Vermithrax? Galen peered into the gloom, squinting against the vapors rising from the lake and, although he saw nothing of the dragon, he could not rid himself of the feeling that he was being watched. The skin moved on the insides of his thighs and on his buttocks; but there was no turning back. He stepped from the muck at the water's edge—his shoe making a small reluctant sound as he did so—to the first of the stones.

Something trembled; he could not be sure whether it was merely the flat stone, or whether it was the ground beneath the stone, but something had definitely moved. He took the step to the next stone, and then to the next. Still no Vermithrax. He had, he thought, been standing at exactly this spot when the dragon had risen before. Could it be . . . was it possible that the lance had in fact struck deep, inflicting a mortal wound? Could it be that Vermithrax was sinking into death even now, curled in some remote crevasse? As if in mockery of this thought, the ground trembled again, and concentric ripples shimmered on the lake's surface.

Hands shuddering, forcing himself to move deliberately, Galen untied the thongs on the packet containing Ulrich's ashes. He extended the pouch arm's length, holding it while he searched for the precise Latin, and then flung the contents in a wide arc. *"Nunc magister reverti iubeo! Ulrich appropinqua!"*

The ashes drifted in a falling band, reflecting the flames; as the first of them touched the water, the earth quivered again, nor did the trembling cease till they had dispersed amidst the circles of flame.

Holding his breath, Galen had watched their descent. But aside from the tremor and the fact that the shapes in the dark water suddenly congregated and then, just as suddenly, sank from sight, there was no change. For a moment his arm remained extended; then it fell to his side. Nothing. So he had been wrong again, and the vision that he had had was simply a whim, the delusion of a romantic child.

Then suddenly a small whirlwind appeared on the surface. Drawing all adjacent flame into its vortex, it spun ever faster, soon rising into an undulating pillar four feet high. Then, broadening funnellike, the top grew denser and more stable, slowing while the bottom of the little tornado gathered speed. Even as Galen watched in astonishment and growing excitement, the thickening at the top took on a distinct shape. A *man* was reclining on this spiraling column of fire, reposing in complete tranquility even as he had on his funeral pyre.

Ulrich!

Galen could now see that it was definitely the old sorcerer—the white beard, the familiar stern brow, the disheveled purple gown. "Ulrich!" he cried, clapping his hands. "You did it! You did it!" His cries echoed in the cavern, *Ulrich, Ulrich*.

The figure on the column moved. His hands lifted and lightly massaged his temples in the manner of a man with a ferocious headache, and then he touched a finger to his lips and moved a slow, quieting hand in Galen's direction. "Shh," he said. "Don't shout." Very slowly he turned and tipped upright until he was standing on a flagstone only a few feet from Galen. His eyes opened He lifted a finger. "That Latin you just used, Galen . . ."

"Yes, Magister?"

"*Appropinqua*. Rather pretentious, wasn't it? Why not a simple *veni?* You were always erratic, Galen. Always."

"Yes, Magister." Galen was weeping with disbelief and joy.

"Galen, did you bring food?"

"I . . . I'm sorry, Magister."

"Hm. Oh well, no time anyway. But you were improvident, Galen, weren't you? Always. Running around laughing and enjoying yourself. Living for the moment. But you were bright. Flashes of insight. You had the Talent. That's why you've brought me, and not Hodge. Correct?"

"Yes, Magister. You see . . ."

Ulrich again waved the quieting hand. "It's a long story, isn't it?"

"Yes sir. You see. . . ."

"There's no need to tell it, Galen. I know it all. In fact, there's no *time* to tell it." He stepped onto the farthest of the stepping stones, and behind him the spiraling funnel dissolved back onto the surface of the lake. "Are you *sure* you have no food?"

"Yes sir, quite sure."

"Hmm. Pity. I'm very hungry. Famished, in fact."

He peered around the cavern. It all seemed to be familiar to him—the tunnel ascending from the world above, the faintly flickering lake, the vaults and arches that stretched into interminable recesses. For several seconds, his attention was caught and held by something upward, at the roof of the cavern and beyond. Ulrich stared grimly at this area; as he did so, his shoulders straightened, and his white beard lifted and protruded challengingly. Then he nodded slowly. "Yes." He spoke so softly that Galen scarcely heard him, and yet his whisper echoed into the farthest recesses of the cave. "Yes. It's time." For a moment Galen believed—although it might have been only the effects of the ceaseless echoes, of the susurrations of the lake—that there came a sigh of consent, a shuddering exhalation. Ulrich heard it too, for again he nodded.

"Come," he said, turning stiffly to Galen. "Come, my boy. It's very close, now. We must be on the surface. Give me your arm! I forgot my stick." Leaning on Galen, he turned his back on the lake and started up the sloping corridor. Although he moved slowly, his step was light and ten years younger. Galen kept glancing anxiously at him. He was filled with both anticipation and foreboding. He had seen such light in other eyes, in the faces of young knights, Saxon and Briton, who had passed Cragganmore on their way to distant conflicts, stopping to take a meal and a flagon of mead, to rest awhile and then go on. They had never returned, none of them. The purpose that had moved them contained their own destruction, and the knowledge of that destruction. *They knew that they would die, and it made no difference.* For a little time they lived intensely, and their radiance had suffused the lives of all around them. So now, with Ulrich. It seemed to Galen that this journey to the mouth of the cave, which even now he could see ahead, was a short life; and yet, if there was anything the old sorcerer had taught him, it was that life and death, the two partners, journeyed always together, and that the one was eternally born from the other.

When they came to the place of slaughter, Ulrich cast a single pitying glance at the body of Elspeth and the corpses of the dragonets. He did not pause. *Death,* his glance said. *Decay and transformation. Good and bad together.* In fact, Galen believed for a moment that the master had spoken, although Ulrich said nothing until they were only a few paces from the cave's mouth. Then he stopped. Beyond, in the almost complete dusk lay green and tranquil hills. Looking at these hills, not at Galen, Ulrich asked, "Do you have the amulet?"

"Yes, Magister." Galen removed the talisman from his neck and placed it in the old man's outstretched palm. Still gazing at the pastoral green of the far hills, Ulrich closed his fingers and smiled.

At that precise moment, outside, Vermithrax crossed the southern edge of the Blight and, losing altitude, becoming indistinguishable from the hills behind, it saw Valerian alone on the ledge of its lair. Its spines rose. Hot phlegm gathered in its throat. Its mouth opened fractionally. Its descent was perfect and almost silent, except for the smallest whistling of wind on scaly encrustations and the protruding splinters of the lance haft in its neck. It was a hundred yards away; its mouth opened wider.

At that moment Galen and Ulrich emerged from the cavern and Valerian, her back to the approaching dragon, saw horror on their faces.

Later she would be unable to say what she actually heard first, the whistling descent or the raucous cry of warning. She heard both, and both caused her to whirl and look into the very jaws and glowing eyes of the dragon. She was so close that she could see in those eyes what Melissa had seen and what generations of other Chosen had seen, so close that she saw the gout of flame that would envelop her already forming, a bright spiral, deep in the creature's throat.

But that flame never reached her. The shrill cry of warning had been uttered by a white bird that, by the time she had spun around, had plummeted to within inches of the dragon's face, claws extended.

"Gringe!" Galen's shout mingled with Valerian's shriek and with the roar of the dragon as it veered to protect its eye, sending a lash of fire spattering into a thousand globules down the hillside.

"Gringe!"

Carried past by its momentum, the raven turned and looked at them, crying again, a long cry of terror and triumph and farewell. Then the dragon twisted, lithe as an airborne snake, and caught its small tormentor with a lick of flame. There was a puff of smoke and Gringe vanished; what was left, tumbling to the boulders where Jacopus already lay, was a charred lump, trailing a black wisp.

"Here!" Ulrich commanded Galen and Valerian. "Come to me!" As the dragon whirled over the Blight, preparing another assault, he gathered the two young people to him, embracing them with astonishing strength. "Do not be afraid." His eyes turned upward. He muttered a charm which Galen had never heard before, and they rose.

They rose effortlessly. Airborne, they saw the Blight begin to revolve beneath them faster and faster, until it was spinning in a dizzying whirl. Valerian screamed, but Ulrich's arm clasped her firmly to his side, and Ulrich's calm words soothed her. "All is well, my child. Our journey is very brief."

A moment later the whirling slowed and ceased. They found themselves on the highest crag, overlooking the Blight, overlooking the river and the village. Vermithrax was far below, circling, rising.

The eclipse was complete.

"There is something you must do," Ulrich said. "A final service." His arms were still around them. His eyes glittered like crystals.

"Anything, Master."

"You have borne the stone well and you have kept it safe."

Galen hung his head, but Ulrich went on, shaking his head slightly.

"But you know that you are not a sorcerer. Not now. Perhaps the fault is mine. You are many other things. You are brave, and kind, and generous, and pure of heart. But you are not a sorcerer. You are not One with this stone, as I am. You have the Talent, and someday, perhaps, in another place, another time . . . But my time is now, mine and the stone's. You must help, Galen."

The sun was a circle of beads around the darkened moon. Time had stopped. The Blight lay dark and silent. Vermithrax rose inexorably, neck arched in challenge, on its mighty wings.

"How, Magister?"

"Take the stone. Here. There will be a moment when you must destroy it utterly and forever. You must release into me that power which my ancestor placed in it at its creation. You will know the moment. You must act while there is life yet in me."

"But . . ."

"No! No questioning. No thought! You must! It is my command!"

As he spoke he detached himself from Galen and Valerian and waved them to the safety of a nearby crevasse. Then he strode to the edge of the precipice and his voice rang like a benediction across the Blight and far out to the fear-ridden villages beyond. "Know the time! Peace be with you now, forever!" He poised on the very extremity of the ledge.

The dragon had climbed in wide spirals. Now it turned, not in the convulsion with which it had attacked Gringe, but in an incredibly graceful movement. For an instant it seemed suspended; the head tilted down toward Ulrich, and the body followed. The body stretched to a lean arrow guided by wings almost folded. Clearly, Vermithrax did not intend to kill Ulrich by fire; it meant to seize the sorcerer and lift him triumphantly aloft. Even the twin sickle claws on the edges of its wings stretched eagerly for him and almost sank into him—would have done so, had not the magician flung out his folded arms as if to push the dragon back and away. Galen could not hear what he said; the words were drowned in the rushing of Vermithrax's wings and Valerian's screams as she cowered beside him, pressing her face against the rock wall. But Vermithrax uttered a scream of pain and missed almost entirely on this first pass; one talon snagged the shoulder of Ulrich's gown and tore a strip of it away. It fluttered like a pennant as the dragon rose again, and then drifted free and down, to be lost amidst the boulders of the Blight.

Ulrich remained poised on the brink of the cantilevered ledge, his palms-out gesture changed now to two raised and defiant fists. He had not flinched from the claws. He continued to shout even as the dragon retreated and rose again, and Galen heard in those shouts the exultant defiance of a young man testing his power for the first time. He wanted to scream, *Kill it, Ulrich! Kill it! You don't need the amulet!* But he said nothing. He was not sure that he believed that. Ulrich, though staunch, was very frail, while the dragon seemed to have drawn strength from pain; it was darker, leaner, larger.

"Why don't you *help* him?" Valerian asked. She was wringing her hands and sobbing. "You said you would. Why don't you smash the amulet?"

He held the stone close. He could feel its pulsing. Its radiance bathed them all like the glow from a tiny sun. "I can't," he said.

"Are you afraid? Give it to me, then. Let me do it."

He shook his head.

"Why *not?*"

"Because," he said, looking at her through eyes that were clear and wise with an old, old knowledge, "that will kill them *both.*"

Again the dragon came. This time it swept from a higher pitch, steeper, faster. It was upon Ulrich with terrifying speed, and the sorcerer's curses and extended palms had less effect, for Vermithrax dropped screaming through buffeting air and fell half on the old man, half on the ledge. Only the lance, embedded in the dragon's neck, saved Ulrich, for had both claws seized him the battle would have been over. As it was, Vermithrax's torn muscles failed it. One claw grappled Ulrich while the other missed the ledge completely. The beast landed heavily on its belly. Ulrich's head and neck had been raked by one talon, and another had stabbed into his thigh, paralyzing him with agony. But, in the seconds during which Vermithrax scrambled to regain its balance, Ulrich twisted free, wrenching at the talons until the dragon released him with a scream and half pushed, half fell from the ledge. It was still screaming as it glided down parallel with the slope of the hill, almost to the floor of the Blight.

Galen, however, was not watching the dragon; he was watching Ulrich. The sorcerer's torn gown was bloodsoaked and he was stiff with pain. When he tried to walk, his arms flailed helplessly as the wounded leg buckled. For a moment he was a bent and broken insect, a travesty of the man he had been but minutes before. But then, miraculously, he managed to straighten and watch the descent of his enemy almost to the valley floor. As Vermithrax rose, he shook his fist and bared his teeth through a bloodstained beard in a grim parody of laughter. "While there is life," he said, turning to Galen. "Remember!"

The dragon rose again, magnificent against the darkened sky and with an obscene languor, as if it knew that it could finish off this prey at leisure. It rose, spiraling, and once more descended.

As it did so, Ulrich raised his arms, although the left one would lift only part way because of his grievous wound. Galen saw that this time instead of repelling it, the old man was actually summoning the beast!

Gripping the amulet hard, he watched.

The dragon swooped, its neck a sinuous arc, its claws extended. Wind whistled on its scaly protuberances. Despite his horror and terror, Galen thought: *You beast! You are magnificent!*

Indeed the dragon was. Its hurts had scarcely slowed it. For that moment, its lean shape gliding across the crags of the Blight conjured another time, a timelessness. Its scream of defiance became all other screams long faded to silence. It was all dragons. Dragon!

It swept down with the speed of a whirlwind and its great claws seized Ulrich cleanly. They opened and clenched with unerring accuracy while the leather wings beat upward. For moments, Ulrich dangled limp and helplessly, like a rodent in the clutches of a hawk; but then, as the dragon rose, it drew him tight against its belly. Its cry was almost pure triumph—almost, for it contained something else as well, such a hopeless yearning that Galen's blood chilled to hear it. Nor did the creature descend. Instead, it veered away over the center of the Blight and began to climb. Its cries mingled with the screams of Ulrich writhing against its belly.

Horror pierced Galen like cold steel. He sank to his knees. "No!" he said. "Ulrich! Oh, Ulrich, no!" He scarcely noticed that the amulet had grown so hot that he had dropped it among the stones, or that its radiance was brighter, steadier than it had ever been. He felt nothing but utter dread and loss, saw nothing but the diminishing dot that was Vermithrax and Ulrich.

Behind him Valerian wept.

The amulet shone with dazzling brilliance. Yet, when at last he looked at it, he found that he could gaze through that brilliance and into the vision beneath. What he saw he had seen once before, in Ulrich's conjuring bowl on the very morning of the Urlanders' arrival: Ulrich dispersing, released from a body tired and old. He knew then with absolute certainty what he must do.

Desperately he searched for a boulder on the narrow ledge, found one the size of a man's head, and lifted it above the amulet. Then, with a final glance at the soaring dragon and its dangling prey, he flung it down on the glowing talisman with all his force.

Much, much later, when Galen and Valerian began to talk about that day, they tried first to describe the sound of the amulet as it broke. Valerian said that it was like a tornado that had passed down Swanscombe

Valley when she was very young, a shrieking, howling wind that had descended suddenly upon them and vanished just as quickly, leaving ruin in its wake. It was, she said, the most awesome of all sounds. Galen had never heard a tornado; but he had listened to the howling of a wild cat passing in the night. That sound, he said, magnified a thousand times, was what he heard when he dropped the boulder.

Both looked up at the soaring dragon, dark against the dark sky, and both sensed what would occur. So brilliant was the flash that they thought the sun had suddenly emerged. Then the roar came, and then the concussion knocked them sprawling backwards on the ledge.

The explosion seemed to feed on itself, with many small explosions bursting out of each other faster and faster until they became the merest puffs of smoke a great distance from the center of the blast. Sudden winds swept this smoke away and allowed Galen and Valerian to see that, incredibly, the dragon remained intact, or sufficiently intact to be recognizable; there were the spade tail, the angular wings, the elongated neck. For seconds it hung suspended, and then it crumpled, tumbled, fell faster, trailing fluttering strands of itself like cerements, a thing suddenly ghastly and pitiful, utterly and irrevocably ruined.

It came to earth in Swanscombe Valley at the edge of the Blight, near the road. It did not literally strike earth, for it landed in a pond, a wide place in the River Swanscombe. From their vantage point, Galen and Valerian saw the huge splash of its impact, and then the maddened boiling of the pool, as if it revolted with every drop of its being against the presence of the dragon's corpse. Immense clouds of steam plumed up, obscuring sections of the Blight and the hills beyond; but then they began slowly to dissipate, tugged and swirled by freshening breezes, so that, when the sun emerged from behind the moon, there were only a few wisps of vapor left to catch its gleams. It shone briefly like gold, this mist, like golden dust blowing in the wind, and then was gone. All was peaceful. The river flowed again. The sun shone warm. Somewhere close by the ledge, a sparrow broke into full-throated song.

Galen sank slowly to his knees. He was shuddering violently. A part of him knew that he should be jubilant, that he should celebrate with the little group of Swanscombe villagers whose whoops and incredulous laughter he heard even now, coming from the edge of the Blight below. But he was not jubilant. What he felt was a sense of loss so enormous that he could not tell whether he contained it or it him. When his tears began to fall, they mourned all that had come together and passed together in those moments. He wept not for Ulrich alone. He wept for Vermithrax too, and for the amulet and the splendid swirling magic that would never be again, and for the poor, diminished, sunny world before him.

He could not stop. He covered his face, but the tears spilled through his fingers and the dumb animal sounds bumped in his chest and throat. Valerian had knelt beside him. She was embracing him; her wet face was pressed against his neck, her hand was caressing his back, and she was uttering the wordless sounds of maternal comfort. All of this he knew, but it was still a long time before his sobbing had exhausted itself and he began to relax from the clenched position into which his shock had thrown him. Finally he sat up. "Quite a show," he said.

She was still embracing him. Her face was in his hair.

"I don't know why. I . . ." He had begun to say that he was sorry, but she put a hand over his mouth.

"You came back," she said. "You did what had to be done. You killed it."

He nodded. "And Ulrich. He really is dead now."

"He was an old, old man," she said.

"And everything has died with him."

"Not everything . . ."

"All that knowledge. That wisdom. I could have learned it. I could have kept it and passed it on."

"Perhaps," she said, "there is room for only so much wisdom in the world. Perhaps it changes. Perhaps it has to die in some ways before it gets born in others." She was looking down across the Blight and into the valley. The little crowd of villagers that had gathered when the eclipse began and had witnessed the final struggle between Ulrich and Vermithrax was advancing hesitantly on the dragon's corpse, a shapeless heap half-submerged in the river. They were led by a big, red-headed man carrying a large cross. Even at that distance, Valerian recognized her father. Behind Simon, urging the others into song, walked Gregorious. Pieces of their singing drifted up.

Galen had heard and also was watching. "Christians," he said. Some were carrying pikes and cleavers. A few bore bows and quivers. Most were weaponless. "Trusting," he said.

"Galen," she said. "Let's go." He felt her shivering against him. "Let's leave this place. For good. Let's go where there is no . . . no power."

He was smiling, shaking his head. "Take me there," he said.

They climbed slowly down from the ledge and picked their way through the Blight. They did not look back. Neither spoke for some time; both were watching the activities of the Christians. They had surrounded Vermithrax, some hip-deep in the discolored river, and were hacking at the carcass. Some had begun to dig a huge pit, and others were stacking chunks of Vermithrax on the edge of it for burial.

"That's good," Valerian nodded. "Get rid of it forever. Back to earth." She could see Simon quite clearly among the others. He had leaned his cross against a tree, and he towered in the midst of the butchering, his stout arm lustily wielding a seax in exactly the way that she had seen him, a thousand times through her childhood, wielding his hammer at the forge. For a moment she wanted to run to him, as she would have done as a small child, and throw her arms around him; but the impulse fled. She had said goodbye, and so had he. He had chosen a new life, a new Faith that did not include her. And she, for her part, had also made a choice. She clung to Galen's hand and led him obliquely across the Blight, on a path that took them back to the road at a point out of sight of the celebrating villagers, who, in any case, were much too busy hacking at Vermithrax to see them.

Once they reached the road and turned westward, their pace quickened. With the Blight and the violence behind them, and with a clear blue sky and an empty road ahead, it was possible to believe at last that they were leaving Urland.

But the road was not quite empty. They had gone only about half a league when Valerian halted suddenly, tensed and listening.

"What?" Galen asked. "What?" And then he heard what she had heard: Horses. Many horses were approaching cautiously just beyond the rise ahead. They froze, their hearts sinking. They wanted no horsemen. They wanted only to cross the Varn at last. Exposed, vulnerable, they stood and waited.

The first rider appeared. He was scouting off the road on their right. He looked so like Tyrian that for a moment Galen believed the centurion's death had been a dream. This man had the same stocky build, the same ready hand on the sword hilt, the same black epaulettes and gauntlets, the same rampant dragon on the black chest. But when Galen blinked away the illusion, he saw that this rider had a thick, sandy moustache. He was close, now. There was another on the other side of the road, and behind and between them came two more, side by side, and then another. In the midst of this troop rode Casiodorus, followed by a small train that included Horsrick. When the two outriders had reached Galen and Valerian, they stopped, eyeing them suspiciously and keeping their distance until the king came up. No one spoke. The horses stamped and blew softly. For a long moment they looked at each other, the resplendent king and the filthy, tattered, proud young man.

Neither spoke.

Then, head high, Valerian began to push through the horsemen. "Good-bye," she said. "We're leaving."

And so they did. Hand in hand they walked past the king's retinue and down the road. Once, when Galen looked back, he was surprised to see Casiodorus looking after them, a tall, sad figure. By the time they

climbed to the top of the hill, however, the king's
party had reached the dragon's corpse. Very faintly
but unmistakably over the distance, mingled with the
barking of dogs and the shrieks of excited children,
came shouts of "Hail, Casiodorus! Hail!" The king
had been helped down from his horse, and Horsrick
had provided him with a bared sword which he now,
with some difficulty, lifted above his head and let fall
on the cadaver. This gesture aroused fresh cheers, led
by the cavalrymen. "Dragonslayer, hail!"

Galen and Valerian turned away and began their
descent down the long slope that led to the Varn and
Heronsford. The river was visible through the trees, a
glittering ribbon in the new sun. When they reached
it, Valerian would have splashed across the ford that
minute, but Galen held her back.

"Why?" she asked.

He shrugged. "This way," he said. "There's a better
place where no one ever goes." He led her upstream
and into the shadows of the forest. As they walked,
they felt sometimes the springy humus of the forest
floor and sometimes the more solid earth of an old,
overgrown path. Soon they came to a deeply shaded
place where the water ran slow and deep. "Here," he
said.

"But we *can't* cross here. There's no bridge, and it's
deep."

"Um. All the more reason," he said, stripping off
his clothes. Then he was in the water, and the cold,
hard river water was cleansing him, soothing his
wounds, and he swam beneath its surface for as long
as he could hold his breath. When he surfaced, Valerian was swimming toward him, and they allowed the
current to carry them a little distance downstream before they leisurely swam back against it to the place
where they had left their clothes. On their backs then,
kicking, they carried their clothes and packs across
and dressed on the other side.

From the shade of a great oak a somnolent bat regarded them indifferently.

"Where are we going?"

"I don't know," he said.

"But on a journey? A long journey?"

"I think so, yes."

"In that case," she said, "I wish we had something to ride. I wish we had a horse."

Galen laughed. "When I was very small, before I was taken to Ulrich and taught serious things—incantations and charms and so forth—I could call horses just like *that*." He snapped his fingers. "I would think, *white horse!* and snap my fingers and there it would be." He shouldered his pack. "But that was when I was a child, and innocent."

Nearby, just ahead along the old path, came a sound like gentle laughter. There was a thudding of hooves, and a moment later they both glimpsed a white flank amidst the dappled leaves.

Galen laughed with delight, but Valerian spun around, closing her hands over his fingers that were about to snap again. "Enough!" she said.